Do the Right Thing

ALSO BY SHYAMA PERERA

Bitter Sweet Symphony

Haven't Stopped Dancing Yet

SHYAMA PERERA

Do The Right Thing

S

SCEPTRE
Hodder & Stoughton

Copyright © 2002 by Shyama Perera

First published in Great Britain in 2002 by Hodder and Stoughton
A division of Hodder Headline

A Sceptre book

The right of Shyama Perera to be identified as the Author of the Work
has been asserted by her in accordance with
the Copyright, Designs and Patents Act 1988.

2 4 6 8 10 9 7 5 3

A CIP catalogue record for this title is available from the
British Library

ISBN 0 340 72822 1

Typeset in Sabon by Palimpsest Book Production Limited,
Polmont, Stirlingshire
Printed and bound in Great Britain by
Mackays of Chatham plc, Chatham, Kent

Hodder and Stoughton
A division of Hodder Headline
338 Euston Road
London NW1 3BH

For Anyusha and Tushara

Be right, not righteous

Part One

Once upon a time on the Indian subcontinent there lived a gloriously handsome young man called Shyam, which rhymes with charm, and is particularly appropriate because, as well as being cute and stonkingly sexy, our hero was a good man. Unlike most techies one meets, he had an innate sense of right and wrong. A moral crusader with a peculiar sensitivity to those around him, he understood that happiness cannot be bought in bottles and applied liberally to affected parts. As he sat at his screen, his tie loosened against the humidity of a poorly air-conditioned office, Shyam surfed the sites of human weakness: greed, neglect, foolishness, pride, divorce, poverty. Bill hadn't just opened the Gates for him, he'd marked the path with a series of icons.

Somewhere left of Shyam, on that same continent, in hillier parts which are cooler and more still, worked a stunning girl called Chita. Her long black hair was braided in an elegant French pleat but her loose clothing was draped carelessly around her slender curves as, returning to her desk, she found a large pile of stock reports dumped by the paean. Sipping lemon tea, she wished, as ever, that a knight on a white charger would come to rescue her. Or, given the location, a Hindi film star lookalike in a studded white catsuit, matching boots and halo. A man who could invigorate her and give her life a purpose. 'Why do you ignore the offers you get, child. You keep looking for a prince and they don't exist,' her mother often chided. Chita smiled, her almond eyes shining. 'Then I'll make do with a prince among men, Amma.'

Chita's dream was no more and no less than that of most young women, but her sisters in the West would temper that romanticism with a large pinch of realism. They have learned the hard way that you can never be certain of anyone. That we all have dark corners of the soul that are inaccessible, sometimes even to ourselves. But Chita was still innocent. As she limbered up in readiness for Cupid's all-encompassing hit, she saw only hope and beauty and happiness ahead of her.

MESSAGE FROM RAMA: *Hi, Sita, want to talk?*

MESSAGE FROM SITA: *Sure. Where are you right now?*

RAMA: *In the office :-(You?*

SITA: *In the office also. I work for a tea exporting business. What do you do?*

RAMA: *I'm in software. Have spent most of today ironing bugs out of a new retail programme.*

SITA: *Ironing bugs? I hope they didn't scream too loudly!*

RAMA: *I'm the only one who feels like screaming :-) It has to be up and running by the end of next week . . .*

SITA: *What a shame you can't be up and running – then you could escape it! Does your job light a fire in your belly?!!*

RAMA: *A fire? I haven't thought of it like that. If fire is purifying and a test of will, then yes, there are flames in my belly, as you put it :-) I like problem-solving. I think it's my destiny.*

SITA: *You believe in destiny?!!*

RAMA: *Don't you? Perhaps you're my destiny? Who knows? Listen, I have to go. Maybe chat again tomorrow?*

Shyam's three brothers were already home when he arrived. Sitting around the dining table they ate chapatis and dahl and four different types of vegetable curry made by Aunty Sujata. Trading stories about their day, each was convinced he could do the other's job in half the time and twice as well. Well, they *were* blokes.

Bobby, the baby, was the only one who'd made a break for it. He'd escaped the clutches of C+ and C++ to become an accountant. Not, it must be said, an exciting chartered accountant, but a safe certified accountant. Nonetheless, around here that was rebellious!

Sometimes the boys had competitions to see who had the most boring job or the most ridiculous office anecdote. This week, Lucky was winning hands down. His head of department was running a time-and-motion study at the water dispenser. 'I drank a full cup every twenty minutes just to irritate the old fool. I spent half the day in the toilet. I won on both time and motions.'

Tutting crossly, Aunty Sujata rose from the table. 'I am going to watch *Doordarshan News*. Then I shall be retiring to my room for private meditation.'

'You're sure it is meditation and not mediation, Aunty?'

'I need both living with you, Lucky.'

The boys pulled out the whisky. 'So, Bobby, how was the girl in the video shop today? Was she on fast forward or long play?'

Bobby coloured. 'I don't know. She wasn't there.'

'She must have found another casting couch.'

'At least I'm not like you and Shivan. Changing your minds with the weather.'

It must be said that the guys were all mouth and no trousers. Despite the horseplay, all four of these boys were chaste, believing their love should be saved for only one woman. No wonder Shyam spent his lunch-times 'whispering' on Inderdates. Soon he would inherit their late father's massive rubber estate. He needed someone to ease both his filial and biological burdens.

'I saw the most sensational girl in the canteen,' Shivan said.

'You should have asked her for lunch.'

'She'd already got her lunch, Lucky.'

'Then you should have offered pudding.'

The twins, Lucky and Shivan, both worked for a Microsoft subsidiary. Each day they were differently smitten with one of the girls in their sales and marketing department. There was Indira with the eyes, Hashida with the hair, Mayuri with the smile, Fatima with the dimples . . .

Meanwhile none of them was getting any younger. They all needed suitable and dutiful women. But none more so than the uncompromising Shyam: 'Marriage is a lifelong commitment – it cannot be entered lightly.'

The brothers were only flirting with the standard nudge-nudge, wink-wink vocabulary, but the nightly serenade of the cicadas underscored a certain tension in their musings.

While they talked, the family's pet monkey, Honeybun, leaped around the furniture, stopping momentarily on the shoulders of the twins. The monkey had been passed to the family by some Bangalore Christians after it deliberately emptied its bladder into a cup of tea being served to a visiting rector from the Church of England.

It had bedded in well and slept at the foot of Shyam's old camphor-wood bed. Now he settled on Lucky's shoulder.

After a couple of drinks, the chaps fell to their favourite pastime: flicking balls of Sellotape on to the ceiling. Tonight Bobby was on form. He secured five balls within the one-minute limit. But, as ever, Shyam wasn't satisfied with merely getting a hit. He needed to make the game harder. He'd ask for markers – little stains or part of a shadow, for which he must aim. Three times in a row, he hit a dark spot where the servant had caught an insect with the fly whisk. His brothers teased him. 'The real Robin Hood, eh, Shyam?'

'Don't you mean William Tell?'

'No. He's Rama. Blessed by the gods.'

* * *

SITA: *Why do you call yourself Rama?*

RAMA: *It's to do with the story of Rama hitting the moving apples – a boyhood game with my brothers :-) Why are you Sita?*

SITA: *Because I wanted to meet you??!! No reason! It's a little like my real name and I loved the story of the dutiful wife when I was little.*

RAMA: *The dutiful wife and her warrior prince.*

SITA: *But I'd argue she was the more interesting!! Are you here to meet a modern-day Sita, Rama?!!*

RAMA: *On Inderdates? Unlikely :-(Do you really expect to meet a suitable boy here?*

SITA: *I haven't joined to meet someone. All the girls in the office log on to flirt with strangers and then go home to be good daughters!!*

RAMA: *I like talking to people overseas – women and men. A lot are in the same type of work.*

SITA: *A friend of mine at Air India knows a stewardess who met a German man through one of these services. They had a coffee in Munich and three months later married.*

RAMA: *A German? Sometimes, perhaps, it's easier to express yourself with those who live by different rules. But I like our rules. It's very important to me that I perform* dharma *– my moral duties and responsibilities.*

SITA: *And to me!!*

RAMA: *Then perhaps we are both wrong, and we were destined to meet on Inderdates? :-)*

SITA: *Perhaps! Rama, my boss is coming. I'd better go!!*

Chita undid her braid and pulled a brush through the blue-black waves. Her father knocked and came into the room. As always he was filled with wonder at the sight of her. How could he and his wife, both quite plain, have produced such a lovely young woman? On this cool November night, backlit by a full moon at the open window, she was suffused with golden light. His daughter: the beauty, the graduate, the business analyst.

Of course, all fathers have romantic fantasies about their little girls. In Papa's eyes, even a child with buck teeth, crossed eyes and a backside like a giant ham is a veritable princess. But Chita really was a mega-cool babe. At uni, they roped her into the drama society, hoping to put her in a wet sari and upset pulses across the southern hemisphere. But, as is often the way with true romantics, Chita was unaware of her sexuality. She assumed they wanted her to move trees round for the singing scenes. And left before the first production.

As it was, even now the servant boy disappeared into a quiet room every time he glimpsed her through the keyhole in a state of undress. The morning bus conductor had constantly tried to feel her up until she boarded with a fork and stuck it in his hand.

It was, thought her father, time to discuss age, fulfilment and love. Again. 'You know, Chita your mother and I are getting old.'

'Papa, you are both fifty-two.'

'And you are twenty-four, child. It's time you thought of settling down.'

'I am very young by today's standards.'

'Without a life partner, the future is bleak. That is not what I want for my flesh and blood.'

'All this talk of gloom and doom. What will be will be.'

Vigorously she bent her head and shook it so the newly brushed hair doubled in volume.

'We just want what is best for you.'

'I too, Papaji. I want what is best. If that were not true, I would accept the offers that have already been made to this family.'

'The Kerala boy—'

'No.'

8

'He's a doctor. His family—' Sensing her tension, her father paused and then said softly: 'Wouldn't you just see him? There will be no pressure. We have always said it is up to you. But it's foolish to object because he's a gynaecologist. Somebody has to—'

'Ugh.' Then, seeing his face, she relented. 'All right, Papaji, I will see him. But that is all.'

Shyam got the rickshaw driver to drop him by the old palace gates and wandered alone into the empty grounds. In the old days princes had ridden out from here to hunt for tigers through miles of jungle. Now, haphazardly placed towns and shanty villages had osmosed into a filthy, noisy, crowded but energising – almost enchanting – whole.

The gardens, once the talk of the subcontinent, were overgrown, and as he walked he disturbed dozens of fat frogs, who jumped across his path, brushing against his long, bare legs.

No sign now of the liveried retainers with their gold-threaded epaulettes, each charged with the welfare of one of the Maharajah's eighty dogs. None of his many children being chased, squealing, through the courtyards by ayahs.

The building, rejected as a possible flagship in the north-east by the Taj hotel group, was in such a state of disrepair that even the local bandit queen, Rukshana, had given up her base under its crumbling moghul edifice to move to the grounds of the old British consulate. As he walked down to the dilapidated boathouse where, since childhood, he had come to meditate, Shyam again thought how fantastical it all was.

'Chitaji, you are even more lovely than they say.'

Chita tried to smile. The doctor was a good-looking man, clearly cultured and well placed; but the thought of his daily work, examining the private parts of strange ladies, repelled her.

She watched as he popped a juicy gulab jamun into his mouth with a surgeon's manicured fingers. She wasn't naturally squeamish – but there was something strangely unsavoury about it.

On the way to the meeting, Chita had agreed with Papa that she was sometimes unfocused. 'I put everything into my job. I don't have the energy to map my future.'

'Just use some imagination when these suitors come calling, Chita. Don't always take people at face value.'

'When the right man comes, Papa, I will know.'

She knew instinctively that this Adonis with his formal double-cuffed shirt and Hong Kong Armani suit was not for her. He is a stickler for detail. He would never break the Hippocratic oath. I would spend my life at polite parties wondering which of the women had been . . . splayed . . . on his table.

On the way home, she leaned across from the back seat and whispered tenderly in her father's ear: 'Papaji, I've done as you asked. Now, please, let us leave alone. Fate, I am sure, will take her course.'

Shyam sat looking out over the murky water. In the dusk light he could make out the silhouette of old boats abandoned on the opposite bank. One was rocking from side to side with the activity of rats. He pushed his thick hair back with strong, square hands and squinted as the dying red sun flashed suddenly; blindingly.

He pulled a blade of grass and blew against its edge so it whistled. A bird in a nearby tree sang in response. In a few months I will take charge of the estate. What does that mean? It means I can change things: update retrieval methods; restock where we've lost ground; improve the living conditions of estate workers; make the whole operation ecologically sound. There will be plenty to do. The grass made his lips sting. He put it down. I'll get Bobby to check all the books, make sure nothing's gone amiss in the months of probate. Apart from that, does anything need to change?

His left leg had gone numb. Shyam got up and started walking back towards the road. *As the boys marry they'll move into houses on the estate. Our children will play together just as we did. If I marry. Of course I'll marry. We'll move out of Aunty's home and into the big house. My wife can oversee the renovation.*

Back in the throng, he bought himself a cold drink. *If everything is so clear cut why am I still filled with trepidation?*

RAMA: *Hi. Long time no see :-(.*

SITA: *One week only! My cousins from Madurai came to see us. Are you well, Rama? Working hard??*

RAMA: *Too hard . . . We're trying to digitise maps of all the major cities for the emergency services – it will allow them to locate disturbances and attend them more quickly. The technology is all very new. But exciting. It's the twins' birthday tonight. Aunty is putting on a feast for the neighbourhood. No office girls allowed :-).*

SITA: *How dull!! Though better for the girls, I expect, than being pitted against each other like ponies at the gymkhana!! Your brothers sound so sweet, Rama. And the strange monkey that is always playing tricks.*

RAMA: *Sita, why don't we meet?*

SITA: *You don't even know my name!! We are strangers.*

RAMA: *We are Rama and Sita, like the Hindu myth. That in itself is an introduction. We have shared thoughts for three months now :-).*

SITA: *But only thoughts, Rama. Not dreams.*

RAMA: *:-(What are your dreams?*

SITA: *Where do I start? I want to change lives. Including my own!! My job is interesting, but progression is limited. For women,*

even now, much depends on who we marry. What I'd like to
do is find the right man and make a difference together.
RAMA: *Those are my dreams too, Sita. To meet the right woman,*
I mean :-) Let us meet. Please.
SITA: *Perhaps you should phone me? By the way, my name is*
Chita.
RAMA: *Chita . . . It's like a whisper. A kiss. Give me your number,*
Chita, and I will call you tomorrow evening. My name, by the
way, is Shyam . . .

Like a kiss. It was an unexpectedly poetic line. Chita, with
her feminine sensitivity to nuance, read more into it than,
perhaps, was intended. That said, clumsy and untutored in
matters of the heart, Shyam had unwittingly revealed a romantic soul.

In love, the smallest gestures and coincidences knit together
to make a blanket of misadventure that tucks itself around
each successive hero and heroine: Antony and Cleopatra;
Napoleon and Josephine; Edward and Mrs Simpson; Bill and
Hillary.

Rama and Sita fought their demons in a peculiarly mythic
way. For Shyam and Chita, living in modern India and brought
into each other's orbit by the magic of the microchip, things
must necessarily be different. Like lovers the world over,
they visualised the first chapter, and left the book to write
itself.

Mrs Dhoti had the finest tandoor in the town. When she
arrived at Shyam's home with two boys bearing giant dishes
of chicken and lamb, the party really began. The twins,
celebrating twenty-five years of duality, had demanded that
their aunt make vats of their favourite vegetable curries –
okra, brinjal and cauliflower quick-fried with saffron and
mustard seeds. There was pilau rice and plain rice, and plates

of chapatis, rotis and parathas. Mrs Mangheshkar had brought two bottles of her famous onion-and-chilli pickle and, for later, bowls of full-cream rasmalai.

At the party's height there were at least fifty guests demanding food on Noritake china, drink in pewter mugs and constant entertainment.

Poor Aunty! Her CDs of Hindi film soundtracks were stacked on a shelf and replaced with Madonna and Iron Maiden. The young people were openly drunk. She went outside and turned on the coloured lights, strung through trees in the garden. The effect was almost magical until she noticed a boy and girl being over-friendly by the back wall.

Before she could exclaim aloud, Mr Pathak came out to congratulate her on the spread. He wanted to know about a row over miracles at the local temple: 'Are the statues really weeping milk or is it another case of mass hysteria incited by the Bannerjee woman? Everybody knows, Sujata, that she has never been the same since her daughter eloped with that low-caste motorcycle messenger.'

The video-shop girl had given Bobby a copy of *The Poseidon Adventure* and they put it on in the sitting room for the children, who argued noisily through the whole film without once removing their gaze from the screen.

Lucky, who had grown a goatee beard for the occasion, and Shivan, who hadn't, looked on and laughed. They never stopped smiling.

'This family has the finest-looking men in the whole province,' sighed one young woman wistfully.

At that moment Honeybun, the monkey, tweaked her and she spilled Coke on to the bodice of her white dress. Immediately Lucky was at her side, offering a crumpled serviette and a solicitous arm with which he guided her to the bathroom to effect repairs. The monkey winked at their departing backs and ran to Shyam.

The different sounds and smells and light brought the house alive so it seemed to pulsate with activity. Shyam went out on to the verandah, where a guest was sitting on the wall, smoking.

'Ah: Shyam. I love this time of night. Finally the town starts to settle. There is a semblance of peace.'

Shyam nodded. 'And you notice the heavy smell of the flowers. When I was little I loved to bring my bedding and sleep out here.'

'I still do, sometimes. My wife scolds and warns I'll get a chill, but people have slept in the open for thousands of years without meeting any harm. Certainly, I am as fit as a fiddle.'

'That's because you get a good breakfast in the morning and want for nothing. It's not the same for those who have no choice.'

'Perhaps not. Cigarette?'

Shyam shook his head. I wonder if Chita smokes? No. She doesn't. I have a feeling about this woman. She's right to say we're strangers. But when we message each other, our inner terminals connect. Everything she is, is stored in me, unopened. How can that be when I know nothing about her: the colour of her skin, the look in her eyes . . . the cadence of her voice? It is irrational and ridiculous.

And yet, and yet . . .

This time tomorrow I will have spoken with her.

SITA: *Shyam, I'm so glad you're on-line. Papa is having a business colleague to dinner this evening. I'm going to escape with my friend. Can we postpone for 24 hours?*

RAMA: *Of course.*

SITA: *You're not cross?*

RAMA: *How could I be cross with you, Chita? :-)*

SITA: *Did the party go well? Are you hung over? Naughty boy!!*

RAMA: *Last night, lassi and passion fruit juice . . . The party was a great hit. Lucky thinks he is in love :-) I slept on the verandah.*

SITA: *How romantic!! Both Lucky and the verandah. I wish I could sneak on to our verandah. Sometimes, even with the window open, the heat in my room is oppressive. The sound of the fan stops being a soothing hum and becomes a constant buzzing in my subconscious.*

RAMA: *I like the way you say things, Sita. No: Chita . . . To be frank, I have a stiff back today – perhaps it's best to keep some ideas untested . . . :-(*

SITA: *Perhaps!! A better reason for not following instinct in the hills is the huge number of poisonous snakes. Shyam, tomorrow is our busiest day so I probably won't log into Inderdates. We shall speak . . . after seven?!!*

RAMA: *I'm counting the hours, my princess.*

Chita pulled on black slacks and a pale grey sweater as, outside, Manju skidded to a halt at the gate.

Chita's parents were wary of Manju. She was quick witted and outspoken. She was considered fast. They suspected she was a bad influence on their virtuous daughter. But she'd turned down better teaching jobs to care for her widowed mother, a woman who, after years of crying wolf, was finally dying of a degenerative condition.

Tying her hair into a high ponytail, Chita added a smear of conker lipstick: 'All right, all right.' She ran out to where her friend was tooting wildly in her ancient gold Humber. 'What's the hurry? The road is empty!'

'I just like irritating your old man.' Manju grinned as Chita climbed in. 'Hey, those trousers are terrific – very nice curve on the hip, yah? Iced coffees at the Meridien?'

She pulled away with a squeal of tyres and drove into the upper reaches of the landscape where the big hotels commanded the views, the pony trails and the golf courses that brought the rich in search of isolation. Well, relative isolation, because the Indian subcontinent is like a London bus – oversubscribed and under-resourced.

While the uplands may be less built up and populous, you will still find encampments in unlikely places and some old geezer asking for socks or Biros or change. As Manju zigzagged the car through descending mist, Chita said: 'Heaven is probably a little like this.'

Of course there were boys in the bar. And of course Manju couldn't resist looking. 'Is it likely, Manju, that you will meet the right man by chance in an up-country hotel? Stop simpering.'

'Don't be a bore, Chita. I am merely admiring the scenery. I know that boy in the sports jacket – his father works for Tata. And his friend, the one in blue, flunked his exams and was rewarded with a Mercedes-Benz and a year in the States. Typical rich boy.'

'Who cares, Manju – they're just local.'

'It's interesting.'

'Well, tonight I have something more interesting to impart – and not Gucci fakes or new face powder.'

Never have iced coffees tasted so delicious. The hotel crowned the glasses with a soft peak of sugared cream, sprinkled with roasted coffee chippings. Chita caught them on her tongue and savoured the moment. 'I am having an assignation with a man from a chat room.'

'Are you mad?'

'We've been talking with each other for months – just about silly things . . . our day in the office, our families, the things we like doing . . . Don't look at me like that, Manju. We're not actually meeting. He's just going to call.'

'And you tell me off for looking at what's right here in front of us? At least I know what I'm doing. Do you?'

'I'll talk to him, that's all.'

'But it's not all, is it? Honestly, you're Miss Goody-Two-Shoes ninety-five per cent of the time and then you do something crazy.'

They ordered more drinks.

'On the basis that you both chose the names of the mythical lovers, you think you've been drawn to this man by fate?'

'There's something in it, Manju.'

'Rama and Sita? Better to be Romeo and Juliet.'

'We're not Rama and Sita, we're Shyam and Chita. Why can't two ordinary people who also believe in duty and virtue meet on a website?' Chita ignored her friend's grimace. 'Why can't there be resonances? Anything is possible.'

'Get real, Chita. What if he's a psycho killer?'

'Honestly, Manju, it's just a little adventure. It's fun. I'm not a total goose. This is quite harmless. I'm not tempting fate.'

'What do you know of these things? You've never let a man near you. It's all very well saying you're not tempting fate, Chita: but what happens if fate tempts you?'

In the office the next day, Chita got an e-mail from Inderdates telling her there was a letter in her on-line mailbox. Logging on to the site, she found a note from Shyam: 'Chita, I'd forgotten that I have to go out of town to talk some people through a system install. Hopefully I'll be back in time to call you, but you know how the train services can be . . . I thought you should be warned. Don't work too hard. Best wishes, Shyam.'

Best wishes. What does that mean? Chita mused as she went for a walk in the botanical gardens during her lunch break. It's so strangely formal. He can hardly say 'love, Shyam'. I might get the wrong idea . . . but 'best wishes'? Why not 'talk soon' or 'missing you'? Yes, 'missing you'. That would be affectionate without being presumptuous. And yesterday he called me Princess. Best wishes is something you'd write to . . . an acquaintance or perhaps an old lady who's getting a Diwali card!

Sitting down on a bench alongside waxy purple orchids, Chita remonstrated with herself. You know what the men are like on Inderdates. All in IT. The only languages they're comfortable with are Java and HTML. But that's what makes Shyam special. He has . . . an inner passion. An impatience.

Returning to work with a chocolate cornet, Chita laughed at her own intensity. Why can't I let things go? I always have to see a project through. Lighten up, Chita. This is only fun. A game of chance. Nothing more.

All human emotion is a function of chance. That's why even the most jaded women fantasise about love at first sight. Where Chita lived, a first sighting was often all that convention allowed. So the concept was romantic actuality. And, actually, often worked. Or was made to. Her idealism, then, was not entirely misplaced.

'Chita, there is a boy called Shyam on the phone.'

'Thank you, Papa.' She waited until her father removed himself. Her heart was in her mouth. She swallowed before speaking. 'Hello?'

Her voice was husky but clear. Shyam was dumbstruck.

'Hello? Shyam? Are you there?'

'Yes, Chita. I am here.'

In the silence she felt the colour rise to her cheeks. Touching them with the back of her hand, she discovered they were burning. 'You got back without a problem?'

Shyam tried to pull his thoughts together. He was over-whelmed by the strength of his feelings. Her voice had set off a series of unexpected chain reactions, both physical and emotional. He tugged at his hair: this is madness. I'm being utterly stupid. She's probably some toothless old hag playing the fool.

'Yes, I had to stand the whole journey, but I'm home now. Everything happened as it should.' I sound such a bore.

She liked his modulated tone and transatlantic delivery. She understood the meaning of the silences. But she had an urge – a woman's urge – to fill a meaningful silence with . . . meaning.

Slowly she tried to get him to talk. 'Are you calling from home?'

'Yes – I'm on the verandah.' That sounds so stupid.

He's shy! I'll tease him. 'Are you being furtive?'

'I wanted privacy.' Too serious. Help . . .

Chita wanted to giggle. Better not . . . he might misunderstand.

Shyam wanted to punch the air with joy each time he managed not to sound like a starched idiot. 'You know, this house is so full of people, it makes the train seem half empty.'

And so they teetered on, bending this way and that as potential lovers do, umming and ahhing, deliberately misconstruing odd lines in order to provoke debate and keep the conversation moving until one of them could muster the gumption to progress things.

Shyam, being an air sign, was a man more comfortable with ideas and theory than practicality. He'd choke on favourite Western lines like 'Get your coat, love, you've pulled'. So it was Chita who tried to steer a course that would result in . . . a result. 'Has your brother seen the girl from the party?'

'I don't know. I think he plans to call her. Some time.'

'Oh. That doesn't seem very enthusiastic.'

'No. He liked her. I'm sure they'll meet.'

'If he doesn't move quickly, she might think his interest is only lukewarm.' Are you getting the hint?

'For him, it's quick.'

A new line of attack was called for.

'Doesn't Honeybun ever get lonely?'

'There's always someone in the house.'

'But monkeys are like humans. They need a mate.'

'What you don't have, you don't miss.'

'Don't you miss it?' Now I'm spelling it out.

And something in her tone made the penny (or is it the anna?) drop.

'Perhaps we all need a mate.'

'It is nature's way.'

'I should enrol Honeybun in Inderdates . . .' Is she interested?

'Why should Honeybun be any luckier than you?'

'Who is to say I'm not the luckiest man alive?' Short dramatic pause. 'Chita: I am being so stupid. We must meet.'

'How? We're hundreds of miles apart.'

'Do you want to?'

Her dramatic pause. For effect only. 'Yes, I'd like that.'

'Do you think you may feel what I am feeling?'

Chita took the biggest and boldest step of her life. 'Yes,' she said. 'I think I may be feeling the same thing.'

Shyam and his Aunty Sujata spent thirty-six hours travelling to Chita's town. After flying to Mumbai they were driven south for the best part of an afternoon before stopping overnight in a guest-house. The following morning they started the four-hour journey into the hills which would lead them to Chita.

In the previous month, the usual exchanges of information had taken place. The two families were broadly equivalent in status and outlook. Even so, Auntyji had grave reservations about the enterprise. 'Soon you will inherit your father's estate, Shyam. The paperwork is almost complete. You will be a very rich man. How do you know this girl is not chasing your money?'

'Without boring you with detail, Auntyji, the computer matchmaker doesn't operate in the same way as standard agencies.'

'How is that possible? It's the first question asked by any decent matchmaker! You should have told me you were looking. Mrs Das has brought together so many couples over the years. She could have found you a lovely girl from your own district. These hill-country girls can be very parochial, you know.'

The old lady sniffed as the taxi drew up outside a gracious plantation-style house. 'There is a dog sleeping on the swing seat,' she said disdainfully.

'We usually have a monkey in ours, Aunty.'

Chita's father, an elegant man in his fifties, came to greet them. He studied Shyam with approval and then talked about the weather and seasonal flowers as he led them to the huge reception room where Chita's mother was waiting.

Shyam could not make out a single detail in the room. It was as if everything was blurred. He fumbled a hello and left it to his aunt to make conversation. He was rigid with fear. Turning away from the elders, he went to the window, pretending to admire the grounds while wiping a cold sweat from his brow.

Suddenly the hum of conversation stopped. He turned around.

She was there in the doorway, in a green silk sari. The fog slowly started to lift. Blinking, he focused on her face. She smiled.

She smiled, and Shyam felt as if the breath had been smashed out of him.

*　　*　　*

Chita had dressed with care. Normally she wore frocks or slacks, but convention on this day called for the adoption of native costume.

She had last worn the green silk sari to a wedding and had been much admired. It suited her willowy frame; her pale colouring. As she draped it around her, she thought of it as a security blanket.

That afternoon she was so sensitive to every movement that she heard the taxi a full half-minute before it drew up outside. She noted that their dog, Pancho, didn't bark as he usually did at strangers.

As the visitors entered the house, she recognised the rhythm of Shyam's voice, though she couldn't hear the words. He is twenty-six and all I know is his name and occupation. And I am crazy for him. There is a wave of heat coursing through me that I have not felt for any other man. Perhaps I've gone mad.

Only last night Manju had asked: 'What if he looks like a young Moraji Desai?'

'What if he does?' Chita had answered. 'What matters is what's inside.'

Taking one last glance in the mirror, she made her way to the sitting room. Ah well, let's find out. It's now or never.

As she stopped in the doorway, she was suddenly aware of him at the window. Tall, straight backed, with thick hair, wearing a sage linen suit that was too cool for these parts. The elders stopped talking. Slowly he turned around. She looked curiously into his eyes.

She looked curiously into his eyes, and all of time stopped.

Neither of them spoke. They couldn't find the words. Chita's father said: 'I have never seen that child tongue tied.'

'And I have never seen my nephew with red cheeks.'

'Would you like more tea, Sujataji?'

'Is it local? Nothing like fresh tea to whet the palate.'

Watching Chita and Shyam was like witnessing two halves of the ripest fig being placed together to make a perfect whole.

'I wish I was blessed with the powers of augury,' Chita's mother said.

'If it is written in the stars, what will be will be,' Sujata replied.

The boy and girl underscored and enhanced each other's beauty. You can imagine how Chita's mother was projecting! Their sons will be gods, their daughters like queens . . .

Sujata forgot questions surrounding Shyam's inheritance and wondered how quickly this glittering prize could be installed in their home. Once the other boys saw her, the blood would rush to their heads. No normal man could be near this woman and not wish a woman for himself.

I'm getting old, she thought, nearly seventy. I cannot care for them much longer. They need wives to make them into men.

Chita's father said: 'Darling, why don't you show Shyam around the grounds?'

Grounds was the appropriate word because, in that climate and at that altitude, the three acres were stepped and the greenery, bar endless eucalyptus trees, unadorned. Not that Shyam cared as he followed his wife – for he already thought of her that way – to a lookout point from which there wasn't very much to see because the clouds were descending.

It was only here that, finally, they spoke.

'The view is stunning.' Like you.

'It's my favourite place.' Now.

'Will you miss it?' I can't believe I said that!

'We'll come back often, won't we?' Oh my God!

Suddenly he pulled her to him, overcome with a need he could not contain. He covered the top of her head with kisses, holding her so tightly she started to suffocate. She pushed him away, laughing. 'Shyam, let me go. I cannot breathe.'

After that, the conversation came easily, so that Chita's father, seeking them out after two long hours, was led to them by the sound of their voices on the wind.

Suffice to say that a marriage was arranged almost immediately – this was India – and six hundred guests dropped all other arrangements, pulled out their finest suits and jewels, and made their way in a caravan of ancient cars to celebrate a union that was as glorious as it was inevitable.

Shyam's brothers did indeed suffer a rush of blood to the head at the crucial moment when the bride lifts her red-and-gold veil and shows her face to her husband. And Shyam, who had not seen her since the fateful day of their introduction, was again struck dumb, but, thankfully, under the weight and density of the bridegroom's traditional headdress, his confusion could not be seen.

Chita, however, being a woman, was absolutely serene. As she perambulated ritually around the ceremonial podium with her alpha-plus male, she felt more in control than she ever had before.

She was already thinking ahead to their married life.

Sujata had booked them the honeymoon suite at the Oberoi. When the bell-boy left, Chita flopped on to the bed. She was like an angel in her delicate filigree going-away sari. Her hair had come loose from its fastenings and fell in a long, slick coil over her left shoulder. 'Oh, Shyam, hasn't it been the most wonderful day? Did you see my grandparents dancing? They were so happy. And your aunt and brothers are lovely. Sujata took me aside and said I was now the mistress of the household! She is so sweet. I told her I was quite happy to be the daughter. Why are you looking at me like that?' As if she didn't know.

She had felt the intensity all day as he stood beside her dutifully, greeting old retainers and barely remembered acquaintances from lives past. Now, as he looked down at her, her husband's eyes were thick with longing.

Without a word – because the pattern of speechlessness that marks the behaviour of most men in marriage was kicking in – he knelt gently over her pliant body, unwrapping and kissing every inch.

Until that night, Shyam's intimate knowledge of female anatomy had been confined to snaps on Internet sites accessed by chaps in the office. The women were strangely bestial. In addition to his general disapproval, the images left him discomfited as a man. He was astounded, therefore, by the softness of Chita's breasts and belly, the perfect curve of her hips and buttocks, the meaty length of her thighs and the neatness of her ankles. She excited in him a hunger that he knew with absolute clarity would last all his life.

He straddled *his* woman in wonder, running a curious finger across her pudenda, admiring the outline of her flesh against the crisp white sheets. Chita is the greatest gift a man could have been given. I will love and revere her always.

His wife, watching him with a sense of joy, was filled with new needs and sensations she couldn't even have imagined. She ran her hand across his broad, lean chest, and down his back to the small, neat buttocks and the muscular legs, sinewed from the cycle ride to work. He holds me in place with the strength of a rock. This is what I've been reading about all these years. And if this is the first time, and Manju is right, it gets even better.

I am a wife. I am a lover. I have given myself to this man.

Being a stickler for detail, she then self-corrected. No, not given. My body is not a gift. It is mine to use as I wish. I chose to save myself as a statement of intent. It is a political declaration about my values.

She looked up into her husband's amber eyes and, smiling lazily, pulled his face against hers and kissed him with a passion.

And that really should be the end of an apocryphal love story: but it's only the beginning. Because true love and true virtue cannot be validated until they are tested. And while, in standard fiction, life can progress in a series of temperate jump-cuts, it isn't half as simple in myth. Or, indeed, in *real* life.

Three months into their marriage, Chita felt she had never known any other way of living.

She had given up work to relocate and spent her time exploring her new environs. 'Tell me about estate life, Sujataji: size, yields, income, expenditure, expectations and priorities. Where is that information?'

'That is not your province.'

'Auntyji, it's my job. It's what I do. If Shyam is going to take over, he needs me to help set clear objectives and expectations.'

'You are a wife, Chita. That is a big enough job.'

'Doesn't that make me an equal partner at all levels?'

The constant questions made Sujata feel foolish. She realised how ignorant they all were about the business. Perhaps this girl is sent by fate, she thought. She was certainly more animated and ambitious than her refined bearing suggested.

'Aunty, I have asked Mr Ladwa to get me the *Financial Times* and the *International Herald Tribune* every morning, so don't throw them when you find them at the gate.'

Would she give Shyam trouble? When he came home, Shyam had eyes only for her. After the evening meal, the two of them sat on the verandah and talked late into the night. But if Sujata had worried that Chita's monopoly of Shyam would cause a falling out between the boys, she was soon reassured by the humour they extracted from watching the cool and collected Shyam pathetically mooning after his bride.

'He's like a dog howling at the stars,' said Lucky, rolling his eyes.

Bobby peered from the window. 'He's nuzzling her ears.'

Shivan put on a Lata Mangeshkar CD. 'Mood music.'

Sometimes they joined the tête-à-têtes: 'Move over, darling, we're gatecrashing.' They enjoyed Chita's stories about Manju and the people in her old office. 'You know, you're a great girl,' Lucky said. 'It's a shame you can't cook.'

'Your own sweetheart can cook for you, brother-in-law.'

'We are just good friends, as they say in Hollywood.'

Shyam, initially confounded by Chita's ability to grasp and manipulate concepts and ideas, had grown to admire her. And Chita, who had found his diffidence difficult to absorb, soon realised that her husband wasn't uninterested but solitary. Occasionally she slipped to bed early, leaving him to meditate alone.

'Chita sleeps like a log.'

'Because you're wearing her out, bridegroom.'

Later – always – they made love in new and different and tender ways. And they were happy.

On the afternoon that probate was finally resolved, the boys trooped off to the family solicitor to be apprised of their various inheritances and Chita went shopping.

Having strict rules about quality and style, she rarely bought things, but loved the ritual: the looking, the sizing up, the feeling, the bartering. She tried on glittery bangles and Bata slip-ons, took great sniffs of the sandalwood soap and stroked the puppies on the pet stall. She found some terrific red buffalo-hide doctor's bags. Chita checked the stitching and the lining before buying one. She got Shyam's favourite ladu for tea and a magazine for Sujata, a new watch strap for Lucky, shoelaces for Shivan and some TDK C90s for Bobby.

It was hot and Chita felt sticky. Even with her hair up, the sweat was trickling down her back. A couple of hours was enough. Hailing a rickshaw, she headed home, sitting for half an hour in unmoving traffic rather than walk the last half-mile in the glare of the sun.

As she entered the house, Shyam came out into the hall looking grave and worried. She grinned and held out her arms. He shook his head. 'We are only just back, Princess. We need to talk. Would you leave us alone for a while?'

'Sure.'

Out of sorts, she took a shower and was changing into jeans and a clean white T-shirt when a commotion started at the other end of the house. Someone was banging and shouting. Leaving her hair wet and uncombed, Chita ran down the corridor to the sitting room. The door was shut and reverberating as someone kicked it from inside again and again. She heard Shyam call out: 'Lucky! For good-ness' sake. It is Father's will – we have no right to ques-tion it.'

Chita kept knocking on the door until it opened. When it did, Lucky stood blocking the way, his face contorted with anger. Without thinking, she gave him a shove. He hadn't expected it and lost his balance. Chita marched past. 'What the hell is going on?'

'Don't panic, Chitaji.'

'I'm not panicking. I want an explanation for this behav-iour.'

Shyam stretched out his arms in supplication. 'My father . . . I haven't inherited the estate, Princess—'

'He's left it to Bobby.' Lucky virtually spat the words. Chita took a few seconds to compute. 'That's right, sister-in-law: he's left your husband's estate to Bobby.'

'Could somebody tell me why?'

'Because of a promise he made to Bobby's mother.'

Unsure whether Chita understood, Lucky went on: 'Our

mother died days after giving birth to Shivan and me. Our father immediately married a distant cousin. Shyam was sixteen months, we were three. She took us as her own. Bobby was born within the year.'

Chita nodded. When told the story she'd thought it magical – changelings placed with an adoring angel.

'A year ago, we are now told, for reasons which are not clear, she got our father to change his will so Bobby would inherit.'

'Shyam has always talked of her with affection and respect.'

'I still do.' Shyam cleared his throat. 'My father never imagined they would die together. But if Kika had outlived him the promise would still have stood. That's the story.'

'Not the full story!'

Shyam stood up. He walked to his wife and took both her hands. 'There is something more. I am outlawed from this house and this estate for fourteen years.'

'You have to leave this house? Why?'

Now it was Bobby who spoke. 'There is no logic. After the fourteen years we are free to do as we wish. Until then, I am in charge and Shyam must go.' He looked pained. 'I knew nothing about this, Chita. Shyam, I've already said—'

'You can say what you like – the will was explicit. He goes, you stay. You've got it all sewn up, younger brother.'

'Enough, Lucky,' Shivan said. 'It's been a day of shocks for all.'

'And where is Shyam going to go? To hide in the forest?'

'He'll go to England.'

All four men turned to Chita. She was smiling. 'The English are always headhunting our software people. I've seen the advertisements. Shyam will leave for London. And I will go with him. Hiding in the forest wouldn't suit my disposition: I'm too frightened of bears.'

'Chita – this isn't what I promised you. I'm a fraud. You don't have to do any of this. It's my fate, not yours—'

Chita put a finger against Shyam's lips to prevent argument. 'Nonsense, Shyam. We're a unit. I'll get work there too. As shadow to substance, so wife to husband. Fate has dealt the hand; how we play the cards is up to us. We both believe in destiny. This need not be an ending. It is a beginning.'

Part Two

It was one of those dark and drizzly days when a grey pall hangs over the city like the curtain on the final act. Except, of course, this is only the second act.

Rushing round the late-night Sainsbury's, Chita tried to remember whether there were enough dustbin bags and Fairy Liquid for another week. I'm not domestically minded, she thought, joining the basket queue.

Letting herself into the flat, she hung up her wet coat and put away the shopping before going in search of her husband. 'Shyam?' He was lying on the sofa, talking on the phone. He mouthed: 'Hello, Princess.' She blew him a kiss. He caught it. She ran up and changed into jeans. When she came back down Shyam said: 'Lucky's coming.'

'To visit?'

'To stay. Three of Flotech's analysts are coming to London next month. There's a long-term project needing extra hands. Also, of course, the Indian staff cost less, but Lucky says they've negotiated good allowances.'

'Will they get a flat together?'

'I don't know. Anyway, Lucky will live with us.'

'With us? Where will we put him, Shyam?'

'In the boxroom. I'll move the computer on to the kitchen table and work from there. You don't mind, do you, Princess?'

She deliberately misunderstood: 'I suppose the table is big enough.'

Frowning, Chita walked to the window and looked down

35

on to the busy road outside. The two-bedroomed flat was just perfect for the pair of them. It took half of Shyam's monthly wage, which would have paid a year's rent in India, but it was bright, modern and perfectly placed for travel into central London.

The station, the supermarkets and the cinema were five minutes' walk; the park and zoo just fifteen. There were two markets, thousands of people, and beggars and stray dogs fouling every pavement. It felt strangely comfortable.

Within three months of arriving and establishing a home, Chita had got herself an administrative job with a management consultancy in the City. It was like a League of Nations, staffed by every type of European and a handful of experts with Third World ancestry. Initially they'd placed her at junior level, but within weeks her efficiency, and the fact that she turned heads, earned her a more high-profile remit.

In the evenings she and Shyam, already equipped with text-book English, went through a dictionary of idioms together, learning the meaning of stock phrases: suck it and see/it'll be all right on the night/lights on no one at home/hot to trot.

Some nights Chita came home with spreadsheets and print-outs and pored over them while her husband caught up with reading after dinner. Within two years she would be earning as much as Shyam and, ultimately, with bonuses, substantially more. Nonetheless, he insisted, and would continue to insist, on paying for a lifestyle he felt was his fault. Fault! This is the making of us, Chita thought. We could never have had this freedom and space in India.

She wrote to her mother: '*I am living the life I always wanted with a man I never thought I'd be lucky enough to find. How my life has changed in just eighteen months!! I know we could have had a similar life at home. We could have moved to another part of the country and lived off Shyam's estate income, but honestly, Amma, I have never been happier!*

'Instead of growing midriff rolls and being a lady of leisure, instead of being dependent and tied to one place, I'm my own woman. Shyam and I feel Bobby is the loser. He is always e-mailing and apologising. We are so lucky.'

Now, a year into this glorious new life, Lucky was coming to spoil it. And Shyam hadn't even given it a minute's thought. He is so preoccupied it hasn't even occurred to him. How can we curl up on the sofa with his brother in the same room? How can we walk naked after a bath? What will happen if one of us needs privacy? How can we make love noisily; greedily? We've turned our lives around and now everything is about to be turned upside down and this . . . this man hasn't even realised.

'Is something wrong, Chita?'

'I love Lucky too, Shyam, but his presence will disrupt everything we've come to enjoy about living here. What about the girlfriend?'

'He is putting us first. He has always been my closest ally.'

'We're not at war, Shyam. This flat has been our solace. Our retreat. Don't you think your younger brother will disrupt that?'

'It'll be fine, Chita. It's my duty.'

She sighed and left the room. And mine too, clearly.

Waiting in Arrivals, Chita felt restless. 'I'm going to buy a newspaper and a cappuccino. Do you want one?' She stayed at the drinks stand watching Shyam hover anxiously alongside cab-drivers holding collection cards and extended Asian families awaiting friends and relatives from the Delhi flight. Every time I get used to something with this man, it changes. The price of love.

She saw her brother-in-law first. And was filled with guilt. As he emerged from customs she remembered how supportive

he'd been to them both. I'm being mean. Lucky's such fun.
He'll bring laughter into our lives.

Chita watched as the boys, catching sight of each other,
embraced with warmth and pleasure. They have always been
a team. Thank God Shivan has found a woman. And that
Bobby can't leave. More than one and I'll be inserting an
opt-out clause. Smiling to herself, she walked over.

Although more bullish than Shyam in every way, Lucky also
topped six feet and shared his brother's diffident charm. He'd
regrown his goatee beard. It made him appear the elder.

'Yo, Chitaji! I haven't seen you in a short dress before.'

'It doesn't suit me?'

'Oh, no. Quite the opposite. Very nice.' He winked mischie-
vously.

'I'll take your case.'

'That's very . . . English, sister-in-law.'

'Is that good or bad?'

He shrugged. 'Neither good nor bad. Different.'

Both bedrooms were on the attic floor. Lucky's, the smaller,
overlooked a garden of climbing roses and flowering shrubs
belonging to the old woman below.

'We've tried being polite to her, but she doesn't like yuppies.
Particularly brown ones. If you're nice to her, though, she will
say "good morning" and hand the post to you.'

'I shan't. I shall growl at her. I like this colour.'

'I painted it myself. Duck-egg blue.'

'So you're wearing the trousers in this house?'

'Only two hours ago you commented on my dress.'

Showing him her own bedroom, Chita was glad for the row
of mirrored wardrobes that added extra insulation to the party
wall between them.

Four steps down from the top floor was a half-landing with
a bathroom. The suite was white, as were the tiled walls and

floor. 'A room from the madhouse,' Shyam had said. Chita had brightened it with towels in primary colours and bags of shells she'd bought from Boots. An airer for drying hand-washed items stood in the bath.

'I like the lacy undies.'

'It's the only way to dry them.'

'It's a shame we don't share a cup size.' He ducked as she swiped him playfully across the head. 'Only joking.'

'The red towels are yours, Lucky. Toilet rolls and toothpaste and things are stored under the sink. The washing machine and drier are here, in this cupboard. I'll show you how to use them.' Because I'm not doing your washing for you.

Down a further eight steps was the main body of the flat. Entry was into a small hallway with the well-fitted kitchen directly ahead. Although small, there was room for a round dining table, where Shyam was now unpacking ready-made sandwiches, tubs of salad and drinks cartons. 'You know your place, brother?'

'So will you. Soon.' They both laughed

It was the sitting room, however, with the elegant floor-to-ceiling windows and Juliet balconies that distinguish Camden's flat-fronted houses, which had sold the place to Chita. Even though the rent was exorbitant by their standards, it felt right. The south-facing room, sunlit all day every day, augured well.

Lucky wolfed down the food. 'Auntyji sends her love. I have presents in my luggage. She is always on meditative retreats these days. Bobby has lost weight and hates running the place. He counts the days to your return.'

'That's a lot of numbers,' Chita said sweetly.

'Even Honeybun has lost heart, sitting in corners chattering alone like one of those old women selling incense at the temple gate.'

'And Shivan?'

'Shivan spends all his time at Kusum's. He's crazy about her, but her family says she must finish her further studies before settling. I think it's a delaying tactic. They hope she'll grow out of him.'

'And no one for you? Perhaps you'll meet someone special here.'

Lucky shook his head. 'I left one behind, because I want to be with my brother during his exile. And it naturally follows, Chita, to be with you.' He got up and bowed tiredly. 'Time for bed. Isn't that what they say?'

The next day was Sunday. Chita woke up and tensed, listening intently for sounds of life, but Lucky was still asleep. He remained that way as she and Shyam warmed croissants in the microwave and layered butter on butter. 'Should we have got rotis or something for Lucky?' Chita asked.

'When in Rome . . . Don't fret, Chita. He'll find his own way.'

Reheating the coffee, Chita felt a rush of warmth towards her husband. He has read my anxiety! 'We are one,' she said aloud.

'One what?' Shyam wiped his mouth. 'I'll get the papers.'

The flat had come fully furnished and most of the furniture was blandly nondescript. But both loved the old leather chesterfield in the sitting room and took position at either end with the broadsheet supplements and the *News of the World*. Shyam worked his way through international news, the technology sections, sport and reviews. Chita devoured lifestyle features, the horoscopes, travel and business pull-outs.

In the afternoon, they had a shared ritual of putting aside an hour or two to write to her parents, to Sujata, to the brothers, to Manju and others with whom they maintained contact. After that they played gin rummy or Scrabble and went out to one of the many nearby restaurants for dinner.

Today, of course, that was not to be.

When Lucky finally came down, it was lunch-time. 'Croissants? Delicious. Is there any Coke? I need a buzz.' Afterwards
they pulled on sweaters against the chill spring air and walked
past Sainsbury's and round the corner to Camden Market.
'These people look like the weirdos you find at Pondicherry.'

He exclaimed at everything: 'Why a candle shaped like a
penis? Do they really buy these things? And then just burn
them and throw? My God – these tie-dye T-shirts! Pink and
purple . . . such rubbish. Look at these moccasins – they
must have cost two rupees to make. How much? Fifteen
pounds! What is the point of the wind chime, Chitaji? A
lucky crystal? How do they know? And this plate. People
buy chipped china? Chi!'

They walked the canal towpath past the zoo and on to
Little Venice. 'This canal goes up into the heart of the
country, Little Brother.'

'Have you followed it?'

'We've been out of London only once. Perhaps we'll make
more trips now you're here.'

At Warwick Avenue they caught the bus past Lord's and
back along Albert Road, where the Snowdon aviary, its netted
peaks like a series of Toblerones in the tangerine light of the
sinking sun, caught Lucky's attention. 'It's the zoo again. Can
we go in?'

'Aren't you too old for the zoo, Lucky?'

'I suddenly thought of Honeybun.'

Chita squeezed her husband's hand. The monkey had an
immovable place in the brothers' hearts. Often Shyam regaled
her with stories of its cleverness or naughtiness or humour,
and tears filled his eyes. 'He's one of us.'

She rested her head on Shyam's shoulder. God, I love this
man. In many ways we are so different. I'm warm; he's cool.
I'm impetuous; he plans. I'm tactile; he's contained. But when

41

he feels, he feels to the core of his being. He is my soul mate; my other self. No wonder we were drawn together.

Lucky stayed out of their way for the next week. Each day he set himself a series of tasks, not returning until they were completed. He travelled to the ends of every Tube line, memorising names and marking key stops: Paddington, Baker Street, Waterloo; Marble Arch, Piccadilly Circus, Westminster; Chancery Lane, Bank, London Bridge.

Unwilling to take Shyam's word for it, he timed the journey to and from his new office in readiness for starting work the following Monday. He visited the main sites – Buckingham Palace, the Houses of Parliament, Tower Bridge – and quickly picked up the geography of central London. At the end of seven days, he was confident and, most importantly from Chita's point of view, independent.

Indeed, within seventy-two hours she started to appreciate that Lucky's presence worked in everyone's favour.

Shyam had, and always would, do anything she asked. But she had to ask: because much of the time he was pre-occupied, his mind racing through ideas and probabilities to which she was not offered access. She had to tease and cajole him into sharing confidences – not because he was secretive but because he felt it inappropriate. Detached like this, he was often impervious to the little things that irritated her. And, it must be said, the little things that thrilled her.

With Lucky's arrival, a window somewhere inside Shyam opened. His brother, more hot headed and confrontational, pushed him into corners and delighted in making him talk his way out: 'You can't just say that, bro' – you have to prove it. Ha! See, Chita, the secret is to not let him get away with it. Don't let him pull rank.' Lucky got up and swaggered across the room. 'Isn't that so, o Righteous One?'

It's going to be all right, Chita thought as she and Shyam made love that night. In fact, everything's just wonderful.

Within weeks they had settled into new routines. Lucky's Indian bearing could have worked against him in such a politely xenophobic city. Instead it made his strong opinions and tendency to play practical jokes all the more attractive.

Unlike Shyam, whose professionalism earned respect, Lucky's work was secondary to his personality. He earned friends. Soon he was out two or three nights a week. Chita didn't ask where he went or what he did, but it was clear he was in a mixed group that enjoyed eating, drinking, playing snooker and nights at comedy clubs.

'You know, these girls here are so fast. Yesterday one asked me if I'd like to go home with her. For once I was stuck for words.'

'Yes is a very short and simple word, Lucky.'

'I was tempted, sister-in-law, but I had a hole in my sock. I don't want people thinking I'm a beggar. Would you darn it for me?'

'I'd be too tempted to stick the needle in *you*.'

'Perhaps you're having too much fun, Lucky?'

'Is that possible, bro'?'

Shyam, catching his wife's eye, smiled and winked. She smiled back and wondered whether he realised quite how . . . progressive the girls were in England. Even the Asian women in her office talked openly of relationships they'd enjoyed. Or endured.

Her favourite was Ambreen, who often invited her out: 'You'll have such a laugh, Chita. We can go to Wheelers or to Maxims or L'Ecu de France. It's all respectable.'

'My place is at home.'

'How can you hold down such a high-powered job and then

go home to act the little woman? What sort of a life is that? You're a total contradiction.'

'Nonsense. I'm loyal. Both to my job and my man.'

'It's hardly disloyal to have dinner with your friends.'

'But I'd be changing the rules.'

'You know, Chita,' Ambreen said, 'you say you're a traditional woman because you do everything with your husband and his brother. But if you were home you'd be on a constant merry-go-round of friends and relatives. What you're actually doing is cutting yourself off. You're not being Indian at all. You're being un-Indian.'

Am I un-Indian? Chita finished the washing up and joined the boys in the sitting room. She picked up the listings guide and circled possible movies for that evening. With Shyam insisting on paying the bills, her income was entirely disposable. She enjoyed using it for outings and presents and dinners and treats. She turned to the style section, wondering again whether to splash out on a Mulberry handbag.

Shyam didn't understand. 'It's a bag. Just something to keep your tissues in. It's a crime to spend two hundred pounds on that.'

'But month after month my wages are just accumulating.'

'Does that mean you have to spend every cent?'

Not wishing to cross her husband, Chita put away thoughts of the handbag for the time being.

Suddenly they all went into overdrive. The project on which Shyam was working was pulled forward on the same day one of the other team leaders resigned on health grounds. Everyone was asked to do extra hours in a desperate bid to meet deadlines. 'I'm sorry, Princess, there will be some nights I come home and go straight to bed. I'm effectively doing two jobs till they find a replacement.'

Lucky, having spent months putting together the framework

for the new software, was told that they'd changed the brief. 'It's like they built a building in Ealing and then moved to Tooting,' he said, pretending to pull out his hair with frustration.

Chita was put on a team modelling new point-of-sale systems for a supermarket giant. This required two or three days a week out of London, staying in Copthorne and Moathouse hotels across the south of England, sitting at her laptop till the early hours to stay ahead of the game. 'We're all in the same boat,' she said, philosophically.

'So we sink or swim together?'

'Those may be your options, Brother-in-Law. I'm cruising.'

'I like a firm hand on the tiller.'

'It may not be so firm after the wrists have been slapped.'

After four or five weeks the charm began to fade. Chita got bored with evenings alone in Brighton and Eastbourne and Bath. She played a bit in chat rooms – Hindi movies, style and leisure, a few games of Tetrus – but she was lonely. I miss the boys. I want to go home.

Lucky usually worked late and ate pizza at his desk, leaving Chita and Shyam alone. They balanced plates of ready-made meals on their laps while watching *Newsnight* and went to bed having exchanged no more than a few sentences.

The weekends became more a time for rest than discovery. Sometimes on a Sunday, despite Lucky's enthusiasm for Hampstead pubs, canal walks and art galleries, she and Shyam didn't leave the flat at all. 'You go, Lucky. You don't need us to hold your hand.'

'I don't need *your* hand, big brother. I'm offering mine. Don't be old before your time.'

One weekend, Chita dragged Shyam to a West End hair salon. His hair was so long the thick waves were turning into long, tight curls. 'You're looking like Shirley Temple. I'll have to buy you a frock.'

The teenage shampooists, who'd thought, in their limited way, that the only good-looking Asians were those sprinkled with stardust – Shashi Kapoor, Imran Khan, Mark Ramprakash, Biddu – were in a state of giggling delirium around him.

Chita, meanwhile, was having her waist-length hair, normally worn in a braid or prim coil, lopped off.

The young man with a thick Northern accent had suggested 'getting rid of the weight'. She'd misunderstood, thinking he was referring to her late appointment. When she looked up from *Vogue* five minutes later, the hair on her right side had been blunt-cut to her shoulders.

'Oh my God!'

'What's the matter?'

'I look . . . very different.'

'You look very . . . beautiful.'

Lucky was on his way out when they came in. 'Yo, guys! You look like Rekha and Amitabh Bhachan, only twenty times better. Can they do the same for me?'

'Do you have a date tonight?'

'I have a multiple date, bro'. But as ever, not one of the girls is as lovely as your wife. Or indeed, if I were that way inclined, as you.' He grinned as Chita rolled her eyes. 'Have a good evening, folks.'

Chita attended her first board meeting. She'd noticed some glaring inefficiencies in her travels around the country and drawn up a damning report. 'I think you'd better make the presentation,' her immediate boss, Monica, said. 'Your recall is much faster than mine.'

Chita wore a sleeveless violet dress with matching box jacket, her newly bobbed hair tucked behind her ears with little diamante clips. The whole was set off with her latest favourite, a matt cerise lipstick. As she entered the room there was a frisson among the men. Her heart sank. They know it's bad news. Such innocence!

Her presentation didn't ignite the place. Staff examining other procedures within the supermarket group had already started the litany of misadventure. One also needs exceptional oratorial skills to make restocking practice and the movement of supplies sound anything more than tedious. But they liked Chita's attention to the small print. She was thorough. Well she would be, as an earth sign. Detail is second nature. Hence the brown Mulberry handbag leaning against her chair.

They liked the way she spoke – husky and exotic, a bit like Benazir Bhutto, although, of course, she was from the other side of both the geographical and religious divide. Most of all they liked the way she looked: intelligent grope-on-a-rope.

Over lunch Monica held the post-mortem. Ambreen came and sat with them. 'Did it go well?'

'Chita was a star. Spelled it out in words of one syllable. Lots of jobs on the line, unfortunately. They're ridiculously overstaffed.'

'So you're a star sacker of men, Chita?'

'Thankfully, Ambreen, most of the staff are part time and others are close to retiring age. We'll shift them gently. Business is business.' Chita got up. 'I'm going in search of chocolate. Any orders?'

Chita, as you will have noticed, was always practical. She'd decided what sort of a man she needed, and found him by most unorthodox means. She'd come up with the plan to emigrate, researching work possibilities and visa restrictions thoroughly enough to guarantee trouble-free passage from one lifestyle to another. She'd chosen the expensive Camden flat against her husband's better judgment, and its centrality and convenience had considerably eased their integration into English society. She'd accepted Lucky's presence rather than fight it, and the result was they were even happier than before. Now, in a lively work environment, she was extending that instinctive gift for strategy and organisation to others. Unwittingly, she was bringing doubters to heel. She was operationally efficient.

Shyam, meanwhile, was also effecting change in a more passive, below-the-line way. He never joined his posse for drinks unless it was a leaving do, but when, after a few months, he realised that the British like camaraderie to be tangible, he'd found a way around it. Their regular Monday lunch became a two-hour fixture they all valued. The odd sickie brought on by stress soon became a thing of the past. The meal and conversation set them up for the week.

Indeed, it was only as they neared the end of their project – a whole new system for collating GP records – that his team realised his value. There had been no arguments, no misunderstandings, no ritual humiliation. This strangely silent Indian man with the startling eyes had led them from A to Z without rancour or cock-ups.

'This has been a much happier office since you came here,' one of the bosses told Shyam after yet another set of tasks was finished ahead of expectation. 'You instill an extraordinary calm in everyone.'

Dear Amma, Shyam has nearly finished his project, often staying in the office till eight or nine at night . . . The good news is that his boss has insisted he take three weeks' holiday when it's over! From me, also, good news. My report to the board has been taken up and Monica says she's going to find me something a little more interesting. I treated myself to an Asprey's purse, and Shyam to one of their credit card wallets.

*I know: I must stop spending!! But why not? You're only
young once!! Did you get the Hermès scarf? Anyway, there's
a huge new contract coming up and Shyam will be leading a
team of twenty so they're keen that he doesn't take a break
for at least six months. As you know, trying to get Shyam to
take a break is like . . . getting Papa to take a break! In the
last two years we have enjoyed just one week in Cornwall
and ten days in Scotland.*

*But . . . here's the really good news!! We thought, even
though it's such a short time, that we would come over and
spend those weeks with you and Papa. Would it be all right if
we also asked Sujata Aunty to join us as Shyam is not allowed
near the family home under the terms of his father's will? I
know the answer to all of this will be yes and can't wait to
see you!! As soon as I have some details, I'll telegraph you
or e-mail Manju and get her to ring you as we never seem
to have any luck getting through on the phone. Your loving
daughter, Chita.*

Monica called Chita to her office. 'As promised: no more
supermarkets. Kingswood Pyms want to acquire a leather
warehouse in the East End. Very small – about a hundred
and fifty staff, turnover around two million. They think they
could double that. When you return, take Ambreen and Mark
and give me lock, stock and barrel on the place.'

'Am I in charge? Oh, Monica, that's great!'

'I like your style, Chita.'

'I learn from you. Though I'm feeling increasingly guilty
about the downsizing and redundancies that go with most of
the work.'

'Have you thought about specialising? Perhaps change
management? You've a wonderfully compartmentalised mind,
Chita. Instead of recommending losses you could be devising
the strategies that cause least pain.'

'I'll think about it.'

'You're only twenty-seven. There's plenty of time.'

Even as they got off the plane, Chita was aware that exile had changed her. The heat, the people and the smells were so familiar, but she was not of them. She held on to her husband's arm for confidence as they cleared passport control and went into the baggage hall. 'Is it just me, Shyam, or do you also feel somehow removed from everything?'

He smiled and sqeezed her hand against his side. 'We have been removed, Chita. It will be like this every time we return: a little fear, a little foreboding. Everything here is fixed, but you and I have been sent wandering like nomads. We are unsettled.'

'Yes. A rock was thrown into the depths of our happiness and splashed us on to the opposite bank. We have changed by default.'

'Can we put profound thoughts away for a few days, Princess?'

'Because only you are allowed them?'

'Because I want to enjoy myself. Don't you?'

'I'm always enjoying myself these days.' Since we married, I've never been happier, Chita thought. Shyam is the one whose expectations have been dashed. He is the one who has been let down. Yet never once have I heard him complain. Never once.

It was only when she saw her parents waiting at the barriers that she relaxed. But instead of re-enacting the joyous scene she'd played out in her mind time and again, Chita collapsed, weeping like a baby in her mother's arms. 'Oh, Amma, I've missed you so much. I'm so happy to be with you again! Take me home.'

They took a taxi to the Mumbai Taj and she had her first iced coffee since her hen night with Manju, three days before the wedding. It was like infusing the past through an intravenous drip. When they emerged in the noonday sun to find their driver and start the long journey home, Chita felt as strangely Indian as she'd felt strangely English just four hours before.

She woke up next to her husband in the large bed that had been hers since childhood. A gecko was running up the newly whitewashed walls. She smiled to herself and, rolling over, ran a finger the length of Shyam's spine and into the small of his back. He didn't stir. *And he says I sleep like a log. How lovely to see him at peace.*

She rested her cheek against his arm and listened to the sounds outside. The verandah was being swept, and someone farther down the street was shouting. Familiar early morning sounds that had been replaced in her consciousness by the squelch of London traffic on wet mornings and low-flying aircraft going west to Heathrow.

It must have rained in the night. There's eucalyptus heavy in the air. Mmmm, that cleansing uplands smell. Papa will be leaving for work at any minute. Amma will be waiting for us.

She stretched lazily and rolled back to watch the little lizard which had come to a halt by the window. She heard her father's footsteps on the gravel outside and the car drawing up in the street. Closing her eyes, she let it all wash over her.

When she opened them again, two hours had passed and her husband had pulled down the straps of her nightie to kiss her flawless wheatish shoulders.

Sujata arrived two days later. 'Auntyji!'

'Hello, daughter. You look well.'

And you don't. 'Was it a hard journey?'

'No. I set out ten days ago and met a number of social obligations on the way. Ah. Shyam!' The old lady put out her arms and her nephew virtually lifted her off the ground. 'My greatest sadness, my son – for that is what you are to me – is that I will die before you return to your rightful home.' She mopped her brow with the dupatta of her sari, and sat down. 'Bobby is unhappy on the estate. Of the four boys, he was always the free spirit. As the youngest, we all indulged him. Now he is made prisoner by his mother's greed and his father's foolishness.'

A little ball of spittle gathered in the corner of her mouth and the dupatta was re-employed. 'Lucky has left his girl and come to you. Shivan is obsessed with Kusum. They marry later this year. A small affair only because her brother has just been killed on the Kashmiri border.' She shook her head. 'Nothing has happened as I expected.'

The next night, Manju came. 'Wow – dig the hair, penpal. How nice to see you in the flesh.' Hugging her friend to her, Chita was overcome by the familiar smell of her perfume: Dune, Christian Dior. I would recognise this smell anywhere in the world . . . 'I've lived for your e-mails, my dear.'

'What nonsense, Manju. All you write about is your social life.'

'It fills the emptiness. Can't you find me a man?'

'One of Shyam's brothers?'

'Heavens, no. One with some life in him.'

'They're brimming with life, Manju.'

'And duty, Chita. I want love and lust, not elderly relations, temple visits and curry for breakfast.'

'Goose.'

'Moose.'

'I've missed you so much, Manju. Let's walk.'

In the garden Chita said: 'Come to England. There's a desperate teacher shortage. You'd love it. The Asian women I work with are just amazing. Totally free. They do what they like – they have flats and boyfriends and go out dressed in virtually nothing.'

'Do you?'

'Only in the bedroom!'

'And is it good?' She smiled as her friend blushed. '*That* good, huh? But how would you know, anyway, Miss Armour-plated Knickers? No: don't answer that. I'll get jealous. I miss you, Chita.'

'Come.'

'And my mother? We really are near the end now.'

'After your mother.'

They sat in silence, listening to night sounds under a harvest moon.

Chita watched Manju in profile, drawing on a cigarette like Marlene Dietrich: ravishing but so alone. The woman who led us all with a battle cry, trapped now like a rare butterfly in a jar. What right do I, someone who has always played by the rules, have to tell my dearest friend to leave her home and obligations and start again? For the second time since her arrival, she found herself crying uncontrollably.

Manju turned. 'What is it, Chita? What's set you off?'

Chita shook her head. 'I don't know. I really don't know. All of a sudden all the people and the values I hold most dear seemed so . . .'

'So bloody sad?'

The next day the strangest thing happened. It was Saturday and Papa was home. The five of them went for lunch at the Meridien. On the way back they stopped to visit her grandparents. Tea had just been served when Uday, the servant boy from Chita's house, arrived in the front garden saying he had a message for Shyam.

After several minutes Shyam had not returned. Chita peered out of the window. She thought she saw her husband sprinting into the middle distance, but the boy was sitting calmly on the front step, so she guessed Shyam couldn't be far. Perhaps getting the lad a drink. I hope the office hasn't called. He promised not to give our number.

She had another cup of tea. Still Shyam didn't return. While not wishing to seem anxious, Chita was out of sorts that her husband hadn't come in to explain what was happening. Again she went to the window. The boy was still there. 'I'm just going to check on Shyam,' she said. Outside, she shook the teenager by the shoulder. 'Where is the young master, Uday?'

'He's gone back to the house, madam.'

'To my parents' house? For what?'

'There is a man there, madam. With a monkey.'

Chita wondered whether he'd gone mad. She gave him a shove. 'Isn't it your job to keep our house secure? For all you know you've led my husband to a madman! Hurry back now!'

In a state of agitation she returned to the sitting room. Her father said: 'What is it, child?'

'Papa, Uday says Shyam has gone back to the house. He has left some strange man there. With a monkey.'

'A monkey?'

Suddenly Aunt Sujata laughed out loud. 'With a monkey? That's no strange man. It can only be Bobby.'

The two brothers circled each other with wonder. It seemed to Shyam that Bobby's new responsibilities had given his brother a maturity never previously possessed. His luminescence was dimmed by worry, but as we grow in years and experience the outer glow becomes an inner light. During his brother's absence Bobby, babied all his life, had completed the transition and become a man.

In turn, Bobby admired the change in his older brother – who wasn't, of course, that much older. Shyam, conversely, had put on a little weight – a thirty-two-inch waist – which made him less angular; softer. A softness Bobby saw reflected in his brother's demeanour. He was more relaxed, more at ease with himself.

Running between them, around their feet and then jumping on to Shyam's shoulder with bewildered joy, was Honeybun. Shyam hugged and kissed them both in equal measure. 'I am lost for words, Bobby. I cannot express my joy at seeing you. I think every time I enter this house I am destined to be tongue tied. It is an auspicious place.'

'I love you, brother. It isn't right that I'm running the estate. It should be yours. It *is* yours.' He opened his arms. 'Please come back, Shyam. I have done my part, you have done yours—'

Shyam moved across and kneaded his brother's hunched shoulders. 'You know, Bobby, we can never take anything in life for granted. Even the stars are constantly moving, albeit infinitesimally. Our father's wish remains our command. In another twelve years, I will come home. Until then, we are bound by blood to meet his wishes.'

They sat in silence for a while. Time had changed things. Bobby was no longer raging and embarrassed by his unwanted elevation; Shyam no longer righteous and controlled about his social humiliation. In that unlit room with the cicadas singing wildly outside, the men reached a tacit understanding. A line was drawn under the subject and both sides withdrew with their love, honour and decency intact.

Chita was woken by Honeybun nuzzling her ear. She rubbed her soft cheek against his warm fur and, reaching out, pulled him into her arms and held him like a baby.

The previous night, while Sujata, Bobby and Shyam rejoiced together in new-found unity, she had gone with her mother to the sewing room, where a bed was hurriedly being prepared for the new guest. They'd gossiped and giggled over disputes between neighbours and Uday's eccentric grandmother, who'd started hallucinating after getting a betel nut stuck in her left nostril.

It was in the middle of a story about a local woman and her eight children that Amma had suddenly asked: 'Chitaji, is everything normal between you and Shyam?'

'Normal? What do you mean? Oh, you mean *normal*. Yes, all is very normal, Amma! But I'm on the pill. What is the point of starting a family if you know you're going to uproot again?'

'A husband and wife come together to have children.'

'There is no hurry. Shyam and I have our lives ahead of us.'

'The chances diminish as you age.'

'It will happen one day. I am surrounded by older women who are only just starting to think about it.'

'It is different in the West.'

'And that is where I am.'

Bobby and Sujata left two days later. The last time they'd parted, there had been a cold logic to it. This time, it was just pure pain. 'It's a good emotion,' said Shyam. 'It shows that all our routers have been re-established.'

They themselves had only four days left at their hilltop idyll before heading for home. They used that time to go pony-trekking in the forests and on long walks through the botanical gardens, where Chita had once spent happy hours eating sandwiches, watching the world go by, and working through the various permutations for her unmapped future.

'What would have happened if we'd never joined Inderdates?'

'I would be a dull man living a lonely life in exile.'

'You'd have met someone else. Some cute little chick from Udaipur or Ootacamund. A honey with money parading with her poodles on Juhu Beach. An architect, perhaps, from Agra.'

'Don't play games. I was destined to meet *you*, Chita. If it hadn't happened I believe I would have died alone.'

Lucky met them at Heathrow. 'You two have caught the sun. Guess what? I've bought a car. Come see.' It was a smart six-year-old executive toy. 'It's a horny beast, isn't it? Yo! It charges like a stallion. I have to watch the speed cameras. No duty-frees?'

He was surprisingly confident in his new machine. A charm to ward off the evil eye hung from the mirror. The back seat was strewn with copies of *Autocar*, *Men's Health* and *Loot*.

To accommodate their cases, he moved a sports bag from the boot. 'Oh yes, I've joined the local gym. You should come, Shyam. I've already improved my pecs. Not specs, Chita, pecs!' He tensed his arm like Charles Atlas. 'It brings out the warrior in me.'

The new sound system blasted Hindi film songs at ten decibels for forty-five minutes. 'You know,' Chita said, 'we've been hearing nothing but this stuff for the past three weeks.'

'Then sing along,' he said, turning the volume up even higher.

In the back seat she switched off mentally, aware that the boys had slipped into work talk. She watched the outskirts of London slip by in a haze of grimy terraces. Just a few days ago we were riding in a beautiful wilderness – now we're back in the urban jungle. She perked up as they came into the centre and she could recognise the landmarks. It's good to be . . . home.

It wasn't long before Lucky skidded into Camden Road and started to circle in a search for parking. Saturday; market day.

This is one way of curing jet-lag, Chita thought, as they

finally found a space and got out with their cases to walk the half-mile back to the flat.

The place looked as if a bomb had hit it. 'Oh, hell. I know that look. Honestly, Chitaji, I really tried but I never realised how much work you do without us noticing. And I'm sorry for all the washing in the bathroom. I fell behind. I'll iron the shirts on your bed right now.'

She walked into and out of the kitchen.

'I'll empty the bin later.'

'And the washing up?'

'Oh, yes.'

In the sitting room, he'd made an attempt to tidy. Chita bit back her impulse to plump and straighten the sagging cushions, move back the armchair, untangle the skewed fringes on the rug and pick up the newspapers. There were four coffee cups on the coffee table, one of which was growing mould. Even Shyam could not mistake his wife's body language at this point. 'Lucky, you've done nothing. It isn't fair that Chita should have to tidy all of this.'

'Who said I'm going to tidy *any* of this?'

'That is what I said, Princess.'

'No, Shyam, what you said was that I shouldn't tidy all of it. But I will not tidy any of it. You and I have just had three weeks' rest. I haven't come home to put on an apron and get out the duster.' Before either could speak – she walked to the door. 'I think, "little brother", you'd better get one of your copies of *Loot* and find us a cleaner.'

On the train the following Monday, Chita gave up trying to read the *Guardian* and made the decision to specialise in change management.

Shyam decided to join the gym: 'Just one hour three times a week.'

'For what?'

'You have a different metabolism, Princess. You're naturally slim. I've seen you jog in three-inch heels. I am a typical Indian man. I'm unfit; thickening round the middle. Everyone at home remarked on it. I never move from my desk.'

He sighed. 'You know, when I was a boy there were always games to play, adventures to be had. The four of us were so close in age, we went out in the morning with a picnic and didn't return till nightfall. Our mother, Bobby's mother, would always scold, but next day we did it again. We were so active.'

Chita rolled over on to her side, ready for sleep. 'Typical boys.'

'We never stopped. We had an airgun. Shivan would swing apples on pieces of string and I would hit them. Every time. Now the best I can do is throw things into bins from a ten-yard distance.'

He turned and held her in his arms: spoons. 'If I start regular exercising, perhaps I can get back some of the vigour. I don't want to be your fat and cumbersome husband.' She laughed, half asleep. 'Chita – you don't regret marrying me, do you?'

'Why should I?'

'I don't know. You're so beautiful and I'm so . . . I don't have the energy for making love to you every night. Lucky says I'm becoming dull. All I do is think and talk work.'

'Have you looked in the mirror recently, Shyam? I'm amazed all the women in the office don't throw themselves at you. You're never dull. You're serious. You always have been. I love you that way. But *I* was more fun. Now I'm overworked and complaining. Monica calls it growing up, but I wonder you don't tire of *me*.'

He kissed her neck. 'I could never tire of you, Princess.'

Part Three

Chita let herself in and immediately opened all the windows. It was a stiflingly hot August day and the loft, with its two walls of continuous glass, was like a pressure cooker ready to blow.

She got a Diet Coke and caught the headlines on *Channel Four News* before throwing off her clothes and going for a cold shower. This is worse than home, and it was bloody hot there during our last visit.

Twelve years away from India and my body can no longer stand the heat. I am otherwise acclimatised.

Have we got beers? Yes. Music . . . An old favourite, Michael Nyman, *The Piano*. The intensity of it gets me even now. Checking the next day's schedule on her personal organiser, Chita dispatched a couple of e-mails and sank into the sofa. Against the far horizon was the dome of St Paul's and the ugly silhouette of the NatWest Tower.

Five years after relocating to Docklands, and a flat they'd bought with accumulated savings and a large mortgage, Chita still found the emptiness of the landscape strangely moving. She missed the hustle and bustle of inner-city life, but they were as centrally placed here as in Camden. It just *felt* like the middle of nowhere.

She heard the key in the lock and Lucky's silly, familiar line: 'Hello, honey, your boys are home.'

'Ah, the team leader, and my husband the programme director. Have you had a busy day, darling and darling?'

'A very slow day. One proposition only.'

'Proposition or preposition? I hope the same is not true of you, husband?'

Shyam laughed. 'Thankfully not. I wiped a few million off the share prices with a single blip but the problem was corrected before the investors noticed. Panic over.'

'What's for dinner, honey?'

'Chicken. And I've left the veg for you to do, Lucky.' The giant living space in which they stood took up half the top floor of the old spice warehouse. Sometimes, Chita was sure, despite all the timbers being replaced and the walls restructured, she could smell nutmeg and cinnamon. It was strangely reassuring.

'Is there a beer?' Shyam, a little greying at the temples now, took off his jacket. He looked like a demigod with his contoured shoulders and slim waist. 'Trying to merge ten dot-com companies into one gives me a dry throat.'

'Don't boast.'

He let his hair grow these days: too busy for a cut, and Chita liked its youthfulness. The blue shirt she'd got him in the Harrods sale reflected his brightness so that he was almost dazzling. He looks edible.

Lucky, clean shaven now, was getting jowly. He was like a cross between Omar Sharif and a footballer: suave but solid, cheeky but sleek. He still refused to wear suits, preferring instead the Indian style of a blazer. He'd left his measurements with a tailor in Lucknow who made and sent to order.

The woman at whom they looked was mid-thirties and quite remarkable. Chita had lost her coltish lines. Her bust had increased – dropped, she would have said – and her hips were more rounded. Her hair flicked up on her shoulders. She wasn't so much sexy as sensual – like a slice of cake layered with cream and chocolate and cherries dipped in Cointreau. There was an ooze from her that made you want to taste whether she was real.

She could still excite her husband with one sideways look. Indeed, she could still unintentionally excite quite a lot of men that way.

Which would prove unfortunate.

That autumn, Manju flew over from Michigan. 'I come empty handed. What can you offer the woman who has everything?'

'Offer yourself, Goose, that's enough.'

'How was Norway?'

'Cold. I was there just two days: most of it in an office where the staff were in a state of total panic. It's so dark there, no wonder Scandinavians are so sombre.'

'The Vikings weren't sombre – all that rape and pillage. I hope you didn't push the longboat out? Or indeed the long anything?'

'I read that size didn't matter.'

'You're still at the theory stage, clearly.'

Chita took Manju's case and slipped her arm through hers. 'I feel like I haven't seen you in years.'

'You haven't.'

'Only four. That's nothing when you're at different ends of the world. Tell me about your new life. Have you got photographs of the school and the end of term concert?'

'Let me breathe first. Did you get the week off?'

'Yes. There's trouble afoot, but nothing I can do about it.'

They explored every inch of London, though Manju retained only snapshots because they talked so much.

'No boyfriends at all?'

'None that count. Ships that pass in the night.'

'Can't you find one that will set anchor?'

'No. They're all listing.'

They went to Madame Tussaud's, the Mansion House, Trafalgar Square, and got a bird's-eye view of the city from the London Eye. 'Look, that's the Dome over there. You must remember all the fuss? The flashing light is Canary Wharf. They built that stupid building to dwarf St Paul's. Such a shame. Can you see Hampton Court? It's just lovely, Manju, but we can't do it all in one week. I love the history here. This afternoon, let's do the museums and then we can shop. I wish we had time to take you to Hay-on-Wye and Wales, and to the Northumbrian coast. Or the Lake District, so you could see Wordsworth's house – I always remember you marching around the playground reciting "season of mists and mellow fruitfulness".'

'That's Keats.'

'Oh, you know what I mean!'

'Any news from home, Chita?'

'My father's much better; he has daily medication.'

'In a way I'm lucky I only had my mother. My life is in America now.' They got off the pod and walked through Jubilee Gardens to Westminster Bridge. 'No host of golden daffodils? What a shame.'

'You never want to go back?'

'I've done my time, Chita. Hold the yellow ribbons.'

In January, the rumblings that had been sending ricochets of fear through Chita's office turned into a roar. The collapse of their biggest British client, Premier & Gulf, led to the Serious Fraud Office being called in to investigate. 'There are allegations of mismanagement, profit syphoning and insider dealing,' Chita told Shyam. 'Fingers are being pointed in all directions, including ours.'

The share price had fallen from an £86 high to £5.50. She held Shyam's hand as they walked through Colombia Road flower market, choosing spring flowering plants for the huge pots on their balcony. 'It's all rubbish, of course.'

'Do we really need a miniature fir tree, Princess? No flowers . . .'

Chita laughed. 'I love you, my husband.'

Later, wrapped in warm coats, they potted the plants together. 'Will it affect you, Chita?'

'Not personally. I've never been involved with P&G, but in-house they've asked me to look at ways of cost-cutting on staff.'

'What are your thoughts?'

'It's utterly unfair that people should lose jobs because of a City rumour.' Chita pulled off her gardening gloves and put them in the trug. 'I want to try and find a different way of approaching the problem. I've sent a memo to Monica, who's doing the operational side, suggesting we work to a three-year plan and make the cutbacks on the milk round.' She straightened up and they walked along the balcony, admiring the final effect.

'We normally take on around two thousand Oxbridge and Ivy League graduates with golden handshakes, cars and bonus schemes. If we cut that indefinitely to five hundred, and initiate a lower-strata intake who come in at eighteen and work an accelerated three-year training scheme, we save a fortune. Of course, our US arm has to agree. It affects them too. But . . . there is no alternative.'

She stopped to dead-head one of the old plants. 'It looks lovely, doesn't it? Our own little Garden of Eden.'

'It's a great idea, Chita, but we employ graduates because they're more skilled, better educated and have demonstrated diligence.'

'I'm not suggesting any student can walk in, Monica. We want straight-A students who are Ivy League material anyway. We'll only send recruitment packs to the five hundred top schools in the league tables.'

'You know what they say. You pay peanuts, you get monkeys.'

'Monica, we're not paying peanuts. And even the best graduate was once a monkey. Anyway, in my country we appreciate a primate's wisdom and speed of thought.'

'Like the three wise monkeys?'

'I think they may be Chinese, but the principle is the same. Shyam has a monkey called Honeybun. Come on. Lunch is on me today.'

Chita was on a high. She knew this idea would work. There was no choice anyway. The company had become the target of scaremongering quotes from City analysts and stock-market pundits. The ripples went to the banks of the pond and back again.

That weekend a two-day 'getting to know you' exercise with their American counterparts was refettled as a crisis management conference. As Monica drove them to their hotel in the Brecon Beacons, Chita said: 'If this is how we deal with a crisis, no wonder the share price hasn't recovered.'

Monica laughed. 'They couldn't unbook the place without losing most of the money. That said, I'd planned to bring my cozzie but decided that would be decadent.'

Chita's recruitment idea was debated for several hours. 'We can't let sophomores – A-level students as you call them – loose in the offices.'

'We don't let *graduates* loose in the offices. Human Resources have mapped out the major training areas. It *can* work.'

Late on Saturday afternoon, an outline was finally agreed.

'You've done it, my darling.'

'For a moment, Monica, I thought I'd lost.'

'It didn't show.'

'We all learn to wear masks, don't we? Especially when the ground is threatening to open under our feet.'

Later, over dinner and drinks in the homespun lounge, the teams relaxed and befriended each other. They swapped gossip and jokes and ended the evening playing charades. Chita deliberately wrote out the names of Indian books and films, knowing they wouldn't be able to act them, let alone guess them: *The Perfumed Garden*; *Amar Akhber Antony*; the Rig Veda; *Shakespeare Wallah*; the Mahabharata.

When Lena from the New York office attempted to do *The Kama Sutra* in a single series of actions, Chita laughed till tears rolled down her face.

Chita was relieved when, in late spring, her plan turned out to work rather well. She'd dispatched information pamphlets and applications to schools with the most consistent sixth-form results in the country. As a result, a number of top students who were ambivalent about university applied to join the accelerated training scheme later in the year. It would take them to the same level in the same time, but they'd be earning and learning instead of studying.

'It's how people got on in the old days,' Monica said. 'The large companies and utilities made staff sit aptitude tests. The top scorers were put on HND, degree and management courses. I've been impressed by the standard of the monkeys, Chita. Well done.'

Simultaneously, changes were announced in the upper echelons.

A new mission statement was posted on company noticeboards. To compound the spirit of optimism, a huge thank-you dinner for key staff was organised to coincide with the Annual General Meeting. Attended by the directors of their American arm and various European big shots, it was a show of corporate strength and unity.

'I'm afraid I'm distracted by a different show of strength and unity,' Monica told Chita. 'I'm pregnant.'

'Oh my God! Congratulations!' Chita hugged her friend and then drew back as if she might harm the baby. 'How far are you?'

'Three months.'

'Does that mean you'll leave?'

'I can't afford to. I'm the main breadwinner. Peter's going to move to supply teaching so he can be more flexible.'

'If I'm honest, I'm glad,' Chita said. 'We've been a team so long.'

The baby was a portent of improved morale. The SFO inquiry into Premier & Gulf continued apace, but improved performance had pushed their share profile back up and people were smiling again. Indeed, they were partying.

The AGM was on the fifth of November. The ball was that same evening at the Grosvenor House Hotel. Bonfire night. Gunpowder, treason and plot. It was an extravagant attempt at bridge-building. It was also a clear message to the City and the outside world that all fireworks were external.

That night, Chita decided to wear a sari for the first time in years. The same green silk she'd worn for her introduction to Shyam.

'I remember feeling I was going to explode,' he said, watching her as she deftly pleated the folds. 'I had no idea what you looked like, no idea how you walked or smiled or smelled. When I saw you I had no breath left in me.'

'Maybe breathless from walking up the hill?' Chita teased.

'I came by car.' He laughed.

'Do I still leave you breathless?'

'Yes. You do.' And then from a man who prided himself on honesty, a blatant untruth: 'You know, you haven't changed a bit.' But Shyam meant it metaphorically. Like many men, he hovered on the cusp of romantic autism, which often meant he genuinely didn't notice the specifics of a given situation. Or person.

He pulled on his tuxedo while his wife went in search of the purple silk bow tie and cummerbund she'd bought him in New Bond Street. 'Come on, husband, pretty up. The cab's here.'

It was a glittering occasion. Chita was comparatively under-stated, but her slim arms were accentuated by a dozen fine gold bangles from home. My husband is the only adornment I need, she thought, watching Monica and Ambreen teasing Shyam.

Each of the tables was hosted by a director of the company or a head of department. 'We're on table sixty-nine,' Ambreen said with a wink. When Chita looked at her blankly she burst out laughing. 'Let's get down there before someone else tucks into our salmon mousse.'

Their host was someone Chita knew well from telephone conferences on international contract law and working-hour directives. Recently appointed to the US board, Sam Raven was one of the bigger movers and shakers, a qualified lawyer who was Global Head of Utilities; a man whose name spelled power. And indeed, as they now discovered, whose presence emitted it.

He was no taller than Shyam, but he had a weight-lifter's physique: broad shoulders, strong arms, a muscular heaviness that kept his body centred. Chita noticed the cut of his tux and the detail of his hand-stitched dress shirt. He was in his mid-forties, ruggedly handsome with skin the colour of acacia honey and a lick of thick dark brown hair that fell boyishly across his forehead.

He grinned, showing perfect American teeth. 'Monica, Chita – we've spoken so many times. It's so good to meet.' He indicated a striking blonde in her late thirties with Clara Bow lips and a cleavage like a tanned ski jump on which nestled a red Moschino heart necklace: 'Meet Brina – Sabrina – Raven.'

Brina nodded coolly, and turned to Shyam, who was placed next to her, with a dazzling smile. The ultimate professional wife, Chita thought, watching Brina devouring her husband's every word. Thank goodness Shyam's company has so few functions. I spend too much time as it is being polite to suits. The woman is a star.

A warm hand on her bare arm. 'Am I boring you?'

'I'm sorry, Sam. I was daydreaming.'

He threw back his head and laughed. 'At least you're honest.' There was a devilish twinkle in his unexpectedly dark and heavily fringed eyes. Like a camel, Chita thought. He's rather cute.

'You're from India originally, Chita, right? My heritage is Sri Lankan – not too far across the water from you, I guess. Been in the States a few generations, though.'

He did most of the talking and the women were glad of that. They liked the rhythm of his voice and his attentive body language. He was compellingly charismatic. Very American, in the way his workings were clearly visible. There would be a lot to discuss in the office on Monday.

Shyam, meanwhile, had scored a hit with Brina Raven. She leaned into him like a helpless sapling blown by the wind. Barbie in distress.

When, during coffee, an Abba sound-alike band moved on to the stage, Brina insisted Shyam dance with her to 'Waterloo'.

His pained expression was ignored. His wife, unable to help, wanted to giggle – especially when her husband, quite incapable of rudeness in any circumstance, was literally dragged out of his seat.

On standing, Mrs Raven revealed an evening dress split almost to the crotch and a set of supermodel legs. Across Sam Raven's magnificent torso, Monica raised an alarmed eyebrow.

Chita shrugged: this was an evening on which, it was becoming patently clear, the turn of events was entirely out of their hands.

*   *   *

'You're a very attractive man, Shyam.'

'Thank you, Mrs Raven.'

'I'm not Mrs Raven. I'm *Ms* Raven. Sam's stepsister. I live here in London. Neither of us is married.'

'Oh, I see.' With difficulty Shyam tried to appear diffident, but he was embarrassed both by his inability to find a rhythm and, simultaneously, to escape his dancing partner's physicality.

If he moved his eyes from Brina's swollen bosom, they fixed on to her quite sensational pins. As an Indian boy of the old school, he found blondes peculiarly interchangeable and didn't like their artificial sexuality. Nonetheless, he had to admit she was unquestionably engrossing. Even if you don't like cars, you can appreciate the line and torque of an XK8!

In a vain attempt to show his indifference, he moved his focus to her face and was immediately terror struck. The message in her unflinching gaze was far more troubling than the overt message from her body. As the band played on, his legs splayed in all directions like a newborn giraffe. Fixing his eyes to the floor, he tried to contain his growing panic.

After twenty frenetic minutes he concocted a reason to stop. 'I'm very hot, Brina. I need water.' But before he could run away, Brina Raven took his arm. 'It's quicker at the upstairs bar. This way.'

Shyam followed her up the ornate stairs into the red-carpeted lobby. There was no bar. 'Brina, I think you have it wrong.'

'Not at all, Shaaarm.' She tucked her hand farther into the crook of his arm. 'Come on, I'll show you.'

She led him up another flight of stairs to a drinking area in the main body of the hotel. 'It's much calmer here – you see? Let's order a couple of drinks and get to know each other in comfort.'

'We already know each other.'

'We've been introduced. That isn't the same thing.'

She was standing so close to him that, at this point, any other full-blooded man would have put his hand inside the split of her skirt and tested the heat. Or run a mile.

Shyam, being Shyam, could hear the warning bells but, torn between good manners and an instinctive need to seek his wife's protection, he sat down with Brina at a small table. 'Are you sure that the service is faster upstairs?'

'Is there a hurry?'

'Well . . . um . . . I'm thirsty.'

'For?'

'Water.'

'Only water?'

Shyam looked around anxiously. 'Ah, here's a waiter.'

He fiddled anxiously with his bow tie until it came undone. His collar stud was open. His slicked-back hair, heated from action on the dance-floor, was unruly and rakish.

He looked hot: in every sense of the term.

Brina put a cool hand on his forehead. 'Hey, you're running a fever. Is it because of me?' Her leg was pressed against his like a throbbing bolster. She felt the back of his neck. 'With your clothing askew you look like you're preparing for action.' Shyam sat absolutely still. 'Don't you like me, Shyam?'

'You're very attractive, Brina. But I have a wife.'

'She doesn't have to know.'

Shyam pretended that he could not see the pale pink outline of her nipple, which had magically escaped from her bodice. She put her head close to his. He moved away. His water arrived. She put her hand on his fly and squeezed. He choked. The liquid spilled down his shirt front. 'Oh, no.' Brina rubbed his back and surreptitiously put her tongue deep into his ear. 'Brina! Please!'

Her hand gently stroked. 'More? Why don't we find a dark corner?'

It was only then that Shyam put convention aside and fled to his wife as if his feet were on fire.

Afterwards, while Brina Raven was cranking up a vixen-like obsession with the couple, and what she perceived as their charmed life, Chita was crying with laughter, begging Shyam to repeat details of the episode again and again.

'You're such a goose, Shyam – I wish I'd seen your face.'

'You can laugh, Chita.' But safe with his wife, he too laughed at his ineptitude and innocence. 'I really didn't see it coming.'

'Why should you? As a married man with his wife down-stairs, it was unexpected. These people have no morals. Don't worry, Shyam. I know you love me. I know you're loyal. It's our way.'

'Our way and our destiny.' He rolled her on to her stomach and kissed the back of her neck in a way that always turned her to jelly.

They did not fear the serpents in the undergrowth though plenty had circled. Chita, being single-minded, tended only to see what she wanted. Thus she rarely noticed the effect she had on men, and when she did, she always misread their interest – which confounded them.

The same was true of Shyam, who did not recognise sexual attention. When women eyed him up on the Tube or the street, he'd misunderstand and adjust his tie or jacket.

'I suppose you can't blame Brina for trying,' Chita said, woozy with longing. 'You *are* the most wonderful man. In my office there are plenty who have succumbed in similar situations. Next thing, their partners find out and the marriage is over.'

'Too much time on their hands. In my office everyone is so busy they don't have the time or energy for flirtation.'

It struck Chita that the evidence suggested one could always make the time and find the energy for flirtation, but it was hardly important. Backlit by a full moon that flooded the uncurtained sleeping area with a white light, they made love with a peculiar tenderness. Chita was filled with wonder that, after so much time together, it could be this good. Next spring it will be thirteen years. Whoever said thirteen was an unlucky number?

At the ball, Sam Raven had been enraptured by Chita. She had a way of looking at you that was absolutely mesmerising: an invitation and a rebuff in one. To top it all, she was so damn smart!

He'd always been impressed by the way she grasped facts in their phone conversations, but her speed of thought in conversation was both surprising and exciting.

That night, lying in bed at the Savoy, in a suite overlooking the Thames, he was filled with bog-standard post-party fantasies about ravishing her. You know, all the usual stuff: splayed wantonly for missionary, grunting appreciatively during doggy, feeding him her tits while bouncing on top, and always, of course, happy to swallow.

That was all. Nothing out of the ordinary. Within a few days, he'd have put someone else's face on the body when he went to sleep. But we're not allowing here for Brina. Living proof that hell hath no fury like a woman scorned.

When, the next morning, Sam pitched up at her place in Chelsea for a late breakfast, she was scathing about Shyam. 'No pump action. And so dull. He can only talk software and the Taj Mahal.'

'She loves him.'

'What a waste.'

'She's beautiful, isn't she?'

'That's exactly what I mean.' Her brother listened with half an ear as he wolfed down his bacon and eggs. Exasperated, Brina said: 'Well, what did *you* think?'

'I told you. I thought *her* the most beautiful creature that ever walked this earth. He's just arm candy.'

'Well,' Brina said, a plan instantly formulating itself, 'if that is true, she's the one for you. The girl is sweet. Right up your street.'

'She's a colleague, Brin.'

'If she's your colleague, get her to work alongside you.' Sam yawned and stretched. 'You need a wife, Sam. You know that. You need a place to hang your hat. What is money without the honey of a woman?'

'Don't worry about me, Brin. I have a great time.'

'Think of that goatskin rug in Aspen. The log fire. Imagine a day out on the slopes – a girl in a ski suit, cuddles, gropes . . . Laughing eyes, long brown thighs: now there's hot chocolate.' Mid-incantation, Brina idly got up and refreshed the water in a huge vase of lilies. She watched her brother in the mirror. He was restless; disturbed. Ah. He's listening now. 'Shucks, just a silly thought.'

Suddenly Sam's mind seemed to explode with the look and the imagined scent of Chita. His sister's words reverberated in his ears. Shyam started to crystallise as a rival who had stolen Sam's rightful prize. He relocated Chita from the realms of fantasy to the forum of the possible.

Sam tried to think himself out of this mindset, but it didn't work. His senses had come uncontrollably alive. Imagine what we could achieve . . . Oh, to wake up to that face on the pillow next to me.

Brina replaced the flowers and started to give her brother a shoulder massage. 'There's nothing to stop you, Sam. Spirit her across to the States. Unless she's stubborn or idle or frigid, you'll soon find her husband will bore Chita rigid.' She whispered in her brother's ear: 'It's not as if they've children. You're not breaking up a happy home.'

'No, I suppose I'm not,' said Sam Raven with a sense of surprise. 'Well, I mean, I suppose I wouldn't be. *Were* anything to happen. I'll think about it. I have to be certain of what I want.'

The next few weeks passed in a high-speed blur.

Sam started calling Chita with minor enquiries. Chita, busy managing a client who was threatening to go into liquidation, gave it no thought. She was also preoccupied with her new love: driving.

In England, she and Shyam had initially been too broke to buy a car. By the time they could, they'd found that public transport was faster, cheaper and easier. They'd turned down company cars as too much responsibility, but after missing vital meetings because of a long-running train dispute, Chita agreed to a company Saab.

'When I put my foot down and turn up the radio, Monica, it's like being in heaven. In India, I hated driving. We live by the horn. Here, I can't get enough of the open road.'

At Christmas she turned down the usual offer to spend it with Monica and Peter. 'I've decided that it's time to have an adventure. Why don't you both come with us?'

'I'm pregnant. You've got to be joking.'

She told the boys: 'What's the point of having a car if we don't use it to get out of London?'

'I've always had a car, Chita.'

'But I have to sit in the back, Lucky. That's what put me off driving all these years. This time I'll do the driving.'

She booked them into a little inn on a rise in the Peak

District. On the twenty-fifth they sat in a dining room full of elderly strangers and ate a passably pleasant lunch before, to their surprise, falling asleep in the lounge, their hats askew.

'It must have been the sherry,' Chita said afterwards. 'I didn't realise it was alcohol.'

They travelled on to York and across to Cumbria, spending New Year at a family-run hotel in the valley at Grasmere. Returning home, Chita said: 'I told you it would be good.'

If the boys noticed the speed at which she was driving, both were far too sensible, or scared, to say.

On Valentine's Day a bouquet of one hundred red roses and a single white rose was delivered to Chita at the office. It was so lovely people came to look at it. When her secretary first entered her office, hidden behind the sweet-smelling profusion, Chita had been nonplussed. 'What is this, Kelly? Another admirer? Can't you keep them in your own space?'

'They're for you.'

'For me? From who?'

'One of *your* admirers. It *is* Valentine's Day.'

It is? Kelly placed the flowers on the table and passed Chita the accompanying card. She opened it with amusement. The message was brief and shed no light: 'With Love'.

'Is this a joke?'

'It'd be a bloody expensive joke. Come on, Chita, who're they from? You must know. Is it your old man?'

'I don't think Shyam knows about Valentine's Day.'

'You're not having an affair?'

'As if.'

'Well, someone's got the hots for you.'

When she returned from lunch there was a note to call Sam Raven in New York. 'Chita. How's it going? Did you get the flowers?'

'They're from you? Yes, I did. Of course. Thank you,

Sam. How kind of you to remember me. What did I do to deserve them?'

'You deserve them just for being you.' She didn't know how to respond. 'You've been in my thoughts. I'm impressed by you. Initially I wasn't sure about your sophomore idea, but these kids are not only sharp, they brighten the office. You know, Chita, you should think about coming over here some time. We could use your experience and expertise. Think about it.'

'You mean full time?'

'Sure. Why not?'

She laughed. 'That's very flattering but this is my domain. Thank you again for the flowers, Sam. They're beautiful. Kelly is in a swoon.'

'Beautiful flowers for a beautiful woman. Think of me when you look at them.'

Chita forgot his words within minutes of finishing the call, but she did think of Sam each time she looked at the roses. Which means she thought of him quite a lot over the next ten days.

It didn't, at all, make her feel differently towards him, because she hadn't felt anything but generally positive in the first place. But it meant that, even in her busiest moments, he had a place in her consciousness. And that would make it easier for him to launch successive forays into her time and space without immediately attracting suspicion.

Over the next few months, Chita came to both love and dread the days when she'd walk into her office and find a little package on the desk – never anything too expensive or too personal. Just little 'tokens', as Sam called them, of appreciation.

'Another gift of love. He FedExed it on his own account.'

'What does that mean?'

'That it's personal. Are you sure he knows you're married, Chita?'

'Of course. He met Shyam. Sam's sister made a pass at him. He ran for his life.' She giggled.

Kelly rolled her eyes. 'Men are strange, aren't they? Once they've got something into their heads, you just can't derail them.'

'Is that true?' Chita opened the package. 'Look: it's only a notebook. What a relief.'

'Handmade paper. *Très* expensive.'

'He's just generous, Kelly. Don't read more into it.'

'But he's only generous to you, Chita.'

'No. Don't forget the lovely box of baby clothes he sent Monica when she went off on leave. The smock, and the socks, and the cardigan and the OshKosh dungarees . . .' Kelly didn't respond. Her expression said it all.

Chita was already a little uncomfortable about the cus-tomised scent, the hand-made fountain pen and the box of lace hankies. But while it was unorthodox, the gifts were sent openly and with innocuous messages. She was confused by the politics of it.

'It's beautiful, this notebook.'

'Golden.'

'I can use it for all my lists: work, shopping, domestic, goals, ideas, ideals, arrangements . . .'

'You and your lists.'

'It hones the mind.'

Jez and Shola, her monkey trainees, turned up at the door for the morning meeting. Chita put the book away. 'Hello, team.'

'I don't think it's your mind Sam wants honed, Chita,' Kelly said, picking up the discarded packaging and exiting the room.

*　　*　　*

81

Chita booked a cottage in the Cotswolds for the spring
bank-holiday.

'Why can't I drive?' Lucky demanded. 'It's always you.'

'Since you got glasses, brother-in-law, I don't trust you.'

'The whole point is that I see better.'

'And, therefore, you take more risks.'

The cottage was on the edge of a wood in one of the
few villages not entirely spoilt by coach parties of tourists,
double yellow lines and twee attractions. Locating the key in
a flowerpot by the front step, they entered to find a fire in
the grate and Rachmaninov's second piano concerto playing
on Classic FM. The two double bedrooms were rhapsodies in
chintz. 'Very girly,' Lucky said.

'But nobody and nothing for half a mile.'

At some point, she knew, they would have to discuss Sam
Raven's latest 'pass', as Lucky had started calling them. 'So
the suitor is again plighting his troth, sister-in-law?'

The moment came sooner than expected, over dinner. 'Did
Sam call today?'

'Of course, Shyam. He calls most days. And before you get
cross, Lucky, always for a legitimate reason. Remember that
he is also a director of the company. Even if he rang to enquire
about the weather, I wouldn't be rude to him.' I'm sounding
defensive – but why is there always an unspoken suggestion
that I encourage him?

'It's gone too far this time, Chita.'

'I know that.'

'Perhaps you should raise it with someone on the board?'

'What will I say, Shyam? You know how they view claims
by women employees. They'll agree that he shouldn't send
presents but privately they'll say I'm overreacting.'

'But a pearl necklace . . .'

'A *seed* pearl necklace. He's always the right side of the
line.'

'Methinks,' said Lucky, 'that the lady doth protest too much.'

Sam had sent her the necklace to mark a year since the monkey initiative had been launched. 'It worked. You saved us millions. Well done.'

'You can't pretend he hasn't got the hots for you any more,' Kelly had said. 'I've asked. No other department head has even had an e-mail from him. When he can't find a reason to send you presents, he makes one up.' Chita said nothing. Kelly leaned across the desk. 'He's getting good at this, isn't he? One day he'll grind you down. Mark my words.'

Chita had anticipated the arguments. The night before leaving London with the boys, she'd visited Monica. Sitting cross-legged on her friend's sofa, Chita took Annie in her arms. 'She's so beautiful. Already twice the size of two weeks ago.'

Monica bit into one of the apple doughnuts her friend had bought. 'Hands free for ten minutes. What a treat. But you're right about Sam Raven, Chita. You can't lay any charge at his door without opening yourself up to innuendo and accusation and a whole lot of grief that you really don't need. Tribunals are killing.'

'That wasn't my thinking.' Chita kissed the top of Annie's soft and pink bald head. The baby closed her eyes and was instantly asleep. 'She's so sweet.'

'But you're right. He *is* putting you in an awkward position and ignoring it hasn't worked. That said, he's never suggested anything at any point that could have been misunderstood or misconstrued, like "I'd like to shag the arse off you" or "Bring your best knickers".'

Chita started laughing. 'Nothing like that. It's my problem, and my defence. All he asks is that I go to New York and work for him.'

'Because Luciana Lopez has marched off in a huff?'

'Precisely. He has no senior change person on his team.'

Monica licked her fingers clean and took the baby. 'I get very territorial. She's just morish, isn't she?' Smelling her mother, the baby woke and cried for a feed. Monica sat in the nursing chair and took out a swollen white breast. 'I think your instincts, and Shyam's instincts, are probably right, Chita, but there's no crime in admiring from afar. We all get office crushes. He's breaching protocols but there hasn't been an actual misdemeanour.'

Now, as Lucky cleared the table, she repeated this to Shyam. He nodded. 'That's the problem. This man is devilish. He woos you openly to make it appear like innocent flattery. He wants you, but he cannot have you. It makes him angry. He will keep tempting until you can no longer resist.'

'I'll knock his bloody block off,' Lucky growled.

Chita smiled, but she was sad that she'd never get to wear the necklace. With her hand on her heart she could say she had never considered Sam as anything other than part of the work hierarchy. To précis Paul Newman – why go out for burger when you've got a steak at home? Nonetheless, the pearls were exquisite. And the one time she'd worn them, their gleam had added lustre to her skin.

On Sunday, Lucky wanted to go for a drive and do something active, but Shyam and Chita felt too lethargic. 'You take the car, brother-in-law. We'll go walking in the woods.'

It was mid-afternoon on a warm April day. The foliage was still young; the trees had not yet formed a canopy against the sky. The light was dappled and the ground dry. Shyam, tall and purposeful in a waxed jacket and cords, led the way. Chita, willowy in a designer parka and jeans, followed close behind.

'This reminds me of home,' she said as they reached a clearing and sat side by side on a log. 'All we need is a sunny spot to nap.'

'Do you get homesick, Princess?'

'Sometimes.'

'Only twelve more months, then our exile is over.'

'Just one year?' Is that really all?

'I can't wait. Can you?' She didn't answer. 'Don't you think about it? Make plans?'

'I don't know. I guess somewhere along the line I stopped.'

She savoured the sun on her face, letting its warmth wash over her. Since their loft move, she'd taken to sunning herself on their balcony overlooking the Thames. Even when it wasn't warm, she liked the feel of the wind, which whistled down river and caught you like a cold slap. It was a lot like her part of India, which shared the sharpness and freshness of the British climate.

Shyam sometimes claimed the dampness of London permeated his bones. 'That's because you're a heat and dust man,' she'd say. Chita liked England: there was romance in the air.

'Will you miss what we've built up here, Shyam?' she asked now. 'We both have such brilliant careers and total freedom. I don't remember once being unhappy or wishing things were different.'

He put his arm around her and hugged her to him. 'I'm the same. Every day here has been charmed because of you. I *will* miss everyone and everything, but running the estate is a big job too. Bobby has six managers working for him. In every letter he counts the weeks to his liberation.' Sensing his wife's ambivalence, he twisted round so he could read her expression as well as her words. 'How do you feel about going back, Chita?'

'It's your destiny, Shyam.'

'But you? How do *you* feel?'

'The day I married you I accepted that my own destiny would be inextricably intertwined with yours. Unless you fulfil your destiny, I cannot fulfil mine.'

'You still believe that?'

'I'm a traditional Indian girl. I've been displaced, and that muddies the detail, but the bigger picture remains the same.'

'That's very pragmatic of you.'

She touched his cheek. 'I love you. Whatever will be will be.'

'Perhaps it will be time to start a family.'

'Let's get there first. Let's settle in. I want to help you find your equilibrium. I'm the expert, remember? Then I'll turn my mind to human resources: little Shyams and little Chitas.'

Monica and Annie came up to town for coffee with Chita and Ambreen. 'I'm really sorry. This baby spends most of her time under my jumper. That's the way it is. They feed constantly.'

Ambreen said: 'It's funny how we automatically adapt, isn't it? To anything, I mean. We've been to hell and back in that office over the last year, and the whole bloody Premier & Gulf case still rumbles on. But we put our heads down and keep going.'

'Any more gifts, Chita?'

'I think her frosty charm has put Sam Raven off his stroke.'

'Don't speak about me as if I can't hear! I happen to know he's chasing a big municipal contract. We've had memos. But without Luciana Lopez he's running to stand still. I shouldn't be pleased about it but I am. Recently he's taken his eye off the ball.'

'Has he taken *your* eye off his ball?'

'Monica! There's a baby listening.'

Initially Chita had missed Sam's humour, but she also appreciated being off the hook. Meanwhile she was pushing Jez and Shola, offloading a number of small research projects on to them. Big bananas for my best monkeys. Home by 6.30, she had free time to concentrate on business plans. 'I think all this talk of recession is fallacious,' she said. 'Instead of sitting back, let's be more aggressive about getting clients. What have we got to lose?' She made lists of things to do, and arguments to put, in the golden notebook. The official results of the SFO inquiry into Premier & Gulf were due at any minute. The pressure was on to secure as many contracts as possible before that happened.

Sam, as Global Head of Utilities, and as a director, was kept apprised of her thinking. But he was employing a new strategy of his own and stayed out of Chita's orbit. Until July. Then he made an official request for her secondment to New York.

Chita was taken aback. She made some internal calls and discovered that his idea was being taken seriously. 'I'd have thought you'd love a few months in the Big Apple,' said the Operations Director. 'All that shopping.'

Chita rang Sam and asked what was going on.

'It's very simple, Chita. I'm trying to pull in the biggest municipal contractor in the country. They run virtually all the refuse services in the northern states. The whole set-up is archaic – crushers that went out with the Ark. If they're going to tender successfully for a new contract worth billions, they're going to have to put their house in order pronto. Big competition, believe me.'

'And?'

'If we get the job it'll mean a complete overhaul from the bottom up. I can't deliver that without an expert in your field. I've lost Luciana Lopez. Lena Jay and Brad Allen just don't carry the weight. You're the only one who has union experience. We'll be dealing here with America's toughest commie boys. That's why I went to the top. Didn't want you thinking I'm up to tricks or something.'

'I really don't want to, Sam.'

'You'll enjoy it. It'll be the biggest challenge of your life.'

'I'm sure that's true, but I know you'll find a way around it.'

'Think of the bonus, Chita. And no: there is no other way around it. We get you and we get the job. You stay put, the contract goes phut.'

'I've told them I won't do it.'

'Resign.'

'I don't want to resign, Lucky. I've been with them since we arrived in England. I'm one of their top people. I love my job. I'm not giving up. Particularly as . . . particularly as I'll probably never work again after we leave here.'

Chita didn't want to criticise or complain. It was just that the conversation in the woods with Shyam had reminded her that freedom was limited. In the interim, she wanted to put on a spurt and hit the finishing line with her arms in the air.

'It'll be a different life as an estate wife . . . Until then, I have no intention of quitting.' She put up a hand to prevent argument. 'And it's not just that. On a practical level, I've just had another rise which means my pension, if I stay, is much bigger.'

'What is money, Chita? You don't need a pension. The estate can, and does, support us all.'

'But *you* still work, Lucky.'

'Your duty as a wife is greater than your duty to the company.'

'They are not conflicting duties.'

'You will be put under pressure to go.'

'I will resist, Shyam.'

Shyam poured himself a small whisky. 'How will you resist, Princess, if the board agree with Sam Raven? You saw what happened when I tried to move the completion date on the Durban software. If it's important enough, *you* jump, they don't.'

Chita got up and went to the window. Tower Bridge was open. That was unusual. It would mean tailbacks for the next half-hour. A rowing boat was passing on the water below. The men inside reminded her of Pip and Herbert and Startop attempting to row Magwitch to safety in *Great Expectations*. Who will overturn our boat? she wondered.

Behind her, the boys were still ruminating. It's ridiculous. We've been married thirteen years. He should trust me. More. I've always travelled for work. Sam's request is hardly unreasonable. The company's in trouble and this is worth millions. That I'm standing firm and irritating everyone is surely proof enough of my intentions and loyalties? Chita noticed that one of her balcony plants had been burnt by the early frosts. She thought of Shyam being propositioned by the one truly predatory Raven – Brina. She wanted to laugh. He's so sweet.

Shyam called to her. 'Chita, I fear losing you. That's all. This man has been intent on getting you for so long—'

'Not me, Shyam. Perhaps my attention. I don't know. But nobody and nothing can weaken what we have.'

'That's not what I'm saying, Princess. I know that. It's you I fear for. I believe he has a master plan to which you are attached. You have given an inch. He's coming back for the mile.'

'Then I'll resist.'

'And what if he makes you an offer you can't resist?'

'I will still resist.'

The offer came a week later.

London called an emergency directors' meeting after the SFO finally filed charges of fraud, deliberate mismanagement and insider trading against the entire board of Premier & Gulf.

The City press were having a field day.

From the information available, it was clear that Chita's company had not broken any rules, but lawyers for Premier & Gulf nonetheless issued a statement implying otherwise.

'They're hoping some of the mud will stick,' Chita told the monkeys. 'It puts us in a very difficult position, but the secret is to concentrate on your in-trays and look forward.'

The house lawyers commandeered all and any paperwork alluding to the contract. Sam and five of the US chiefs were flown to help construct the firewall.

'Serious decisions, Chita. The dogs are on our back. All PRs are on twenty-four-hour call and we'll be issuing emergency numbers for staff to call if approached by journalists.'

'I've already spoken to the team.'

'I'll be there tomorrow. I hope they've got an extra-large shredder.' He laughed. 'Is there anything my top operator wants from over here?'

'A reprieve.'

'Have you been indicted along with the Premier board?'

'No. Silly. I meant your request for my secondment.'

'And more important than ever, now. Perhaps I can tempt you with lunch. I'll give you the detail over dessert.'

'I don't eat dessert, Sam.'

'Because you're frightened you'd enjoy it too much?'

'Three courses is excessive.'

'That's what I said, hon.'

Chita tiptoed around the building avoiding Sam for the first two days after his arrival.

'Has anyone called, Kelly?'

'You mean Sam?'

'No. I meant anybody.'

'A little bird tells me there's a lock-in on the fifth floor. They've even put security guys at the lift to make sure we lesser mortals don't get a sniff of what they're up to.'

When, after forty-eight hours, Sam hadn't ventured into her territory, Chita relaxed. On day four she was bending over her desk signing some letters when she felt the hairs on the back of her neck rise. Slowly, she straightened up and turned around.

It was him. Blocking the doorway in a Polo sweater and jeans, every inch the all-American boy. His hair was tousled and he was grinning cheekily, as if he'd been caught with his hand in the cookie jar. 'You've got legs. Last time I saw you it was in a sari.'

Suddenly self-conscious, Chita pulled her skirt down, although, at two inches above her slim knee, it was hardly revealing. Her jacket was on the back of her chair. The slinky singlet she was wearing came to her neck, but she was acutely conscious that her arms were bare and her breasts emphasised by its bias cut.

Her hair, normally pushed back, fell loosely to her shoulders because she'd removed the clips while using a headset. They stared at each other for a second. 'Hello, Sam,' Chita said.

He came into the room. 'So this is how the other half lives. I think we have a much better view from our windows in New York. We're right near the Chrysler building. Do you know it?'

'No.'

'There's nothing to beat our skyline, our coffee and our hash browns.' He stopped to study a chart on her wall. He was so close she thought she could feel his breath. She felt scorched by his presence. He scares me. He's so . . . testosteronic.

Sam tapped one of the icons on the chart and looked across at her. 'I like this idea. It's fun. Yours?' She nodded. 'Why do you look like that, Chita? I'm not going to eat you.' Yet. 'I'm just some regular guy who thinks you're terrific at what you do and wants you on his team. For a finite time. It's called business. We're all part of it.'

'I know, Sam. It's just that my husband and my life are here.'

'And my life is in Manhattan, but when there's a UK

emergency . . . well, here I am.' He shrugged. 'Hey, lady, I'm not going to force you over against your will. I thought you'd enjoy it. I'm about to pull a multimillion-pound contract and need a smidgeon of extra input in the absence of Luciana. That said, I'll bag it anyway.'

'I'm grateful for your wanting me.'

'I don't *want* you, Chita. I need you. That's different. But, hey – your call.' She shivered as he went out of the door. He hasn't actually done anything wrong. Has he?

A moment later he returned. 'By the way, this is for you. I left it on Kelly's desk – didn't see you at first. You'll probably hate it but I thought of you as soon as I got line of sight on Fifth Avenue.'

'Sam, I cannot accept a single other gift.'

'Open it.'

'It's really kind of you, but I—'

'I'm a director of this company, Chita, not some lovesick fool trying to win your heart. Believe me, if that were the case I'd fly you to Aspen in my plane, take you out in the snow and present you with diamonds.' He sensed her continuing uncertainty. 'All I'm doing is saying thank you. Maybe other directors don't do it this way, in which case forgive my style; but don't offend my sensibilities by returning it. No more after today, okay?'

Chita unwrapped the package and was so thrilled by its contents that she reddened with pleasure. In the box was the most exquisite handbag she'd ever seen. It was made of the softest doeskin. It felt like a powder puff and looked a million dollars.

It was lovelier than any other in her considerable collection, including the original Fendi baguette, the red Christian Dior clasp bag and a Lulu Guinness beaded clutch.

She unzipped it and looked inside – wanting to examine the gold silk lining and the little zipped pockets. 'It's exquisite. I don't know what to say. Thank you.'

'They had the jacket too, but I didn't know your size. Anyway, that *would* have been overstepping the mark. It's a shame you won't come over. Then you could buy it for yourself. It'd look sensational with your colouring.' He rummaged in his pocket, pulled out a mobile phone. 'Sorry: it vibrated.'

He reeled down the screen, reading a text. 'Gotta go. The jacket. They have two in stock. I could ask them to put one aside. You know I've told the guys I'd release you after three months?'

'Is it only three months?' Chita said. 'I thought it was more.'

'We never discussed it,' said Sam Raven, 'because you didn't ask.' He sat on the edge of her table. 'Chita, I'll say this once only. I'm not asking you, I'm begging you. I'm begging you to help me, and to help the firm by coming out to New York. It *is* just three months. Can't you do that? See the big picture and not the small?'

'If it's only three months,' said Chita, looking at the bag and feeling terribly guilty for being selfish at his moment of need, 'perhaps I *should* do it.'

Part Four

Is Chita's decision really that surprising? Don't so many lives turn on a sixpence?

Chita, it is important to keep emphasising, because this is the story of a dutiful wife and her virtuous husband, enjoyed a solid marriage. This was as much to do with her working on it as anything else – marriages aren't really made in heaven. But it's not the detail we're examining in this narrative but the broad strokes as presented to the outside world.

So, while the doeskin bag was the trigger that weakened her resolve, it wasn't the presence of beauty that made her risk the security of Docklands life, but Sam's need. Pulling off the contract was within her gift. It was mean to refuse.

Chita also knew that soon this stage of her life would be over and she and Shyam would start again in a country where they'd spent just twenty holidaying weeks over nearly thirteen years.

Six years previously, Sujata had died. Shyam and Chita had not been able to attend the funeral because it was at the family home. Instead, Lucky had gone, placing locks of their hair on her funeral pyre.

In the hills, Chita's father had suffered a heart attack and would be permanently dependent on medication. At the time, Chita had taken compassionate leave and flown straight home. But her endless worrying and remonstrations fuelled Amma's hand-wringing and complaining. Her father sat in bed crossly. 'For goodness, sake, child, if you stay much longer goading your mother, it will finish me off. Go back and do something useful.'

Shivan had married his girl and gone to work at one of his father-in-law's refineries in Malaysia. He had two sons and seemed very happy in the letters and photographs that came like clockwork four times a year. Lucky had been out to Kuala Lumpur a number of times and reported that his twin was fat, well and happy and Kusum was a nice girl who clearly enjoyed her food.

Bobby, meanwhile, like the hermit in the tarot pack, held his lantern aloft and continued his lone walk through the woods. The phone at the main house was rarely answered. The estate accounts were in order. Everything was fine except for Bobby himself.

Little wonder that in the recesses of Chita's mind were caches of great sadness. Details of the unexpected and unsettling that would one day come together and make an imperfect whole. The backdrop to her life, once a tapestry of petit-point perfection, had been passed to a blind seamstress with a blunt needle!

And now, even her current points of reference were moving.

Manju, as we know, was in Michigan. In recent months she'd been dating another teacher at her school. 'He's called Rich, but he isn't. You know the Americans, they have such strange naming rituals.' She sighed. 'If I'm honest it's been building up a long time, but nothing happened till the school play. Love in the final act.'

'You were made to be a heroine. Enjoy the happiness and stability, Manju. You need it. And don't lose your temper or make demands he can't possibly meet.'

Monica was due back in the office soon, but Annie was all engrossing in the meantime and she remained worn out and nappy obsessed.

To top it all, their bosses were at sixes and sevens and the office was cloaked in gloom, doom and upheaval.

There was more to Chita's decision than guilt or impetuousness that morning in early September. Sometimes we need to step outside the charmed circle to remember that we're alive. To *feel* that we're alive.

Chita loved New York from the minute the taxi dropped her off at the company apartment on the Upper West Side. The corner window in the sitting room overlooked Broadway. On the vast coffee table was a huge hand-thrown jug of cut flowers. There was a little note of welcome from Sam's secretary, Eva. 'Relax and enjoy yourself today. We're all looking forward to meeting you in the morning.'

The second half of the room contained a dining table on which was placed a crystal bowl filled with ripe fruit. Chita was suddenly hungry. She picked up an apple and took a bite.

Her bedroom was prettily functional. There was an adjoining dressing room and shower room. She opened a window on to the cross-street below. It was a hot day in mid-August and the air-conditioning wasn't on. There was a haze outside.

A second, smaller bedroom with en suite facilities was squashed between her and the sitting room, which formed a corner bridge in the three-sided apartment. The kitchen was on the far side, compact and streamlined with one of those wonderful white fridges in which you could fit two whole Indian people or half the groceries an American family eats in a week.

Off the kitchen was an office area with a computer and printer, fax, photocopier and stationery. Restaurant delivery menus, cab numbers, useful addresses and home contact details for all the principals in the New York office were fixed to a notice-board on the wall. Chita marvelled at the clever use of space.

After unpacking, she lay on the bed and tried to nap. It was impossible. The street sounds seemed to be screaming at her to come outside. She walked down Broadway, stopping at Zabars to buy provisions, enthralled by the huge choice of delicatessen goods.

She called her husband from her mobile. It was 7 p.m. London time. He wasn't back from work. She left him a message: 'Shyam, it's just wonderful here! I'm in a shop filled with caramellised oranges and crystallised lemons and every type of cheese imaginable. I wish you could smell it. It's amazing.'

Afterwards she went to the Loews Cinema across the road and watched the new Mel Gibson movie. Coming back, she checked her watch: it was one in the morning in London, but she dialled home, wanting to hear Shyam's voice and share her day.

Sam had arranged a team breakfast. Chita had already met Lena and Brad at the Brecon Beacons conflab, and knew the others by name. 'They seem a nice bunch, Sam. A little more serious than their British counterparts. No Jez and Shola here.'

'They loosen up over time.' He walked her around the building. 'Learn the space and settle in. No hurry. You know the terminology. Rest rooms, elevators, Xerox, cash dispenser, that sort of thing?' He was friendly but formal. He is sending a signal that this is strictly business. Of course it is! 'Any questions?' She shook her head. 'You're more easily pleased than I thought, Chita. That's promising. Joke. I'll leave you to it. You know where I am if you hit any walls.'

Over the next few days Chita relaxed into the job. It was very clear that she had a significant role. But a curious aside from Brad over an early morning mocha lodged itself in her head.

'I don't blame you for resisting the transfer, Chita,' Brad said. 'Sam is very changeable. This time last year, Luciana

Lopez could do no wrong. Then, around Christmas, he took against her. He found fault where it didn't exist. Her life was hellish. When she got another offer, she ran. Mind you, the upside is that if she was still here we wouldn't have got you.'

At the end of the first week, Chita had rung home eighteen times. 'We've spoken more in the last few days than we ever do normally.'

'That's because we're missing each other.'

'We've taken each other for granted. Maybe this space is good for us, Shyam. Our lives are going to change drastically next year. My being here provides solitude for rethinking goals.'

'But they are mutual goals, Chita.'

Are they? Chita was unsettled as she put down the phone. So much in a marriage is taken for granted, and, where destiny is seen as the prime mover and shaker, the players often imagine mistakes will self-correct. It is only later they recognise that life is a series of multiple-choice options. And that every tick has meaning.

She tried to sleep. Her first week was painlessly over. Tomorrow she would explore this vast city for the first time. She'd pencilled in a walk down Fifth Avenue to find, without Sam's knowledge, the doeskin jacket. Then she planned to turn back on herself and walk up to the Met and see the new exhibition there.

Rolling on to her back, she stared at a mark on the ceiling that was shaped like a trident. In the evening, I'll probably return here and watch real American TV and eat American Chinese food from boxes. That'll be fun.

Shyam provided a wake-up call at ten. 'Princess?' He laughed at her muzzy grunt. 'Still asleep as always?'

'I couldn't sleep. I haven't got used to the noise.'

'Don't get used to it. Think of the silence in your home and the solid presence of your husband in the bed beside you.'

'That's very poetic.' She sat up slowly. 'Fool. I'm already planning my return. Have you watered the balcony pots this morning?'

'As soon as I put the phone down. What are you doing today?'

'I'm going to look for that jacket. Because I love the bag, Shyam. It would be nice to have the set.'

Shyam was gentle. 'Princess, I'm not going to argue with you. You are there, I am here. It is him I mistrust, not you. Let's not discuss Sam Raven any more. If anything he does worries you, then tell me. Otherwise, the subject is out of bounds.'

'Thank you. What are you doing today?'

'I'm going to a jazz club with Lucky.'

'Since when do you like jazz?'

'In small doses it's all right. Better than cogitating and agitating about my wife and her movements abroad.'

'I'll be back every second weekend. You don't lose me that easily.'

She spotted the shop within minutes of passing Tiffany. The doeskin bag was in the window. No prices. A liveried doorman guarded the revolving door. Inside, Chita rode the escalator to the first floor. There it is. God, it's beautiful. But much too small.

'Hello, ma'am: may I help you?'

'Do you have this jacket in a larger size?'

'I'm afraid it's the last one.'

Chita stroked the pelt regretfully. 'Oh well. That's that.'

'Say: are you Sam Raven's girl?'

Confused, Chita said: 'Yes. Well, I work with him.'

'I should have guessed. He called and said you'd be coming.

I put it away. Chita, right?' She nodded. The woman disappeared through an unmarked door and returned with a larger version of the garment. She held it open. Chita took put down her bag and tried it on.

'My. He has a good eye. Take a look.' She went to the mirror. Sam *was* right. Although brown against brown was technically unworkable, it did something for her colouring.

Like the pearls she never wore, it gave her skin a lustre.

'You like it?'

'I love it. It's . . . exquisite. But probably beyond my purse.' She turned to admire the cut of it. 'How much is it exactly?'

'No cost,' said the assistant, surprised. 'Mr Raven paid for it when he bought the handbag.' In the several minutes Chita stood rooted to the spot, the garment was wrapped. 'Can you sign here please, to confirm receipt? Thank you.'

She picked up the carrier and left the store on leaden legs.

Chita didn't go to the Met. She caught a cab back to the flat, hung up the jacket joylessly and agonised. Oh God, I'm so stupid. Shyam saw this coming and I've refused to believe it. I've walked straight into Sam Raven's trap. No, not a trap. A silly psychological game

Shyam and Lucky think it's sexual because they're men. But if *they* don't automatically pursue attractive women, why should Sam? He may be single, but I'm not. Anyway, according to the women at work, he has plenty of girlfriends.

Chita phoned Manju. 'I've been such an idiot. I shouldn't have listened to him. He's played me like a fiddle.'

'Tell me something, Chita. When he enters the room, does your skin prickle? Answer me! Do you get a shiver down your back?'

'There's a tension . . . that's it.'

'In other words, he has an effect on you. And you on him.'

'Not a positive effect.'

'And not a negative effect.'

'I like him, Manju. He hasn't done me any harm. He's more interesting than the usual chiefs. He's an internationalist. Because of the Sri Lankan roots. It's not what you're suggesting.'

'I haven't suggested anything, Chita. All I've done is question you.' She paused and then spoke into the silence. 'It *is* strange, don't you think, how he's got under your skin? Such a strong sense of who you are, what you like, what you want. More, perhaps, than Shyam?'

'That's it exactly: he gets under my skin. He *does* understand me: though not that well if he thinks I'm a romantic possibility. It's like sorcery, Manju. He has a bag of tricks. What should I do?'

'What can you do? You're trapped by commitments now. Make the most of it, Chita. If you discover you like his tricks perhaps you should inspect his magic wand. Your husband will never know.'

As she opened a tin of tuna, mixed it with mayonnaise and tipped it on to a bowl of green salad leaves, Chita laughed aloud at her friend's irreverence. It doesn't matter, she thought, perched on a stool looking out on to Gap and Banana Republic. I'm no soft touch. Sam Raven has met his match. If he wants to play cat-and-mouse, I'll beat him at his own game.

What she didn't consider was the fable of the tortoise and the hare.

Against Shyam's pained advice, she wore the jacket to work on Monday. 'Wow, what a sensational outfit. A month's money?'

'Sort of, Suzie. Yes.'

After lunch she knocked on Sam's door. He looked up from his desk, clearly pleased to gaze upon this vision in her virginal white linen blouse and fawn slacks. 'Chita. Any problems?'

'Not at all, Sam. I just wanted to say thank you.'

'You got the Ross-Bromnick memo?'

'No, I got the matching jacket.'

'It fits?'

'Like a second skin.' She stood her ground, meeting his gaze unflitchingly and without visible emotion.

'Lucky jacket. It was presumptuous of me.'

'Yes, Sam, it was.'

'But you love it.' She didn't know what to say. 'I couldn't resist. When you see something beautiful and know some*one* beautiful it seems . . . almost cruelty not to marry them together.' He waited for her to respond. She didn't. He looked amused and cocked his head. 'Was that why you came to see me?'

'Yes.' He nodded his head but said nothing. Chita found herself filling the silence. 'I've already acted on the Ross-Bromnick data. Brad has gone through the files and found all the records. I'll draft a letter this afternoon.'

'Good.' He picked up a file and scanned it quickly, then looked up as if surprised she was still standing there. His look was igniter fuel: bright; unreadable. 'Is there something else, Chita?'

She shook her head. 'Nothing I can't deal with.' Smiling tightly, she turned and left his office.

Great ass, Sam thought as she walked away. Can't wait to get my hands on it.

Two days later they had to attend the first official client conference. Climbing into the cab, each took position at opposite ends of the short bench seat. Chita was wearing a grey knee-length dress-suit. The contentious jacket, worn as a statement of rebellion, was back in the wardrobe. She couldn't decide whether to flaunt it or destroy it.

As the cab swung into Central Park, Sam said amiably:

'How's it going? You seem to have bedded in, no problem.'

'New York is a great city.'

'It's certainly that. Well, here we go: Mr Raven and the walking, talking evidence of his gold standard. The Rent-a-Turd squad.'

Chita smiled. I can't help it. He has such a dry turn of phrase.

Rent-a-Turd, or RAT, was Sam's take on the contract that they would rubber-stamp this morning after Chita's presentation. The corporation that was employing them didn't just specialise in municipal rubbish clearance, although that was the main focus. It also owned and managed huge dumps and dispersal sites across the country.

Sam's preliminary recommendations had identified the need for massive reinvestment at the cost of thousands of jobs. 'Their retrieval and distribution systems are so slow and antiquated, they've just paid out zillions for erroneously dumping chemicals into the water tanks of a small town near Atlanta.'

'That's where you come in, Chita,' Sam had said on her first day. 'Evolving change strategy without causing riots among the troops. Some of the biggest American unions are involved. The last thing they need while tendering for contract renewal is posturing Swat team reps.' He'd handed her four box files of correspondence. 'There's going to be a quake around the block. We're talking at least five thousand jobs, maybe as many as ten. So: that's us. Rent-a-Turd, the RATs in the rubbish.'

Leaning into the cab window as they passed the Dakota building, Chita knew that she and Sam must be able to trust each other implicitly to pull it off. She turned to find him dozing; his long fringed lashes perfect arcs against olive skin, the wayward lick of hair down across his forehead.

Shyam looks like a demigod when asleep, she thought. With his chiselled looks and curly hair, he's Michelangelo's David. Sam's features are blunter. He's like a wayward cherub.

Suddenly, Sam's eyes opened and she found herself locked into him. Mesmerised. He was looking both into her and through her, like someone in the middle of a dream. There was no flicker of recognition. After several seconds they closed again, and remained that way for the last twenty minutes of the journey.

Friday night she caught the flight home from JFK on a total high from the week's successes. She slept the whole seven hours, waking up refreshed and full of energy.

She saw Shyam as she walked out of customs with just her Coast hand luggage. Chita's heart flipped like it always had. He looked handsomer than ever, his shirt casually unbuttoned beneath an ochre sweater; the whole slightly frazzled, sexily, with tiredness. Chita was filled with love and longing. Her heart was in her mouth as she walked the length of the barriers to her husband's side.

Shyam wasn't a demonstrative man. Firstly, he was Indian. Secondly, an air sign. He held her to him appreciatively, but briefly. He searched her face for something . . . she didn't know what. Signs of life? Satisfied with what he found there, he kissed her on the cheeks. Chita dropped her bag, pulled his head down to hers and planted a long, wet smacker on his lips. 'For goodness' sake, husband, look pleased to see me.'

Outside, Lucky was waiting in the no-waiting area. 'The first of many fleeting visits, sister-in-law? I just chased off a warden with a promise of favours. May I charge them to your account?'

'Only my husband draws on that account, Lucky. Your own accounts are surely healthy. You're clearly not spending much on wardrobe.'

'I told you she'd make fun of my sweater, bro'.'

'Let's go.'

If Chita detected a certain sharpness in her husband's tone, she didn't say anything.

'Will your admirer be pining this weekend?'

'He's flown to his place in Aspen. He takes no interest in me whatsoever. Are you disappointed?'

'No interest? Look at that jacket. It must have cost a fortune. What shade of green are you, Chita? You're blind to his motives.'

'We haven't even shared a lunch-time sandwich.'

'Because he wants to eat *you*.' Catching his brother's look, Lucky got up angrily. 'He challenges all of us.'

'He's playing a game. I'm just one of the pieces, not the prize.'

Lucky snorted. 'You've clearly never played chess, Chita. The prize *is* one of the pieces: the most precious piece.'

Bounding up the stairs, he shouted to Shyam: 'We'd better stay in shape, big brother. The pawns may be called into battle.'

Lucky loved Chita. Coming from a heritage of extended family where, put at its crudest, what's yours is mine, he appreciated his good luck in his brother's choice of wife. He himself was blessed with looks and character, but when he'd made the decision to join Shyam and Chita in London, he'd left behind a girl who loved him and put his own life on hold for fourteen years. Shyam and Chita's dilemma, then, had reverberations for him. He had a pathological fear of any impediment that might prevent their safe return to India.

So it was that, while he'd have flirtations and assignations, he always made his intentions – or lack of intentions –

absolutely clear. He never knowingly misused or misled anyone. This didn't stop women throwing themselves at him. Indeed, any woman can testify to the aphrodisiac effect of unavailability. It has a smack of macho self-denial; a sniff of bastardliness; a soupçon of come and get me if you can, pussycat . . .

But, unlike his brother, Lucky was wise to these moves. And what made his self-control particularly remarkable was that every refusal went against his genetic grain. We have only mentioned two of his father's wives, but in fact there was a third that has been excluded for the sake of brevity. To avert his gaze, therefore, from the charms of some quite lovely women took a focus of will and spirit that confirms both his virtuousness and his virtuosity.

Within this context, it is easier to understand his pivotal role in the lives of Shyam and Chita, and why his presence, though initially a cause of anxiety to the young wife, was soon taken for granted. He wasn't so much a part of the furniture as one of the foundations on which they had set their bricks and mortar.

Now, as he straightened his tie and came back down the stairs in a smart shirt and jacket, he stopped and considered them both with deep affection. 'I'm going out. We've missed you, Chitaji. Whatever that man Raven throws at us, he will never get to keep you.'

The weekend passed in a blur of sleeping, lovemaking and croissants. Lucky, fortuitiously-on-purpose, had a full schedule of extracurricular activities, and Shyam and Chita were left alone.

They both, in theory, had so much to say, yet they barely spoke.

'Shyam?'

'Yes?'

'Oh. Nothing. It's nice being home.'

Enough had passed in the long nightly calls. It was, therefore, a magical forty-eight hours in which touch and feeling –
an expression of the deepest emotion – took over from words.
It was healing; soothing; like a balm taking away the tension
and the uncertainty.

We are blessed, Chita thought, waking on Sunday in his
arms and smelling the early morning earthiness of him.

They sat in bed sharing out the reviews and the supplements
over breakfast, wiping jam and coffee spills as they went.
Later, they watched an old black-and-white movie – *Now
Voyager* – that reduced her to tears. In the evening they got
a Thai home delivery.

On Monday, Chita watched from the bed as Shyam dressed:
a pale yellow YSL shirt, navy single-breasted Armani off-the-
peg suit, Patrick Cox loafers she'd forced him to buy against
both his taste and better judgment, and a tie she'd got him
in Bloomingdale's one lunch-time: silk, printed with leaping
horses.

On Sunday afternoon, after the film, she'd insisted on
trimming his hair, and this morning he'd slicked it back with
gel. She noticed the flecks of grey striping at his temples. So
sexy. Sometimes you need distance to be reminded how lucky
you are.

He kissed her gently, 'See you in two weeks, Princess,' and
was gone in a slam of a door.

Chita enjoyed the luxury of pootling around in the nude.
The flat wasn't overlooked and nobody on the river below
could see her in her sunny eyrie. She danced to Capital
Radio and sorted out various creams and potions to take
back with her.

She had planned to mooch around Roman Road market,
but by the time she'd finished daydreaming and writing letters
and pining in advance for her husband it was time to head for
Heathrow. Pulling on her jacket, she was suddenly filled with

a sense of emptiness. I love my husband and I love my job and . . . and this is the way people live in the modern world. She called a cab. How can something so wonderfully right feel so strangely wrong?

Or, given that Sam Raven is part of the equation, how can something so strangely wrong feel so wonderfully right?

The next week was lost in the haze of activity. Chita was in the office by eight each morning and rarely home before nine. There had been a slight freeze when she returned on Tuesday morning, but as it also seemed to extend to everyone else in the office it didn't bother her.

She'd set herself the task of getting a feel for both their client's developmental history and the history of unionisation in the US, so she could put it all in context. Her reading was prodigious. On the Friday night she took home books, boxes of photocopies and endless notes. She didn't leave the apartment, living on bagels and using reading breaks to surf the Net and download background and knowledge that might be worth something later.

Chita had an instinct for information. She filed away unconnected facts and figures which inevitably proved useful. By Sunday, she'd filled an exercise book with her spiky upright writing.

During that time she spoke only to Shyam – six times – and Manju, who rang to shoot the breeze with surprising but not unexpected news: 'Rich has asked me to marry him.'

'That's brilliant. You're going to say yes, aren't you?'

'Because I won't find anyone else at my age, you mean?'

'No, you goose, because you love him.'

'I don't know, Chita. I'm thirty-seven. I was resigned to spinsterhood.'

'What an old-fashioned term. What's wrong with you, Manju?'

'He just asked me in the car on the way to work, Chita. There was nothing special about it. He was turning left when he suddenly said: "How about it, Manju, why don't we tie the knot?"'

'Would it have made a difference if he was turning right?'

'You know exactly what I mean.' She started to laugh. 'He said he was too nervous to look me in the eye because he thought I'd say no.'

'So you *did* say yes.'

'I'm too fat for a bridal frock, Chita.'

'Then wear trousers.'

'You're supposed to say, "No, Manju, you're not fat at all."'

Now they were both laughing. 'You know you're not. I'm so busy I'm not thinking clearly.'

'Will you be my maid of honour?'

'If you're not in a hurry. My diary's full till after Christmas.'

'I thought you were in New York three months only?'

'So did I. But there's no way I'll be done by mid-November.'

'Don't kill yourself, Chita. It's only money.'

'With you I can't win whether I'm wife or worker. Manju, tell me that marriage isn't going to make you dull and self-satisfied.'

'I wouldn't steal your crown, my darling.'

They talked about Rich's parents, who'd finally accepted that their son was in love with an Indian girl. And a trouble-some child in Manju's class who had, it transpired, been bringing herself to school for four whole days while her mother lay dead of a drugs overdose in the bedroom. 'Don't our problems diminish to nothing?' Manju said.

'Yes. Why do people tempt fate like that?'

'Because, as I told you years ago, it's ultimately less frightening than fate tempting you.'

*　　*　　*

'I hate asking this, Chita, but is there any chance that you can cancel your trip home this weekend?'

'It's already Wednesday. The tickets are bought, Sam.'

'We can sort that out. It's easy enough.'

'But it's such short notice. I'd rather not.'

'Okay. I just asked. Will you digest the pile of stuff on your desk in time for Tuesday's group conference?'

'I'm taking it with me.'

'Sure. I didn't mean to suggest otherwise. But if you think it might help – all of us, that is – to cancel and put the jet-lag on hold . . . I'm happy for you to have an extra-long break in two weeks' time – say Friday to Tuesday inclusive?'

'That's very sweet, but I've already had two weekends back at home without any problem.'

Monica called from London. 'Thank you for the card. What an irony that the only person to mark my return to work is actually in the States. They tell me you're run off your feet.'

'Mr Raven is very demanding . . .'

'Tell me about it. Half my memos are from your office. But I'm bloody glad I'm back.' Monica lowered her voice conspiratorially. 'The most amazing things are happening. You've heard about the night of the long knives? This morning half the board resigned at gunpoint after fisticuffs at yesterday's AGM.'

'No! It's only nine o'clock here. The grapevine hasn't woken. Is that why Sam was so distracted? Tell me all.'

For a delicious half-hour Monica shut the door to her office and wove a tale of deception and destruction, much of the narrative embellished with conjecture for the pure joy of it. But, as it unfurled, it became clear to Chita that Sam's request, while irritating, was hardly unreasonable. This company is lurching from crisis to crisis. I've been with them too long to disappear at this moment. Everything is in the air. If I were in London I wouldn't budge from my desk.

Chita got a coffee from the machine and took the unusual step of calling Shyam in his office. He was mid-meeting. She distilled the basic information and rang off. Then she went to Sam and told him she'd be staying. He was only grudgingly grateful: 'I'd rather hoped you'd agree without the extra incentive.'

Oh no, mister, you don't get me like that. 'I'm not staying because of the workload, Sam. I could easily have managed that *and* taken the break. I'm staying because I don't want morale in the department to be shaken more than is already the case. On *that* basis, taking time off is unacceptable.'

He nodded, unsmiling. She felt the need to underscore her point. 'I didn't have the full facts at my disposal when we spoke this morning.' Bobbing neatly – almost a curtsy – she excused herself. You can't get at me, Mr Raven, Chita thought. See if I care.

She went swinging down the corridor with such a jaunty step that passing staff commented that things couldn't be that bad after all.

For the next two weeks, they didn't come up for air. Sam worked his way up the spectrum from surly to charming. A couple of times they walked over to the local diner and had eggs and hash. He could mimic anyone. She thawed. He made her laugh.

At the end of each day, Chita was relieved to go home to an empty apartment. She missed the physical comfort and security that Shyam would have offered, but the issues were so clear cut she didn't need him as a sounding-board. Anyway, no matter where she was, Chita always cleared half an hour at 6 p.m. to talk to him before he went to bed.

'You had lunch with Sam? That's twice in ten days.'

'It's hardly a crime.'

'I didn't say it was, Chita.'

114

'*He's* the one you don't trust, Shyam.'

'And now you're cancelling this weekend too? That's a month without seeing you: six weeks between your last visit and your next. No. Don't say anything. Let's not argue.'

'You know how it is. We haven't drawn breath. Nobody knows what's going to happen.' She sighed. 'Pax?'

But soon the fretwork of progression was clear. A new chief executive was headhunted from a UK-centred global media group. There was talk of refashioning the company image – spelling out the name in lower case and changing the logo to something more wholesome like an apple (except Mac got there first), or a heart (but that clashed with the British Labour Party).

New directors were appointed, statements were issued, people were warned not to talk to the press and share prices stabilised. Again.

By the end of the week, Chita was too exhausted to take work home. She slept till noon on the Saturday and walked across Central Park to the Met. The foyer was higher than it was deep. She cruised the galleries in a detached way, enjoying the processes of the displays but not feeling them in her soul.

Part of that was cultural. Oils and large pastoral canvases have a peculiarly Western sensibility about them. Particularly in the West. The card indexes at the Met or the Tate or the Louvre show no proliferation of Syals, Alibhais, Shahs or Pereras. And, while moghul art and its derivatives are revered and reproduced prodigiously on the Indian subcontinent, there are no rows over which of their national art houses should bid for the touring Monet exhibition or a loan of Constable's *Haywain*.

Chita thought of the moghul women, constructed in miniature with the finest brushes and smallest strokes. She loved the intricacy of their adornments: the tight encasing of large breasts; the thick curve of thighs under silk; the mocking

115

challenge in the black-painted slant of their eyes. All sex and power. How romantic!

On the Sunday, Chita took the boat to Ellis Island and found herself weeping. This is ridiculous. I'm stressed.

All around were photographs and testimonies from the hundreds of thousands of immigrants who underwent the exacting medical and financial tests required for entry. These people made America what it is today. I wonder how far back Sam's family goes?

One story Chita later related to Shyam was of a young Polish girl who, to prove her usefulness as a woman and worker, was asked if you washed stairs from the bottom up or the top down. 'I didn't come to America to wash stairs,' the child replied.

She took the boat to the Statue of Liberty and, later, walked home through Battery Park. Getting in at five, she called Shyam. Lucky answered. 'So we don't even get a monthly visit, sister-in-law?'

'Does it make that much difference?'

'Actually it will make three times as much difference, but maths clearly isn't your best subject or you'd know it takes two to make a marriage.' Lucky sighed. 'We told you, Chita. You think you're free to do as you wish, but you're trapped. I'll get Shyam.'

Monica was her first Monday caller. 'That was a remarkably coherent and well-informed report on American union practice you wrote last week. They've circulated it for general information.'

Chita shovelled the last of an M&Ms multipack into her mouth. 'Sorry for the crunching. I'm comfort eating.'

At twelve, she and Sam went to the boardroom for a team lunch and briefing. They'd ordered a Tex-Mex lunch with bottles of beer and Virgin Marys.

'Ready for action, partner?'

'Yes siree, Mr Raven.'

He pushed a stray hair from her face. 'You do the talking. I'll be in the wings if your hand needs holding.'

Aware that everyone was hungry, Chita kept it short and to the point, running through the agenda that would carry RAT through to Christmas. At the end they applauded. Her natural optimism made her a favourite with the Americans.

'You look terrific in that dress,' Sam said, over the cheers. 'Light wool always settles in the right places. You should wear it to client meetings. Schmooze with your ooze.' Grinning, he walked away.

Over coffee Chita watched him work the room. We do gel as a team. He's right. Lena called her over to gossip. Sam came by and leaned into her ear. 'This is so nineteen eighties, isn't it? Like a scene from *Bonfire of the Vanities* or *American Psycho*.'

Two nights before she was finally due to go home for her long weekend, two of the union players asked to meet Sam and Chita for an off-the-record chat over dinner at King Mambo.

As they walked through to the dining room, Chita was genuinely excited. I love the uncertainty and the circling. What are these guys after? I've read so much about the financing and corruption of organisations like the Teamsters. Who's to say which pies our guys have got their fingers in?

She and Sam had agreed their strategy before the meeting. 'No specifics and no numbers. This is just the warm-up.'

'I might run into the bathroom and make the odd note.'

'As long as it's only lists and not graphs tonight.'

The small talk was surprisingly easy. They were interested in Chita's mixed background and her informed take on American politics. Sam did the PR bit, mentioning companies that had increased profitability and, ultimately, employment as a result of their input. Over the main course they progressed to the public service industry in general and finally, over dessert, to theirs in particular. Chita was surprised to find that American frankness stretched to covert behind-the-scenes conversation. When the evening came to an end with handshakes and kind words, a clear understanding had been reached. She felt enormous satisfaction. 'We know where we stand now, don't we?'

'We certainly do, hon. Did you enjoy yourself?'

'It was wonderful. Funny. And the food was good too.'

He burst out laughing. Dropping his case, he whooped loudly and grabbed her by the waist. Lifting Chita in the air, he whirled her round as if she were a little girl. 'We're gonna do this, aren't we? We're the greatest team in this whole damn city.'

She couldn't stop grinning. She was exhilarated. When he put her down it took a second to get her breath back. But in that second he took her breath away again by leaning down and kissing her mouth so lightly, and wetly, that she stumbled back.

'Whoops. That didn't land as intended, hon.' He steadied her, still smiling. Chita looked at him blankly. She's clearly put out, but not, Sam noted, repelled by me. She hasn't wiped her mouth. She's thinking about the sensation. Let's get her home before she thinks too much. He stepped into the road and flagged down a cab.

'You get to bed and have a well-deserved sleep, Chita. I'm so high I'm going to walk.'

As the big yellow taxi pulled away, she watched him loping cheerfully towards 55th Street.

The next two days passed in a blur of notes and queries ensuring that compromises implicitly agreed over dinner were incorporated in the list of priorities and objectives. Sam, as was always the case when Chita was feeling a little sensitive, paid her hardly any attention at all.

He had kissed her intimately but carelessly. So fleetingly that she couldn't remember the detail of it, but with enough pressure for her to still feel its imprint. And, as ever, even though he had not invited the attention, she was forced to respond emotionally. To yet again afford him space in her thinking; in her consciousness.

When, later, they ran into each other in the main office, he greeted her distractedly: 'Hi. How's it going?'

'No change from yesterday.'

'Good. Good.' He walked straight by her.

Eva raised an eyebrow. 'Forgive him. He's preoccupied.'

Chita shook her head. Being around Sam is like being at the epicentre of a series of minor seismic tremors. They don't register until the first crack appears in the foundations. After that, you notice the tiniest shift. *I* notice the tiniest shift.

That afternoon Sam cancelled a meeting with her. 'I'm running to stand still, hon.'

Chita smiled. 'That's okay. I've loads to do anyway.' I'm right: last night's kiss was not confirmation that Sam is still playing with me, but confirmation that he isn't . . .

The long weekend at home somehow wasn't as she'd imagined. The boys were both at work when she arrived in London on the Friday morning, and she got the Heathrow Express to Paddington. The taxi queue was swollen by the fact that it was pouring. After twenty minutes, she was only a third of the way along. Frustrated by the whole exercise, Chita walked to the Edgware Road where, soaked to the skin, she got a minicab to Docklands.

She'd wanted to shop and make them dinner, but, having been dropped at the only cash machine for miles, she found

119

it was faulty. She had just ten pounds – not enough to buy what she needed from the corner shop. Not for the first time she wondered how it could be that such a residentially dense area had virtually no infrastructure. Feeling seriously out of sorts, she dragged herself tiredly home, only to discover, as she rummaged in her handbag for the keys, that she'd packed them in her luggage.

Squatting in the wet, Chita removed her carefully wrapped belongings and placed them on the damp doorstep. The tears coursing down her face mingled with the rain as, finally, her fingers closed around the precious keys, and, after repacking, she let herself into the building and took the lift to the fourth floor.

The flat was strangely empty. It was as if, lacking a woman's presence, the giant living area had transformed itself from home to function room. Technically, everything was where it should be but it lacked . . . warmth, somehow. Thinking this was a literal problem, Chita immediately went and switched the heating on.

She'd been gone ten weeks. It was late October.

Still in her coat, Chita patrolled her space. She'd spent hours telling successive cleaning ladies exactly how to polish and where things went. As she stood in the middle of that vast loft, a trail of drips marking her passage across the blocked-ash floor, she saw that, indeed, nothing was amiss. It just *felt* forlorn and foreign.

She went to the window and looked out on to a river that was almost lost in the spray of water on water. Perhaps, if it's true that walls absorb vibrations, without me here to keep home this flat reflects only silence. Oh God, why did I promise to see this job through? If my part's done by January, it'll be a miracle.

Clever Sam. He had Chita hoist by the petard of professional and moral obligation. Meanwhile, Shyam and Lucky showed scant interest in the detail because it irritated too much to hear it. But to Chita it felt like punishment.

As the wind changed direction and the rain started beating violently against the glass at which she stood, Chita felt an overwhelming fear: a desperate need to be with her husband. She went to the laundry basket and scrabbled about for a shirt that might hold his scent.

Crushing it to her nose, she wept again.

Unbelievably, Shyam had taken Monday off. Chita was thrilled. 'I've never known you to do that!'

'You've never before been rationed.'

They made love twice after Lucky had gone to work. It was the first time he'd touched her intimately all week-end.

Chita had said nothing, but her husband's lack of libido and, indeed, her own hesitance in initiating lovemaking, were totally out of character. She and Shyam often expressed joy or anxiety through passion. His delicate but detached handling of her had left her depressed on Friday.

On Saturday they'd had a falling out when she'd asked if he would mind the fortnightly trip home being commuted to monthly.

'Why do you ask me, Chita? Have I really got a choice?'

'For goodness' sake, Shyam, team morale is so low. We've the biggest crisis in years and all around us are feng shui experts changing everything from the logo to the letterhead to the office furniture because some idiot has said red filling cabinets make the staff aggressive. Everybody's being redeployed. I'm not getting any extra back-up.'

'But I'm the one making the concessions.'

'Does your sense of duty only operate when *you* are directly involved in the proceedings, Shyam?' Chita took his hand. 'If I lay the groundwork, I can leave with a clear conscience.' And then, when he didn't respond: 'Why are we fighting? I haven't seen you in weeks.'

She'd made them a casserole that night but they ate in silence, watching the Sean Connery retrospective from different ends of the sofa. In bed she deliberately rolled away, expecting him to come after her. But he didn't, even though he was still awake when she finally fell asleep.

By Sunday the tension had eased, but when Chita went to bed, Shyam stayed up talking to Lucky. She had no idea what time he joined her. She'd woken with her body aching for him; laden with need. Finally the freeze had stopped and they had made love with a tearing passion, too quick for fulfilment the first time, but wonderfully satisfying the second. Which made the general loss seem even greater.

'Let's go down to St Katharine's Dock and lunch overlooking the marina,' Shyam said. 'I wish we could escape all this bloody pressure. What are we doing to ourselves, Chita? What's happened to us? We've suddenly become old.'

'You're just forty. Life begins. Don't have a mid-life crisis on me, husband. Let me tell you, you still make my heart skip a beat.'

He stared at her intently. 'Why don't we give up? Let's pack our bags, buy a round-the-world ticket and see what life throws at us? We could travel home via all the continents, starting in Australia and working our way back round to India. Would you like that?'

'I couldn't fit my shopping in a backpack.' She smiled, but inside she felt moved; sad. *He's feeling insecure. And it's my fault. I'm his security and I've rocked the boat. It's not about Sam. It's about us. How can I reassure him without making it worse?*

After lunch they took a leisurely stroll to Butler's Wharf, stopping on Tower Bridge to enjoy the views before spending a happy couple of hours slipping in and out of the chichi shops.

'How can you get so much pleasure from this nonsense, Chita?'

'We'll do something else.'

'Don't be silly. I get pleasure from your pleasure.'

He watched her trying on bracelets, draping herself in pink and purple tulle and exclaiming at the workmanship on silly little wooden boxes and monkey puzzles, but it never occurred to him to buy her any of these baubles, because that wasn't in his nature.

Although instinctively generous, Shyam lacked the sentiment for grand romantic gestures. And, it must be said, as she ummed and aahed over peridot rings and silk flamenco tops, it didn't even occur to Chita that it should be otherwise.

Later they caught a bus to the West End. 'Let's get theatre tickets – the new Lloyd Webber. But first I want to go on the Pepsi Drop.'

'It terrifies you, Chita.'

'Well, yes. That's the buzz.'

Shyam bought the picture taken by the auto camera – the two of them terrified but grinning. Many a true thing snapped in jest!

As his wife dragged him downstairs to the Segadrome, Shyam said: 'Why no social life in New York, Chita?'

'I see the occasional film and there are client dinners but I haven't time to make friends and loaf around, Shyam. We're both living the same life, but separated by water. That's all.' That's all.

Before heading for Heathrow on the Tuesday, Chita lunched with Monica at Orso's. 'I'm sorry I haven't seen you since leaving. Oh, doesn't Annie look lovely? She's so big. I hope these things fit her.'

'They're lovely.' Monica ordered pizzas. 'Come back, Chita. I've got nobody to gossip with. Phone calls aren't the same.

There's a ghastly new woman who looks like a stick insect and eats alfalfa sprouts at her desk, and the monkeys have been put on the bonus scheme in return for implementing the new rules at base level.'

'I miss Jez and Shola. The New York crowd aren't so . . . irreverent. So how are you juggling your two lives?'

'By dropping the odd ball every now and then. Coming back to work has given me back a sense of self but I miss Annie. That said, Peter's a real brick.' She sipped her spritzer. 'So how are you juggling *your* two lives?'

'Well, the Sam crisis never happened. He's fun, Monica. He can be sulky if you go against him, but mostly we operate independently of each other.' She smiled. 'I love the work. It's terrific. And of course the bonus will be nice . . . You know, Sam can only penetrate my defences if I let him.'

'Bad choice of words, Chita.'

They laughed till they cried. 'Far from Sam's moods being the problem, it's Shyam,' Chita suddenly found herself saying. 'He can't deal with the separation. I was weak to accept Sam's line about RAT. He could have pulled it off without me. But—'

'Does it matter now?'

'Shyam wants me back here. But I've promised to see through the preliminary changes. I can't just walk out. It's very difficult.'

'You'll weather it. That's the whole point of marriage. You grow together and, occasionally, for a little while, apart.'

Seeing her friend into an airport taxi, Monica wandered down the Strand to Charing Cross station. She hoped Chita and Shyam would resolve their tensions soon. Although both were singular in their pursuits, they were very much a couple: two magnets. Currently they were facing different poles. Soon, they'd pull together. In the meantime, Monica was aware of a change in her friend. Chita's rhythm was gone. She'd lost her groove.

The next Saturday, Manju flew into Manhattan. As soon as she'd dumped her bags in Chita's apartment they went shopping for a wedding dress. By store number seven and dress number ten, which, apparently, accentuated Manju's shelf-like bottom and pinched around the sweetheart neckline, Chita had had enough. 'For God's sake, Manju, can we go back now?'

'No. We can fit in one more shop. Don't look like that, Chita. When I think how I sat with you in old man Thapar's as you turned down sari after sari. And then the jewellery! As if anyone could tell the difference between one hanging gold bell and another, but you made me drive fifty miles to help you find the perfect one. Where is it now – in a box somewhere?'

'Amma has it.'

'So: fifty miles for baubles you'll never wear again. And what about the sandals—'

'For goodness' sake, Manju, I had no choice. Isn't the whole point of marrying this boy that you can do it quietly?'

'I am doing it quietly!'

'And you haven't even set a date or chosen a venue—'

'What difference does that make?'

'It makes all the difference, you goose. If you marry in the winter you must wear a warmer dress; in the summer you can go sleeveless. And what about tradition? Why not marry in a sari? He's the American, not you.'

'When did you last wear a sari, Chita?'

'At a bonfire night party. Exactly a year ago.'

'And before that?'

'My wedding.'

'Exactly! Well, that was the last time I also wore a sari. No, I tell a lie, I wore a sari to my mother's funeral.' Her face fell for a minute. 'All my life I've worn them for rituals: for rites of passage. For loss. The death of my father. The exile of my best friend. The death of my mother. For happiness, let me wear something else.'

The two women walked around Greenwich Village, stopping to laugh at a clockwork couple enjoying coitus in the window of a women's sex shop. 'The whole act is so strange when you observe it from one remove. And yet it gives so much enjoyment. But, Chita . . . enough Rich talk! How is your own Prince Charming?'

Chita didn't mention the residual emptiness she'd felt since returning from London. It wasn't appropriate when Manju was clearly feeling so happy. She dragged her friend into a gift shop. 'You know, Manju, you're the only person apart from Amma and Papa who has been with me through thick and thin.'

'Don't get all sentimental on me, Chita. It's not your style. Are you feeling maternal all of a sudden: getting ready to be your husband's brood mare? Or have you had a premonition that I'll be struck by a truck tomorrow and you want to make your kind goodbyes?'

'Manju.' Chita hugged her friend to her. 'I adore you.'

'Could you demonstrate that by finding me a shop with dresses that don't look like chapatis?'

For three days the following week, Chita was out of town. Although she had often been on the Continent while working from London, it was her first overnight in the US.

She flew early to Denver and picked up the connecting flight to Aspen. The previous evening, Sam had said to her: 'See how you like the place. I've a chalet there, not far from the centre. Great skiing, great views. I'll be spending Christmas in front of the log fire with a glass of schnapps. Good company would be welcome.'

'How do you know I'd be good company when not talking about work? I fear you'd tire of me, Sam.'

'I could never tire of you, Chita,' he'd said, leaving the room without another word.

She was met at Aspen airport, a small strip flanked by mountains, by a driver with a people carrier who took her to her hotel in Carbondale. She sat silently in the passenger seat listening to an argument about Golgotha on the local Christian radio station. *I am so lonely. Isolated. And I can't talk to anyone. Manju is wedding mad and Monica is still baby obsessed. I am in this alone.*

She checked in her luggage, collected her four-wheel-drive and headed along the freeway to the office complex where she'd be information-gathering. The provincial crowd were much friendlier than the usual city slickers, who viewed Chita and her colleagues with mistrust and caution. They were interested in her – pumping her for her thoughts and volunteering their opinions. At the end of the first day, they insisted she join them for a welcoming drink in a local bar.

Returning to the hotel, Chita showered and took a wander down the main street, pausing with delight to peer into the cinema, which appeared to be part of someone's house. The main drag, made up of pizza restaurants, small bars and craft shops, was both lively and subdued. A truck, lit like a Diwali lantern, rumbled through, temporarily blinding her.

Above, the sky was so clear she felt that if she jumped with her arms up she could touch the stars. Pulling her coat around her, she sat on the wall outside the post office, watching people walk by in the dark. *I'd better buy some thermals tomorrow.*

Even in the valley they were well above sea level. It was cold but crisp. It reminded her in a strange way of home. The next day, at lunch-time, she went into the tourist centre and got some leaflets. Why am I doing this? I go back tomorrow night!

She saw that there was a mountain fair in one of the outlying towns over the weekend. There were spectacular shots of the National Monument at Grand Junction: red rocks and swooping lows like something from a moonscape.

'Why don't you stay over the weekend?' one of the women in the office said. 'Unless you've got something really pressing, you won't find a more beautiful state in the whole of the US.'

'Maybe I should.'

'Have you seen much of the country while you've been here?'

'Nothing.'

'Well, there you are.'

That afternoon, she called Lena and asked her to change her tickets for a return late Sunday night. 'Hey, Chita, you're taking time to chill? That's a new one! Report back on Sam's place, won't you?'

She left at 6 a.m. on Saturday morning and got to Grand Junction five hours later. There had been a light snowfall overnight, but the sun was already high. She stopped by the dinosaur museum to buy coffee, juice, chocolate and sunglasses, but then couldn't resist a quick tour. The building was small, but the models were animated and fun. 'I've met some of these in real life,' said one of the staff as she left.

Chita smiled. 'I know. I'm one of them.'

Heading out of town, she turned towards the national park, grateful for her four layers of clothing. She drove up through the red, pink and orange mountains, losing herself in the vastness and sheer beauty of the landscape. The higher she went, the more snow there was. Not too much; a smattering. The bonus of a continuing warm fall.

Parking at a viewing point, Chita locked the car and walked for what felt like miles across rough terrain on the precipice of canyons and cavities stretching downward for several hundred feet. Her black loafers soon became wet, but she barely noticed. What the hell – once in a lifetime. Finding an exposed boulder, she sat down, opened a Snickers bar and felt totally at one with nature.

Shyam would love it, she thought fleetingly, though actually, at heart, he was a town boy. Safety in numbers.

She put her face up to the afternoon sun. No wonder Sam bought a place here, she thought. Tomorrow I'll spend half the day at the winter fair and the other half in Aspen. Before going back, she looked down into the canyon and screamed her name: 'CHITA!!'

The mountain fair was in a ski resort built into the hills outside Aspen. There was a huge concourse filled with shops, stalls and entertainment areas. Chita bought herself native Indian jewellery and, for Shyam, she chose a charcoal alpaca sweater.

Children were taking part in a talent competition on a large stage. She watched one cross-faced little girl singing *The Good Ship Lollipop* and couldn't stop laughing.

Afterwards she drove into Aspen, which was like Bond Street and the King's Road mixed and dispersed within a self-conscious grid. She rode the gondola up the main mountain and bought cocoa and a chocolate beignet. So this is where Sam spends his winters. She watched some youngsters mess around, cross-country skiing. Being Indian, Chita wasn't particularly interested in sport. Certainly not winter sport. I am too lazy. When my waistbands pinch, it's easier to cut my chocolate intake. I don't know how my two warriors in London maintain their gym regime.

Taking the car back down, she emerged in the town ready

for a late lunch in the milk bar of a fifties-style clothes shop. It was surreal. Every second woman had had a face and bosom lift. They are twenty from the back and seventy from the front. For the second time that day, Chita laughed aloud.

On the way back, she stopped at the open-air ice rink and, just for the sheer hell of it, hired some boots and attempted a few circles. She'd only managed a few shaky yards before a beautiful man, like a young Jon Bon Jovi, offered his arm. Chita accepted and found herself giggling and gliding.

In the shadow of mountains she skated with a stranger to Ella Fitzgerald: bewitched, bothered and bewildered am I.

The answerphone was bleeping as Chita let herself into the apartment. Shyam, calling to say goodnight and tell her, diffidently, that he loved her and hoped she'd enjoyed the weekend. 'I tried your mobile but there was no signal. I'll call tomorrow. Some time.'

Chita leaned against the door of the office, suddenly filled with longing. It's crazy that these two weekends without him have been more pleasurable than the single long weekend with him.

She had a long shower to wash away the self-doubt. The bedroom was baking from aggressive centrally controlled heating and days with the windows shut. Pulling on a light slip, she went in search of a cold drink. When she opened the fridge, her heart stopped.

Every shelf was stocked with food: juice, bread, eggs, cheese, jams, yoghurts, salads, ham, steaks, carrots, beans, ketchup, lemon vodka and two bottles of Sonoma Valley Turning Leaf Zinfandel.

Chita stood absolutely still. She clamped her hand across her mouth to stop any involuntary sounds coming out. Calm, calm, calm. She counted to ten. What is this? Who is this? Be sensible. Intruders don't buy food. There is *someone else* in these rooms. Somewhere. *Oh my God.* Calm, calm, calm. This is a company flat. Whoever's here must be authorised. But I wasn't told . . . What if it's a crazed psychopath who found the keys?

Well. Only one way to find out . . .

Spinning on her heel, she scanned the corridor. Nothing. Except the second bedroom door, directly in her line of sight, and usually a few inches ajar, was shut. Without stopping to consider, and relying on surprise as her best weapon, Chita charged down the corridor, threw herself at the door – which turned out to be unlatched – and smashed on the light switch as she skidded to a halt by the bed.

He'd kicked off the duvet and was sprawled asleep on his stomach: big and muscular, his clenched and fully rounded bottom a delicious swell before the fan of his shoulders. Woken by the noise and the light, he rolled over, grumbling, on to his back and then raised his arm to shield his eyes from the light. 'What the hell? What's going on?' Blinking and shaking his head to wake himself, he struggled upright. 'Chita? What time is it?' But Chita didn't answer. She was staring at the enormous erection between the legs of the naked Sam Raven.

Stunned by the intensity of her fear, and now relief, she went silently to the sitting room. He wrapped a towel around himself and followed her. Curled in the chair, Chita was once more startled by his physique – his peculiarly powerful bestiality. It was disturbing.

Sam rubbed his eyes against the light. 'Sorry, Chita. I did actually leave you a note.' She saw the arum lilies and a white envelope propped against the vase. 'I assumed you'd come in here at some point – to watch TV, have a drink . . .'

He pulled the towel tighter, his erection subsiding. 'There was a flood in my block on Friday. I got called out of a lunch

131

meeting. One of the water tanks in our roof split a seal. I'm in the penthouse . . . It looked like a scene from *The Poseidon Adventure.*'

'You could have gone to the company apartment on Madison.'

'No: I couldn't. Jeremy Baines is there at the moment and the British MD has it booked for next week when he arrives for the Fed's banking conference.' He ran his hands through his hair. 'My place is unlivable. The floor buckled and the furniture soaked it all up. It needs a total refit. I'm sorry. I can't live out of a suitcase. I hoped you wouldn't mind.'

She couldn't look at him. 'It is not usual, Sam.'

'No, Chita: it's *un*usual. That's why I'm here. I apologise if it upsets your sensibilities. I couldn't see an alternative.'

'Were any alternatives explored?'

'I just lost half my home, Chita.'

'Of course. I'm sorry.' She forced herself to meet his eyes and found him staring at her breasts, cold and unfettered, nipples fighting the restriction of her slip. Oh God.

The night was progressing in a series of jump-cuts. Even as his attention made her self-aware, Chita felt she was having an out-of-body experience. Inexplicably, in the midst of this confusion, she felt excitement. Goose bumps as he took his time over the detail before slowly moving his gaze upward.

He studied her now. She'd like me to pull off that pornographic top and free her. But she doesn't know it. She's curious, though. And brazen. No looking away. What would happen if I slipped off this towel? Would she take me in her hands? Her mouth? Perhaps. But not yet . . .

Unspeaking, Chita uncoiled and stood. She had only put on the ceiling light, but the brightness of the street was enough to make her nightie transparent. Unwittingly Sam touched himself.

She shook her head – disbelieving. 'Goodnight, Sam.' As she returned to her room, he noticed the way her hair hung in a loose tail to her pale shoulder blades. He was charmed by the bold curve of her hips; the beginning of cellulite at the top of her thighs.

She is all woman.

As a man raised on New York girls who lunch on vitamin pills and correct imperfection by being artificially pumped and sumped, Sam was a sucker for the real thing.

He poured a glass of brandy and sat up watching dawn rise over Broadway. The flood was a really good line, he thought, finally going to bed on the other side of Chita's wall. Should have come up with it months ago.

In the morning Chita applied a slash of red lipstick to match her defiant mood. She practised various arguments to have with Human Resources: this whole arrangement breaches the protocols of civilised living; it is unorthodox for two adults of a certain age and status to share dormitory lodgings; I know he's a director, but that doesn't make it all right. Does it?

Heading for the kitchen, she was dogged by one persistent thought: how am I going to tell Shyam?

She found Sam eating breakfast and reading a stock report. He greeted her cheerily, pointed to fresh coffee in the pot, and returned to his papers. Chita poured a cup and popped a frozen bagel in the microwave. 'You'd be better off having cereal.' She buttered the bagel and cut herself a block of cheese without responding. 'Do you know, until I opened that fridge I didn't know they still sold butter in New York? Thought it was outlawed for fat content by the new administration; far too much like indulgence for us po-faced Yanks.' With some effort, she smiled. 'The full-cream milk is great, though. Never knew it could taste like that.'

It was 7.15. She had a slight earache from grinding her teeth during the night. She could hear herself chewing.

'Not sitting down? Am I putting you off your stroke?'

'I'm not a morning person.'

'Yes, I heard the two alarms. You haven't told me about Aspen.'

'It was lovely.' She bolted down the bagel and, taking the coffee with her, returned to her bedroom. She'd studied the same stock report Sam was now reading on the flight back. Thankful that she'd made detailed notes – because her thoughts were distracted to say the least – Chita shoved it into her briefcase.

She stood for a few minutes looking down into the cross-street, where the sweeper was cleaning the sidewalk. Steam was rising from the road vents. She reapplied her lipstick and pulled on her full-length black cashmere coat. As she stepped into the hallway, he was right behind her. 'Shall we travel together? Bus or cab?'

'I usually take the bus.'

'And I usually take my Ferrari, but there's nowhere to garage it around here, so it's gotta stay at the condo. Joke. Sort of. Let's take the bus. It'll be a revelation.'

'So how's the new room-mate?'

'It's not funny, Brad.'

'Sure. He asked us all what we thought. It kinda made sense the way he said it. It's only for a few weeks.'

Of course. That's what they'll all say. I'm on my own here.

She remembered last night's moment of revelation, the way he'd rolled over on to his back and her eye had been drawn to his extraordinary . . . maleness. Women say size doesn't matter, and in many ways it doesn't. But, like money, it helps.

Thus, Sam's erection wasn't in itself what occupied Chita at that moment, so much as the power embodied in the penis. (And in fairness to Shyam, one must point out as a matter of record that his own was larger than average and well utilised. But . . . it mirrored his overall physique which was slimmer and more wiry than Sam's. A World Trade Tower to Sam's Empire State; a Nelson's Column to Sam's Canary Wharf.) I'm going mad, Chita thought. And I am putting off the inevitable.

She closed her office door and called Shyam at work because she couldn't wait till he was home. Luckily he was at lunch – eating a sandwich and reading the newspaper in his office. He listened in silence until she'd finished. 'What do you want me to say, Chita?'

'I don't know. There's nothing either of us can say.'

'Except, perhaps, I told you so.'

'He's had a flood.'

'And now he wants to enter the Ark, two by two.'

Despite herself, she laughed. 'Isn't it crazy?'

'What are you going to do about it?' Shyam said.

'What can I do?'

'I don't know, Chita. But if you don't find a way of extricating yourself from this man's orbit, I will find a way to do it for you.'

She left the office at nine. She had no idea where Sam was, but told herself she would not let his presence in the apartment affect her normal routines or behaviour.

Tonight, anyway, it was dinner and then bed. With two particularly busy days ahead, she needed to re-establish her natural swing. She got a cab to the Chinese carry-out and bought chilli beef, choi sum and rice. Approaching the apartments, she saw the light on in her fourth-floor sitting room. She entered with a heavy heart, to wonderful cooking smells.

He'd put on a Wagner opera – *Tristan and Isolde*. This wasn't at all what Chita had imagined. Not that she'd given a lot of thought to it, but she'd automatically filed Sam under an umbrella of executive male clichés: dates with blondes

135

and dinner in fashionable restaurants. If she'd been thinking straight she might have associated a full fridge with a home body but she wasn't thinking straight at all.

Her instinct to slip unnoticed into her bedroom was foiled by her three leaking food boxes. The kitchen was empty but steaming. A bottle of red was breathing on the side. As she emptied the bag, she smelled his Givenchy. He'd put on jeans and a burgundy shirt. 'Hey, you haven't bought food? I've cooked. I thought we should have an inaugural dinner. Anyway, I want to hear all about your trip to Colorado. You didn't tell me a thing this morning. That said, I guess we were both sleepy still.'

He swept past her and saw the boxes. 'Can you freeze this or have it tomorrow? I've made us a casserole with sugar snap peas and butter-mashed potatoes. To maintain your cholesterol intake.' He opened the oven door so she could see inside. 'Don't pretend it doesn't look sensational.'

'Yes, it does.' As she stood there uncertainly, he put away her carry-out and found glasses for the wine. He touched her arm. 'Do you wanna take your coat off and freshen up? I'll have dinner on the table in twenty minutes.'

She showered and put on a T-shirt and leggings. He'd laid the kitchen table. 'The diner's too formal.' She waited awkwardly as he pulled dishes from the oven. It is all too cosy. Too domestic. This is what couples do.

He handed her a glass: French red. Chita wasn't really a drinker, but this was heavy and velvety and made her feel immediately better. 'Sit down – or do you eat dinner standing up as well?' She perched on the edge of one of the stools while he sprinkled herbs on to the mash and gave the meat a stir before serving.

'And it tastes good too. Admit it!' He put out a hand and touched her hair as she took a mouthful. Chita flinched. 'Sorry.

136

I just wondered what you'd put on it. Didn't realise you'd just washed it. I like the smell. Camomile.'

He sat down opposite her. Their knees touched under the narrow Formica strip. He crossed his fingers and held them in the air. 'Pax, room-mate? I'm sorry to invade your space. I realise now that it was presumptuous of me, but . . .' She didn't answer, but met his hangdog look with a dry stare. 'Why so glum? You mean the way to your heart isn't through your stomach?'

He batted his eyelids like a sick puppy. Chita smiled. 'It's delicious.' And it was. Really delicious: so much so she had a second helping and a second glass of the wine that, unknown to her, had been chosen with skill and care and had cost him eighty dollars. It was also the first alcohol she'd had in weeks, which, combined with her previously empty stomach, meant she was incredibly relaxed and even bordering on good humour by the time her hair had dried in an upward flick on her shoulder and Sam was preparing dessert.

'Cherries soaked in kirsch. Yum. A couple of scoops of Ben and Jerry's and, for good measure, a soupçon of Cointreau which I burn off like this.' He lit a match and the wet heart of the ice cream flared for a few seconds. 'I think you will enjoy this.'

Afterwards they chilled out in the sitting room. He got her to tell him about Carbondale and Grand junction and Aspen. 'Would you like to come skiing with me one weekend, Chita?'

'I don't ski.'

'You can learn.' She made a face. 'All right, don't learn. We can go sledding or walking or riding or . . . we can stay in and enjoy being in a beautiful place at a very special time of year.'

She didn't respond, but switched on CNN News. She doesn't like this line of discussion. I'll move it to work. That's safe. 'So, Chita, has the Colorado depot earned a reprieve?'

'I think so. I want to check a few things before saying definitely.'

'And those are?'

He already knew the answer because Chita, being Chita, had dictated a series of detailed notes by mid-afternoon, but it relaxed her and . . . And he was happy to listen. 'By the way, did you see your monkeys' upsum of the new UK reporting procedures? I'll show it you.' Sam got up and paused. 'Or should we have a no-work rule?'

Chita shook her head. Talking work makes it all so much easier.

He came back and perched on the arm of her chair, his own arm casually thrown across the back, pointing out the key points he'd highlighted in the document. It was good stuff and made sense.

If Chita felt Sam's arm move to her shoulders, she didn't indicate it. But once she'd read through and made some comments, she yawned and stretched, displacing him without offence, and got to her feet. 'I'm so tired. Thanks for a delicious dinner.'

'My pleasure. May we do it again in a couple of days – once you've got through your chilli beef?'

'Okay,' she said, neither gratefully nor ungraciously, and with no hint of anything other than vague interest.

They fell into a pattern of commuting together. A couple of evenings he went out after work; others they passed in the kitchen. Every third day, he cooked.

Chita never offered to buy the ingredients or to do the work, thinking he would eventually tire of the effort, but by week three – with her first official monthly trip home cancelled when Colorado had a crisis – the arrangement was still going strong.

As a woman who had spent virtually all her married life with a second man sharing her space, Chita soon grew comfortable with Sam. She became familiar with his physicality. In some ways he mirrored Lucky, who was affectionate and tactile and bossy and fun. It was only the *nature* of Sam's proximity which sometimes troubled her: it was not quite so . . . brotherly.

When occasionally he crept up from behind and put his arms around her, she'd laugh and sidestep his hold. If, on the crowded bus, their bodies touched too intimately for her own peace of mind, she learned to twist herself away. Sometimes she enjoyed the charge of him brushing against her in the corridor or entering a room, but at others she deliberately locked herself away because it was too much.

They developed acceptable limits of behaviour. And misbe-haviour.

She didn't mind if he touched her arm or buried his face in her hair to smell 'that gorgeous camomile'. She liked him reading the newspaper over her shoulder or talking through work he'd brought home. She knew his smell; the bulk of him in small spaces; the feel of his breath against her skin. But she knew that of Lucky, too. She kept her romantic focus firmly on England.

'I don't know why you worried, Shyam. It's all under control.'

'Oh, yes – when he's walking around with only a towel *you* have everything under control? I don't think so.'

'I wish I hadn't told you that.'

'Is there anything you haven't told me, Chita?'

'For example?' He didn't respond. 'Nothing has happened that I haven't mentioned. I promise.'

Occasionally Sam teased her: 'Can I put in a special request for your see-through nightie from the first evening?' When she didn't answer, he'd back-pedal: 'I've said too much, right? That wasn't a pass. Really. Just a stereotypically male observation.'

What worried Chita, though she didn't acknowledge it, was

that she enjoyed his observation. For the first time in ages, she didn't feel like a wife or a worker but a woman.

The third Monday night, Sam came home drunk and she had to get up and let him in at 2 a.m. because he couldn't find his keys. She didn't hear the bell. He had to call from his mobile to wake her. Stumbling from the bed, she opened the door in a scooped satin vest that only just covered her.

He stopped and stared. Heavy lidded from sleep and bemused by the alcohol fumes, Chita asked anxiously: 'Are you all right?'

'Yep. I'm very all right.' He dropped his briefcase and reached out to her. 'Give me a hug, Chita girl.'

She'd laughed. He was just like the drunks in sitcoms and on late night trains. As he shambled towards her, she'd put her arms out to protect herself from the impact and found herself in a hug. She closed her eyes: it was like snuggling back into her blankets.

Then she felt the rise of him through his suit.

At that moment he pulled down her straps with his mouth and Chita found herself in the bizarre position of needing to hold him tighter to prevent being bent backward by his height and bulk.

'Sam, let go,' she said gently, but he was mumbling into the curve of her neck and then into the open swell of her breasts and the feeling, as he trapped her against the wall and his hands slipped down to her buttocks and eased under her top, was sweet. He wasn't being overbearing and demanding, just silly and drunk.

'Let go. Please,' she said, trying to locate his ear.

For a split second it was like being with Shyam, but it wasn't Shyam, and as Sam went to take her nipple in his mouth she was suddenly wide awake. 'Sam, get off me! *Get off me now.*'

It was as if she'd hit a switch. He shuffled backward,

shamefaced. He put his hands over his eyes and frowned as Chita violently pulled down her top and closed the bedroom door behind her.

The next morning, he slept in. At work, Chita avoided him. When she got back that night, there was a one-pound box of hand-made chocolates and a huge bouquet of delphiniums and red roses laid at her door. The card bore a single word. Sorry.

How do I tell this one to my husband? I'll wait till I'm back in London on Friday. Face to face. Then he can judge me for himself.

Chita was confused about her own part in the incident. She made a number of observations, and counter-observations, in her notebook.

- If I hadn't answered the door in nightclothes, he would not have made a pass.
- But: I'd been asleep three hours when he woke me up.
- If I had not put my arms out to him, we wouldn't have ended up in a clinch.
- But: I weigh 130 lbs, he weighs 200. If I hadn't put up my arms I'd have been knocked flying.
- If I had told him to stop earlier, events would not have escalated.
- But: I did tell him to stop. He took no notice.
- I should have shouted and made a huge fuss as soon as the situation became sexual.
- But: He is my boss. He'd been drinking. Is it right to demonise a man for being an idiot?
- The incident lasted probably ten seconds in total. Get real.

Then she wrote a number of reminders, in preparation for her husband's cross-examination.

- I did not and have not encouraged him.
- I did not reciprocate.
- I told him to desist.
- He did.

Why, then, she wondered, sitting in the coffee shop at Zabars, do I feel so guilty?

It was mid evening and Chita had slipped away to escape Sam's return. Outside New York's many dog-owners were walking their mutts. A woman in a green Tyrolean coat dragged behind her a dachshund in matching winter attire. 'Wouldn't mind one of those myself,' said the elderly man parked next to Chita with the day's papers.

'The woman or the dog?'

He laughed. 'The coat. I'm too old for anything else.'

'You're never too old,' Chita said.

'That's the sort of remark that'll get you in trouble, young lady.'

She smiled, put away her notebook and wandered down on to Riverside Drive. This weekend I'll be back on *our* river, albeit for a few short days. She did a circuit, cutting back through Riverside Park and buying a bag of groceries. Striding back up Broadway, Chita dreaded entering the apartment in case Sam was in. Not because she felt either pleasure or pain at the thought of seeing him, but because there was continued guilt by association.

As if she had invited trouble, just by being a woman.

On Wednesday, Chita got a Rent-a-Turd call from the client. 'Chita, good morning. Is there any chance of having a meet in the next twenty-four hours? You remember we agreed we'd deal internally with the management seminar in Seattle this coming weekend?'

Chita felt her heart sink. 'Yes . . .'

'Well, after dinner with Sam Raven on Monday, our head honcho thinks it'd be better if you and Sam took the main sessions after all. Sometimes it's easier to hear the unpalatable from those who're on the sidelines.'

'I see. Was that Sam's opinion too?'

'It was his idea. Can you spare a couple of hours to talk it through?'

Sam appeared at her door ten minutes later. 'You heard? Brina's furious. I was supposed to be meeting her in Rome this weekend.'

'And *I* am supposed to be in London.'

'You are? Of course you are.' He hit his forehead with the flat of his hand. 'I should never have let him order the third bottle of champagne. It's got me into too much trouble already. I'm sorry, Chita.' She didn't respond. 'Look on the bright side, hon – it's a weekend. I can charge you out at ten thousand dollars a day and me at fifteen. Though I guess we don't get to see much of it.'

'Why did you do it, Sam? Why suggest we run the seminar?'

'I'm sorry, hon. I was drunk; pie-eyed, as you'd say . . . Anyway, it's the truth. We'll do it better.' Unbidden tears spilled down Chita's face. 'Hey, hon, what's the matter?' She shook her head. 'It's going to get you in trouble at home, right? I'm sorry.' He was embarrassed. 'Look, your next monthly break is at Christmas. How about extending till mid-January?' He sighed. 'Don't be sad, Chita.'

'I'm not sad, Sam,' Chita said tersely. 'I'm angry.'

'You know, Chita, I no longer care why you dance to the tune of this many-headed monster. I would please like you to return.'

'This is a circular argument, Shyam. I know it's my own fault, but there is no escape route here. I have to see things

143

through. Shouldn't we be able to survive occasional up-heaval?'

'This isn't upheaval, Princess. It's a landslide.'

'It's me doing my job. I'd put up with the absence for you.'

'If I was with a woman who had decided to make me her new life partner? A woman who would do anything to achieve that goal?'

'This is all surmise.'

'That doesn't make it untrue.'

Boarding the flight to Seattle with Sam, Chita felt weary from it all. They took their seats and shared magazines, but within minutes of take-off she'd slumped into deep sleep. Sam took the magazine from her hands. He tipped her head on to his shoulder. Gently he kissed her crown, her cheeks, her mouth. His hands hovered where they shouldn't. He whispered in her ear: 'Chita, I want you. I want you so badly. And I will make you mine.'

Chita had quickly learned that everything in America is larger than life, including the weather. When it's hot, it's very hot. When it's cold, it's bloody freezing. She snuggled into her coat in the car to the hotel, listless from being shaken out of slumber.

They travelled in silence, staring out of their respective windows. The scenery was beautiful; breathtaking. In the lobby of their hotel was a huge fireplace with logs burn-ing. Their liaisons, David and Rooly, had already booked in.

Chita went to her room, unpacked, took a hot bath and joined them in the bar, where they were laughing and drinking with Sam.

They'd ordered her a hot toddy with cinnamon and honey, and finally she felt herself warming inside.

'You still haven't told us how you're finding the US of A, Chita.'

'I tell you every time.'

'No. You tell us about this contract and the various work-ings in-house. You don't tell us about *you*.'

'There's nothing to tell. I'm here to work. That's what I do.'

'Sam – you tell us. Is she a secret raver?'

'I'm working on it. Chita hasn't yet learned the art of chilling.'

'I'm quite "chilled" enough.'

'He said chilled, Chita, not chilly.' Rooly giggled.

'I miss having my husband around.'

'Can't you borrow someone else's?'

'Do you think those two are an item?' Rooly said, getting into David's bed that night. 'There's something there.'

'I can't work it out, Rools. A couple of times, the way he's spoken about her, I've thought they're definitely lovers. Other times, I look at them and there's no glue.'

'Like you and me, you mean?'

'We hold together, no sweat. For one thing, you and I plan all our awaydays in tandem. They don't. This is their first trip together.'

David pushed her back head down on to his body. 'But I can't see how two people can be together so much and not do anything: it's not physically possible. It's not natural.'

'Hey!' Rooly looked up again. 'Are you saying if you worked with someone else, not me, you'd be sleeping with her instead?'

'Hell, no, that's not what I'm saying at all.' Again he pushed her back into place and sighed loudly. 'It's just . . . he's not a real man if he hasn't been there already. Godsakes, they share an address.'

*   *   *

Seattle passed without problem. Chita remained cool and Sam ached with longing but they got by.

After talking things through with Shyam, it was agreed that Chita might as well hang on till Christmas week, flying home on Friday the 23rd and staying in London till the weekend of 12 January.

That was enough time, the boys decided, for them to talk Chita into giving up New York. Shyam, whose hands had been tied by the need to oversee completion of two major software design programmes, had already warned his employers that he needed protracted time off.

'If needs be, Lucky, I will resign. We return home in the spring anyway. Chita is right: I cannot ask her to commute her work without offering to do the same. It wouldn't be just.'

'What if she says no?'

'She won't say no.'

'Really? I would have said the word was stamped across her forehead in luminous lettering.'

'We had been together every day for nearly fourteen years. She is my rock. My love. I miss her.'

Lucky was embarrassed by this uncharacteristic sentimentality. 'What are we doing for Christmas, Shyam? If you want to woo her from Raven's clutches, we should make it special. She'll get here too late to go shopping for turkeys and all that other bloody nonsense.'

'We're Hindus, Lucky. It doesn't come naturally. Has Monica not invited us? She usually does. I don't even know. How old is the baby? Chita always organises these things. I have no idea.' He sighed. 'I don't know what she'll say when she sees the pots.'

The two men walked to the balcony doors and stared at Chita's plant collection, which had shrivelled and died, withering from frost burns and plain neglect. It was the worst winter since records had begun. The whole city had come under attack from an eastern front that was moving at a rate of knots but remained unremitting: a caravan of eastern fronts. After four days of severe weather, the streets were frozen and even the river had occasional ice floes.

Shyam, foolishly, had thought this relieved him of his plant care duties – why water when melting snow will do the job for you? But what he hadn't understood was that plants don't just require food, they require physical protection. If they are to flourish, they must be sheltered from the elements or their growth will be impeded.

The miniature fir that Chita had bought with such pleasure a few months earlier had withered to virtually nothing.

With Christmas a week away, there was so much to do, and yet they all seemed to find shopping time here and there; an hour for drinks; an evening for a spit roast. Half the New York staff wasn't native and many were returning home as part of a mass exodus from the city.

Chita found herself spirited away on shopping expeditions and into restaurants. 'You know, Lena, it was a blessing after all that Sam and I went to Seattle. So many of the tasks I'd be doing now were covered there. Every cloud.'

The eastern front had just hit New York. The rooftops were covered in snow. Stopping and watching the skaters at the rink outside the Rockefeller Center, Chita was filled with such wintery cheer she booked in her bags and had a go. This time there was no young man offering a helpful arm, but she was so preoccupied with the thrill of it any diversion would have been unwelcome.

The avenues were decorated with twinkling Christmas trees. She loved the sudden changes of temperature – the way you walked, draped like a mummy, into a department store and were hit by a wave of heat.

Chita returned to the apartment loaded down: clothes for

Shyam, electronic toys for Lucky, a silver horseshoe to post to Manju, the most terrific bunny suit for Annie and sunflower plates for Monica.

She still travelled into work with Sam, but other encounters were rare and centred on holiday chitchat: 'I'm flying myself to Aspen. Brina and a friend are coming on Chrismas Eve. You'd be welcome.'

'But I'll be in London.'

The day before she was due to leave, Brina called in Sam's absence. 'I hear you're coming back to London tomorrow? Well, safe journey. I just wanted to confirm our journey from Boston to Aspen. Could you pass the details on to my brother?'

'Sure.' Chita got a pen and wrote down Brina's dictation. 'We'll catch the early flight as planned, unless events see movement banned. Tell him, if there are no blow-ups, we'll be at the chalet around lunch-time.'

'Sure. Merry Christmas.'

'And a merry Christmas to you, Chita. I hope you spend it with the one who loves you best.'

Chita passed the message to Sam. 'Your sister has a strange way of saying things.'

'Tell me about it. I've never understood that woman. She's like the Tower of Babel – many tongues, and I don't recognise one of them.' He crumpled up the paper and threw it in the bin. 'Don't get me wrong. I love Brina. She's a terrific girl. But she only came into my life when I was ten. My father's second marriage. She was a spooky kid. Grew up great, though. For a blonde.'

He winked at her. 'I've always preferred dark girls. Must be something to do with going back to my roots. I've been to Sri Lanka a few times. The women are a knock-out. And you Indian girls aren't bad either.' Smiling, he hung up his coat and put away his briefcase. 'Do you mind if I take over the office?'

The next morning, Christmas Eve, Chita ordered a cab to the airport. She popped her head round Sam's door to say goodbye. They hugged with genuine affection. 'Hurry back, hon.' She was glad to go home so their relationship could be legitimised by meeting her wifely duties. I'm on my way, Shyam.

JFK was in chaos. Scrawled boards around the airport stated 'All flights to the UK facing long delays. No further information available.' She asked at the BA desk. 'All we can tell you at this stage is there's been a security alert. It isn't looking good.'

Chita called Shyam.

'I've just turned on Sky, Princess. It's very bad. There was a series of bomb explosions at hangars around Manchester Airport this afternoon. Nobody hurt but six planes damaged beyond repair. They've had warnings that all major airports are booby-trapped.'

'What does this mean for me?'

'They've just announced that all international airports will be isolated for at least seventy-two hours. One device has already been found at Stansted. An animal rights group.'

'What are we going to do?'

'What can we do, Chita? Today I bought a turkey and Lucky has practised cooking on two chickens.'

They both started laughing. It kept the tears at bay. 'I love you, Shyam. I so need to be with you. To see you. I miss you so much. I'm sorry I got myself into this mess.'

'I'll rescue you, Princess. I love you too. More than you imagine.'

'It doesn't matter, does it? We're Hindus. It's not as if we celebrate Christmas, so we're all right.'

But, whatever their persuasion, it had been a God-given opportunity for her to have time with him. Alone. Away from New York. Away from stress. Away from Sam Raven.

*　　*　　*

Chita entered the apartment with a heavy heart. There was no food and she had no idea how she'd pass the time when everyone was out of town. What if they don't get the all-clear? What if I don't get back at all? She put her bag down in the hall and went to make a cup of tea. The lights were on in the kitchen. Walking down the corridor, she heard the tap-tap-tap of a keyboard. 'Sam? I thought you'd be gone.'

'Hey! You spooked me. What are you doing here?' She told him. 'That's tough. Do you wanna come with me?'

'Where?'

'To Aspen. It's going to be pretty lonely here on your lonesome.'

'You've got a full house.'

'Four bedrooms. You'll fit. The place will be covered in snow after the last few days: it'll blow your mind.'

'I don't know. I want to catch the first flight home that I can.'

'No problem. Fly from Denver.'

Chita stared at the Xerox as if she might see some revelation there. She was weighing up the pros and cons. Well, actually she was weighing up the cons. There were no pros because any contact with Sam would be problematic as far as Shyam was concerned. On the other hand, New York was iced up and empty of people she knew. There was no one to be with. Better the devil you know?

She called JFK information, who now confirmed what Shyam had heard on Sky News. 'At this moment it's a seventy-two-hour shutdown. I'm sorry, there's nothing we can do. All other European flights are full.'

Sam put the cups in the dishwasher. 'You'll get to fly over the mountains in my Cherokee. And if you think I make great coffee you should taste my hot chocolate.'

What the hell, Chita thought. Shyam can't claim this was

set up. And neither can he grudge me some company. Brina and her pal will probably be awful, but at least they're friendly.

'I'd like that,' she said.

Shyam sat at the table with his head in his hands.

Lucky paced the kitchen area around him: fourteen strides along, twelve strides across. He was counting. 'Let's go and get her.'

'How can we get her? Run in with guns blazing and hold Sam Raven and his sister hostage? Are we going to fly on our own gossamer wings? Can we say this is deliberate on his part? Of course not!'

'It's deliberate that she's there and we're here. That's enough.'

'Fate is conspiring against us.'

'Fate gives us the tools, Shyam. How we use them is in our own hands. Chita will always give the benefit of the doubt – that's what you love about her. It's what we all love about her. She's never judgmental, she will never criticise or make assumptions without proof, but her greatest strength is also her greatest weakness: she assumes that if there is no evidence, there is no problem.'

Lucky took the turkey out of the fridge and stared at it glumly. 'I don't like the thought of putting my hand inside this bird. It's so bloody large. I am half expecting it to take off. Do turkeys fly?'

'Just take the giblets out this time. That first chicken was a disaster. It says the stuffing can be cooked separately.'

The bird was placed in the middle of the table and studied with some uncertainty. Lucky had chosen an organic bird because Chita refused to eat any meat that was not humanely raised and killed, but it seemed to him that this was pointless if you couldn't cook in the first place. 'Why don't they sell ready-cooked turkeys? If you can do it with curry and vichysoise and pizza, why not microwaved Christmas meals?' The thought of Brussels sprouts virtually brought Lucky out in a cold sweat. 'Perhaps, if Chita isn't coming, we should just put them in the freezer.'

'You can't freeze vegetables.'

'Why not? There are frozen peas and corn and beans in there.'

'Ready frozen. You can't freeze fresh vegetables.'

'You mean the vegetables in the freezer weren't fresh when they put them into packets?' The two men stared at each other balefully. 'What the hell. I'll find a way in the morning,' Lucky said.

The flight was exhilarating. Chita was without words as Sam swooped the Piper Cherokee down into the well of white mountains and skittered to a halt on the runway alongside the main airport. She'd never been in a small plane before: had no sense of the wonder, the sheer joy of being at one with the elements. Her pilot had steered them through winds and snow with silent ease, grace and confidence. As he now helped her on to the ground, Chita was filled with the excitement of it: the passion. When Sam grinned down at her, it was all she could do not to hug him.

'Here's Billy with the Jeep.' A young man pulled up a few feet from them and helped Sam load the bags into the trunk. He drove them to a lodge halfway up a mountainside. It was beautiful. 'Welcome home.'

As they came through the front door straight into the main living area, logs were crackling in the huge central fireplace. There was a smell of freshly baked bread. The furniture was big and soft, the carpets thicky and creamy. Billy took the bags up and left.

Chita flopped into the sofa, grinning. 'This is glorious.'

Sam pulled her up. 'Come on, I want to show you your room.'

There was a small hand-carved bed, a chest of drawers with her case on top, and a half-sized wardrobe. The walls were palest pink, the curtains flowered. 'It's like something from a fairytale.'

'The bathroom's opposite.'

Through the window she could see skiers zigzagging down a neighbouring peak. Sam was next to her. 'Good, isn't it?' Momentarily she enjoyed his closeness. His warmth. 'Do you want some food?' She nodded, still entranced by the view from her window. 'I'll pull something together. See you in a sec.'

There was indeed freshly baked bread. He'd cut it into thick roundels. There was a salad and a plate of cold meats. They ate together in silence with Sam getting up every now and then to check cupboards or tweak things around the place.

Chita started to think about presents. She went up and rummaged through the gifts in her luggage. I'll give Sam the dancing ape I bought for Lucky. Thank God I remembered batteries. He'll laugh when it bashes the cymbals together. Brina can have Monica's sunflower plates and I'll give her friend the crystal paperweight I got for Ambreen. She wrote out the cards and, stopping to brush her hair and pinch colour into her cheeks, ran back downstairs.

'Have Brina and her friend gone shopping?'

'I presume they're still at home.'

'Home? Who made the bread?'

'Billy. He always pops a loaf in before collecting me.'

'So when will Brina get here?'

'I thought you said *all* British airports were closed, Chita.'

'Yes.'

'Then I guess she's not going to make it. I've left her a message.' Sam cocked his head and looked at her quizzically.

'She was coming from Manchester. Isn't that where the first bombs went off?'

'She said she was in Boston.'

'*Coming* from Boston. Oh, I get you . . . not Massachusetts, Chita – Boston, Lincolnshire. She was picking up Alice and they were going to fly from Manchester.'

'So we're alone here?'

'Yes, we're alone here. You can't get to the UK. Brina can't get to the US. It's just you, me and Rudolf the red-nosed reindeer. Is that a problem?' When she said nothing, he sighed. 'Chita, I just can't read you sometimes. I don't know what goes on in your head, but whatever you're thinking, remember they are your thoughts, not mine.' He got up and took her elbow. 'Come on, I'll show you where to find books and games and whatever you need to make you happy.'

It was desperately important to him that she should be happy.

Christmas morning, Shyam was woken up by Lucky, who had put on his newly acquired CD of appropriate songs: So here it is, merry Christmas, everybody's having fun. 'What is this bloody torture?' he cried, staggering into the kitchen, where he found his brother back in action with the bird, now splayed open and spilling out packet mixed sage and onion. 'Oh my God!'

'Relax, bro'. Go and have a shower and I'll put on some toast. I didn't realise the stupid thing had to be cooked slowly for five hours. We won't get to eat till three.'

Thankfully the turkey was out of sight when Shyam re-emerged. He helped his brother with the sprouts: enough for eight, even after they'd mistakenly removed all the outer leaves, leaving only the nubby kernels for boiling.

The same happened with the potatoes, which they ignorantly peeled with butter knives. 'What is lard?'

'I don't know.'

'It says I must baste the potatoes with lard . . . Must be some sort of oil. Do we have oil?'

'There's the walnut oil Chita puts in salads.'

'Give it here.' Lucky emptied the bottle over the baking tray. 'What's the time difference between here and Colorado?'

'Seven hours. I won't call her till this evening.'

'Right. In it all goes. Break a leg.'

When Lucky pulled out the turkey at three and did the juices test with a chopstick left over from a home delivery, they ran pink. 'This is bad news. Do we have a Fahrenheit or a Centigrade oven? Oh dear. This is my worst nightmare.'

It was six before they deemed the bird safe for eating. 'Oh . . . Shit. The potatoes are black, the Brussels are soggy and there's no gravy.'

'Perhaps it's fate that Chita isn't here,' Shyam said.

After dinner, he tried calling her. His calls didn't get through.

'Of course they won't,' Lucky said. 'She's in one of the most mountainous regions of America. The signal will be non-existent. You couldn't get through when she was there on business. Didn't she give you a number for the house? No? You'll just have to wait for her to call you, bro'.'

Chita woke feeling happy and light-hearted. Snug and warm in bed, she'd had the best and longest night's sleep in weeks. Opening the curtains, she found the view from her window obscured by freshly fallen snow.

She undid the latch and pushed the glass outward, clearing the sill of the build-up and then rubbing her cold and wet hands over her face. The water stung her awake. This is the finest snow I've ever seen, she thought. I love this state.

There was a knock on her door. 'Come in.'

Sam pushed the door open and looked at the woman who

was slowly driving him crackers. She was in a T-shirt and long johns and looked sexy beyond belief, standing at the open window, a gale seemingly blowing through and around her without causing any discomfort. The framing brought her body into sharp relief. I want her so desperately I could die of longing.

'Good morning, beautiful,' he said. 'Sleep well?'

'As if I was under a spell.'

'Would a kiss release you from that spell?' He waved a branch of mistletoe. 'Billy must have left this for fun.'

When she grinned he felt suddenly reckless. More reckless. So he approached her tentatively, holding the twig comically above his head. He closed his eyes and brought his stubbled and ruggedly handsome face close to hers, puckering playfully.

The touch of her lips when it came was so light and quick he would have thought he'd imagined it, were it not for the instant swelling in his loins. He opened his eyes and her face was just inches from his, smiling and amused.

'I'm crazy for you, Chita,' he said.

For a moment her eyes clouded. She took his face in her hands, tenderly, for the first time. 'I know, Sam. But I'm married; and I like being married. I love my husband. I've never loved another man. I'm an Indian girl. That is my life.'

She saw his despair and kissed him again. 'You're lovely.' He could smell her; feel her breath. He wanted with all his heart to stay like that for ever, but she extricated herself gently. 'I'm sorry,' she said. 'I'm sorry that you can't have what you want. I'm sorry if it's my fault. I'm sorry for everything.'

After breakfast, Sam pulled on a thick coat and wellingtons and went outside. The road was invisible. 'Must have been a bad night. I didn't notice.' Wrapped up like an eskimo and wearing wellies from a selection in the boot box on the front porch, Chita helped to grit the path while he shovelled it. Then he got a sled from a storage shed to the side of the building. 'Have you ever done this? You're in for a treat. Let's hike up the hill.'

They spent two hours trudging up and whizzing down. Each time the sled gained momentum, hitting grassy humps beneath the snow and bouncing them all over the place, Chita's stomach was in her mouth, but she felt safe as Sam, holding her in place, confidently guided them with cries of 'giddy up, cowboy!'

Inevitably it came to a bad end when the sled hit a tree trunk, sending them both flying out in one direction while it continued in another. Sam landed on top of Chita in the snow, pulling her head up and rolling her on to her back so she didn't smother in its all-embracing whiteness.

He leaned over her. 'Are you okay?'

She couldn't stop laughing, half with hysteria and half sheer delight. 'I'm fine.'

He wiped snow from her cheeks and her eyebrows and her mouth. 'Maybe I'm not the finest of navigators.'

'Nonsense! That's the first accident, only.'

He pushed damp tendrils of hair off her face and cupped her head in his hands so she didn't get any wetter. She was slightly breathless from their fall and hadn't moved. He noted for the second time that morning how much easier Chita was with him in Colorado. Perhaps it was the mountain air, the sense of peace and isolation. To him, this was just the best place in the world. It clearly affected her, too. She was relaxed; youthful. Despite her words that morning, he felt greater hope than he ever had before. He brushed the snow off her torso, talking as he did so. 'I should have given you a hat. Wiggle your toes and fingers. Is everything in working order?'

'Of course. For goodness' sake, Sam, we only came off a sled!'

She pulled herself into a sitting position. 'I'm soaked.'

'Let's get you home and dry.'

'Yes. And then I must call Shyam and say hello.'

It was midday when they got back. Sam towel-dried Chita's hair as she made fresh coffee. 'Sam, stop it. I'm not an invalid. I won't die of a cold just because I got wet.'

'You're underestimating the weather, Chita, but so be it.' He turned his attention to warming waffles with maple syrup. 'This will help keep you healthy.' Shyam would laugh to see Sam now, Chita thought, and was filled with longing for her husband. Her first pang for home had taken a little longer than usual to kick in.

Opening the fridge to get milk, Sam said: 'Damn, I forgot to put the duck in the oven. Will you season the bird if I organise the rest?'

They worked together in companionable silence.

'Lucky was going to cook us a turkey this year.'

'Does he cook well?'

'No. He has no idea. But watching him at play is usually fun.' Chita started to laugh. 'I remember one year we spent Christmas in a hotel full of elderly people. He took out *Twister* and had them on all fours. Then he joined in and one old chap went flying. That was the end of that.'

'Funny.'

'And he always cheated in Monica's Christmas quiz.'

'We're all done,' Sam said. 'Shall I light a fresh fire?'

'I need to call Shyam.'

She went upstairs and found that her mobile had switched itself off. 'Sam, my signal's out. It always goes in Aspen. May I use your phone? He'll be wondering what I'm doing.'

'Sure. I guess I should call Brina, but I don't know if she's with Alice or back in London. And she hasn't bothered to call me.'

Chita dialled London. Nothing happened. She tested the phone: no dial tone. 'Sam, does this phone work?'

Sam took it from her and listened. 'I called Billy on this handset last night. Maybe the battery's gone. Try the sitting room.'

'It doesn't work either.'

Fruitlessly they tried every handset in the house. 'It's not an internal fault, hon. It'll be a cable connection brought down by last night's snowfall. Don't worry – they're always fixed within a few hours. That explains Brina's silence.'

'But it's Christmas,' Chita said.

'I suppose that may delay the process,' Sam replied. 'They'll have to pay overtime. But it's a vital service. Just have to keep trying.'

By midnight there was still no joy.

Shyam felt frustrated and out of sorts. 'I'm going to bed.'

'There must be a reason,' Lucky said. 'What if he and the sister are holding her hostage?'

'It's not funny, Lucky,' and then Shyam looked at Lucky and couldn't help laughing. His brother, for reasons known only to his self, was lying on his back on the wooden floor in the belief it might ease the severe stomach pains he was suffering after their turkey dinner.

'It's not like her, Shyam. There will be a reason.'

'Let's hope it's a good reason. Are you going to lie there all night? You look like a bloody fool. At least lie on your stomach.'

Shyam didn't really want to go to bed so he prodded Lucky and irritated him with his foot until he agreed to play Grand Theft Auto series six. They drank beer and battled till 2 a.m., by which stage, as ever, Shyam had managed to creep ahead on points.

'She's not going to call, is she?'

'Perhaps there isn't a phone if it's only a holiday place.'

'Nonsense. The office would insist on a contact number.'

'It is odd.'

Suddenly Shyam jumped up. 'We don't know where she is.'

'She's with Sam Raven, lunatic.'

'But where? I last spoke to her in New York. What if he took her somewhere else? What if he's kidnapped her?'

'Now you are entering the realms of fantasy for which I am always criticised. Is there no way you can find out where this house is?'

'I'll ring Monica in the morning.'

By late afternoon, Chita had stopped worrying about the phone. You must not waste energy on that which cannot be changed. 'If the phone's are still down tomorrow, Sam, may I take your car to Aspen and find one there?'

'Sure, hon. We'll both go. We can have lunch. In the meantime, should we check what's happening to our bird? Smells delicious.'

Despite it being 2 a.m. in London, Chita had another go on her mobile. Nothing. She pulled out the duck. 'Mmm, looking good,' Sam said. 'The vegetables are crispy too. I like something firm to bite into.'

While she carved, he laid the table. She turned to find a little present had been put on her plate. Sweet. She went and got the battery-operated dancing ape. 'To be honest, it's something very silly and I had intended it for Lucky, but I think you'll like it.'

They opened their presents together. In Chita's box was a pair of dazzling jewelled studs. 'Sam – you can't give me *these*. I gave you the ape because it was bought purely for fun. To give me Brina's gift isn't right.'

Sam switched on the ape, which started bashing together the

cymbals in its hands. 'It isn't Brina's gift, hon, it's yours. I had them made in Aspen. Billy picked them up for me. I planned to give them to you later.'

'It's too much.'

He switched off the ape. 'They are a token of affection; a totem of appreciation because you're wonderful and we're a terrific team. But you're married. No need to remind me. All right? Put them on.'

He watched as, bemused, she removed the silver hoops she was wearing and replaced them with the studs. 'Push your hair back off your ears. Yes, like that. You look beautiful. They look beautiful.'

Chita studied her reflection in the door of the microwave oven. 'Find a mirror, Chita. They're yellow diamonds. Flawless. Treat them with respect.'

When she came back, she was flushed with pleasure and embarrassment. 'They're lovely, Sam. Really lovely. Thank you.'

He had poured wine and served lunch in her absence. 'That makes it all worthwhile. Now let's eat.'

After dinner, tiddly and full, they sprawled in front of the fire. Sam stretched out on the bearskin rug and Chita sat with her feet up on the sofa, thumbing through old magazines. It struck her again that they were comfortable in each other's space. Too comfortable perhaps. The thought made her anxious. I must get to London. And this time I won't come back. I'll invent an emergency.

She watched Sam thumbing through the TV guide and felt strangely moved. Frowning, she turned away and stared unseeing at the article in *Vanity Fair*. It's so long since I've been held. He's here and my husband isn't.

It wasn't a question of wanting Sam and not Shyam, but wanting Sam because she couldn't have Shyam. Chita closed her eyes: all the parameters have changed. I think differently in this place. *I must get to London.*

Suddenly self-conscious, she turned and found Sam watching her intently. 'Are you all right?'

She nodded. 'I'm fine. A little light-headed.'

He patted the rug beside him. 'Come and lie with me.'

'No.'

'Okay. You're in charge.'

'Am I?' *Am I?*

'When you say no, I stop.' He turned back to the TV guide. 'Loads of old films and sitcoms. There's a documentary on PBS that might be interesting. Do you have any preferences?' When she didn't respond, he looked up again and saw the indecision in her eyes. And something else. Stay cool, Sam, you're playing it perfectly. 'Any preferences, Chita?' She shook her head. 'Then let's have music instead. Do you know *Madame Butterfly*?'

Returning to the rug, he lay on his back, hands behind his head as the overture started. 'I always lie between the speakers to hear music properly. It's like being in the orchestra pit. Come and listen. I love it.' He closed his eyes. *Your move, Chita.*

But she didn't move.

Until the music rose to a crescendo. Then she got up, strangely stirred by the passion and the intensity, and moved to the rug. She knelt to brush that wayward lick of hair off his forehead and kiss where it had been. He lay absolutely still.

'Goodnight, Sam,' Chita said.

In bed she lay awake till the early hours, listening to him moving first downstairs and then upstairs. For a moment he paused by her door and her heart stopped.

Sam viewed the evening with hope and expectation. She's so beautiful. No man in his right mind would fail to feel her in his blood; wouldn't be obsessed with her in his thoughts. No woman could be like that and not enjoy attention. She's *begging* for it.

He tidied up and went upstairs, stopping momentarily by Chita's door. I could just go in and force it. She's clearly excited. Probably dilated. Just needs a little push.

When she kissed me . . . she must have known what she was unleashing. She'll be half asleep. I could slip into bed beside her. Part her legs with my thigh. Open her lips with my fingers. For a second she'll feel a breeze of cold air in her most intimate place and she'll wake with a cry. That's when I feel deep inside. Prepare for entry as she rocks with fear. And then, excitement.

She'll love it.

His hand moved towards the handle but then stopped. No. Let her come to me. She will come. If I wait. And pump up the volume . . . She won't be able to resist.

Shyam rang Monica at twelve on Boxing Day. She was disturbed by his anxiety. 'I'm sure there's a completely normal reason for Chita's silence,' she said, but she too thought it odd that Chita hadn't touched base. Diligent was her friend's second name.

'I don't know Sam's address in Aspen or his phone number, Shyam. Try ringing one of the monkeys. Jez was on the phone to him last weekend. He may be able to help.'

Jez was having a party. 'Sorry about the noise,' he said. 'Let me have a look . . . I don't know about Aspen, but this is his number in New York. There may be an answering service. Otherwise, take Shola's mobile because she might have it. Happy Christmas.'

Shyam dialled Sam's New York penthouse. A young woman answered. 'No, I'm sorry, I don't have Sam Raven's contact numbers. We've only got his flat on short-term rental so all dealings are through the local agent.'

'I beg your pardon?' Shyam's heart missed a beat. 'You're renting the flat? I thought there'd been a flood there – the water tanks in the roof . . . No. I see. Is it recently refurbished? Not to your knowledge? I probably have my facts confused. May I take the agent's number? Thank you.'

He called Shola in a state of panic. 'There hasn't been a flood in Sam's apartment. The story is a complete fabrication.'

'That can't be true. Listen, Shyam, I'm in town having dim sum with my parents. I'll pop by the office on my way back and access Sam's files. The Aspen address will be there somewhere.'

Shyam called up the stairs to Lucky. 'Brother, something strange is happening.'

Lucky came down carrying a small suitcase. 'As I suspected. Never fear. I told you I'd come up with an alternative plan. I've just called American Airlines. If we get the Eurostar to Paris in the next two hours, there's a flight from Charles de Gaulle to Denver at seven o'clock London time. We can keep in contact with the monkeys while we're on the move. If they find the address, we can be with Chita within twenty-four hours.'

Sam woke Chita with coffee, sitting on the edge of her bed in a black T-shirt and black button-front jeans. 'I thought I should wake you or it'd be bedtime again.'

She sat up muzzy headed and tried to rub her eyes open. Her lids were so heavy she collapsed back down, groaning. 'Give me a minute or two, Sam, I feel terrible.'

He got up and opened her window. 'The house is too damn hot. It's hard to get the heating right sometimes.' She felt him sit back down. He took her hand in his. 'You're like the sleeping beauty.'

'What time is it?'

'It's one o'clock.'

'In the afternoon?'

'Of course in the afternoon.'

'I didn't fall asleep for a while.' This house is strange. Enchanting; witchy. It has a character and momentum of its own. She struggled to sit up, forcing her eyelids open with her fingers. I feel drugged. He leaned across her, body on body, and plumped up the pillows behind her so she could lean back. He smelled good: of coffee and cakes. The smell reminded her of being woken by Papa when she was little. She felt a wave of nostalgia and longing.

'You're not sick, are you, Chita?'

'No. Just tired. Are the phones working, Sam?' He shook his head. 'Can we go into town?' He smiled and nodded. 'Shall I get ready?'

'Drink that first and give yourself a kick-start. There's a muffin on the table. I'll just go and put chains on the four-wheel-drive. I haven't been here since October and we were having an Indian summer then.' He grinned down at her. 'Now I'm enjoying an Indian winter.'

The phones in Aspen were fine. Chita called and left a message at home. She tried calling the boys on their mobiles but Lucky had left his on the coffee table so he would never get the message, and Shyam's phone was switched off because he was in the Channel Tunnel.

Instead she dialled Manju, who was romantically ensconced with Rich. 'We've done nothing but have passionate interludes in the bedroom. Happy Birthday, Jesus, and thank you.'

'Manju. Please.'

'It makes the world go round, Chita. And the date is set for April the first, by the way: two fools playing a joke on everyone else including themselves. Will you be here?'

'Let's discuss this later, Manju. I'm in a fix.'

'Because your husband might worry that you have succumbed to Mr Oh-So-Charming? I don't think so, Chita. We all know you too well.'

'He'll read the worst into my silence.'

'If he was that fearful, Chita, he would be waiting by the phone. Listen, my darling, only a few more months and you'll be back on the subcontinent making rotis and buying bangles in the bazaar. Shyam and Sam are separated by only two letters. Can't you make believe for a little while?'

'Don't.'

'I'm teasing. But do enjoy this while it lasts, Chita. Shyam is fine. He's out making mischief with that crazy brother of his.'

Chita caught up with Sam a couple of blocks farther down in a row of galleries. They walked up to the gondola and rode to the top. 'Hot chocolate first and then a brisk walk to keep in trim.' They strolled through the more sheltered woody areas, the snow up to their knees in parts. Sam lifted Chita over some of the more difficult obstacles.

As the light faded, they rode the car back down the mountain. He snuggled up to her. She rested her head on his shoulder.

For the sheer joy of it Sam let Chita drive the Jeep all the way to Carbondale, where she pointed out her favourite haunts. It was dark and moonless by the time they slowly climbed their way up the icy mountain road to the cabin.

The house was chilly as they entered. Chita shivered. Sam hit the lights. Nothing happened. He went and tried other switches in the room. 'Damn. The power's gone.' He pressed the light dial on his watch. 'It's eight. Too late to get Billy.'

Opening the boot box, he pulled out a large torch. 'You stay here. I'm going to go and switch on the emergency generator.'

She heard him crunch through the setting snow to the large

shed at the back of the building. Standing alone in the entrance like that, she felt like Frankenstein out in the Alps looking for his monster. It is so utterly silent. And empty.

'Shit!'

'Is everything all right?'

'Chita, come and hold the torch for me. I can't get this damn thing started.' She found Sam bent over a small and rusted generator. 'Here, take this.' She held the light while he pulled at things and fiddled and prodded without success. Finally he straightened himself. 'I don't suppose you know anything about this type of machinery? Damn, damn, damn. Well, that's it. We are without lights and heat until I get Billy across in the morning.'

'You're sure it's not a fuse?'

'No, hon. This happens all the time up here.'

Back inside, Sam dug out candles and made a fire. 'The temperature drops so quickly. We'll be freezing by the morning. I'll make us a hot drink. Oh, no. No kettle. I'll find the brandy. That'll warm us.'

'I'm fine. That wine last night knocked me out.'

'That wasn't the wine, Chita, it was the mountain air. Less oxygen. It's tiring until you acclimatise. And you're the heaviest sleeper I know. The alcohol relaxed you, that's all.'

He poured her a half-balloon of spirit. She took a mouthful and choked. 'It's horrible.' Putting down the glass, she got up and wandered around the room, flapping her arms for warmth. 'It's too dark to read and too dark to play games.'

'Then we'll have to talk. Tell me about your life in India.'

She came and sat on the rug with him, back to back, and talked about Amma and Papaji. About the family pets, about university, about Manju, about Shyam . . . 'We met through the Internet. On a dating site. Not what you'd expect, is it?'

'Not for someone so defined by tradition.'

'You don't have to be dull to be traditional, Sam. It was fun.

But once I'd made contact with him, that was it. We arranged a formal introduction and married straight away.'

'Love at first sight. But how could you have known better?'

'It was fate. Karma.'

'Otherwise known as a combination of lust and coincidence.'

'It was neither.'

'So it was both?'

'It's perhaps something peculiarly Indian.'

Chita, gazing into the fire, believed, as we are wont to do when nostalgic, that she was seeing her past in a series of snapshots. But it was just imagination and closeness and brandy – laced by her host with a slightly stronger sedative than he had used the night before.

'You see, Sam, Shyam and I both believed it was meant. Determined. That the element of choice was removed, almost.'

If Sam, who was enjoying the warmth of her back against his, hated the things she was saying, he didn't show it. Hey: I'm not totally stupid. The more she thinks about the situation the more likely she is to realise how ridiculous it all sounds. And all this sleep is going to make the place seem mighty restful.

'Do you think I should join one of these websites, Chita?'

There was no answer. Her body felt suddenly heavier. It's happened. Suddenly still, Sam had a clear premonition that if he did not move quickly Chita would return to London and never be seen again. His mind racing, he picked her up in his arms and carried her to his bed. It was cold upstairs and she gave a start when he removed her top clothing. He stroked her back to sleep, lying over her so she absorbed his heat; an inner furnace.

Sam fondled her heavy, rounded breasts through her T-shirt. She arched her back and moaned. Somewhere deep within her, Chita was stirred. But she was too doped up to protest.

Anyway, her subconscious told her it was a dream – because Shyam was somewhere else. So she didn't wake. Pushing Sam off, she rolled on to her side under his fleecy duvet.

Lying across her, he moved his fingers into the waistband of her briefs. She sighed. But when his fingers went where they shouldn't, she turned on to her stomach to prevent further access. He rested his head on her buttocks and kissed their softness. He loved her.

And because he loved her, Chita's purity acted as her shield. Sam could not besmirch the very qualities he revered.

After a while he went back downstairs. He switched the mains on and found her handbag. He took her passport and her credit cards and locked them in his safe. What am I doing? This is madness. But I have her now and I am no longer willing to let her go. All this damned loyalty, and it transpires they met on a website!

As Chita lay unknowing overhead, Sam got his pistol and gave it a polish. What am I doing? I don't know; but I won't let her go. If she leaves Aspen, all is lost. He loaded the gun with a single bullet. It was as if he was being guided by forces outside himself.

Laying the weapon beside him, Sam stared into the flames where, an hour earlier, Chita had seen her past in a series of snapshots. I'll make a plan in the morning. It'll all come together then.

The sun was already rising when he finally fell asleep.

'My God, I'm tired.' As they disembarked from the connecting flight to Aspen, Shyam was overcome with weariness. The sun was out on the horizon, and as he looked up from the well of the airport, to a hundred mountain-tops glittering with wet snow, he was overcome by the enormity of what they were doing.

Lucky, as ever, was bluff. 'I hope Jez organised the car. It was short notice to say the least.' But it was there, and it was theirs for at least the next forty-eight hours. 'The monkeys have done a good job. The luck of Honeybun. Just think, bro', we'll be seeing him soon.'

'I'd like to see Chita first.'

It took them an hour to find the mountain road to Sam's chalet. Both were struck by the idyllic location and the simple beauty of Sam Raven's winter residence. Like a painting.

In the thick snow, they made a slow and silent approach, stopping the car two hundred yards from the house. Continuing on foot, Shyam looked through the window and saw Sam asleep with the pistol on his lap. His first instinct was to smash the glass, but then he froze. If Chita was safe, he must do nothing to aggravate the situation. He combed the room for signs of a struggle. Nothing. Where is she? He felt strangely calm. As if he had trained for this moment all his life. So this is my rival. We meet again. He will not harm what is mine any more.

His memory of Sam had been of a well-built and handsome older man, perhaps in his mid-forties. But asleep, with that lick of hair falling over the black-fringed eyelids, Sam Raven looked like a child. Unexpectedly, Shyam felt the ugly heat of jealousy.

Lucky, creeping up from behind, took in the situation. 'So this is the man at the centre of this epic? Our many-headed monster. The man who single-handedly turned our lives upside down.'

'He looks so innocent. Except for the gun.'

'No sign of Chita. You think it's loaded?'

'No point otherwise. Listen, Lucky, I'm going to knock. You stay out of sight so he thinks I'm alone.'

Sam pushed the pistol under the sofa. He assumed it was Billy popping by with groceries. When he opened the door to the

Indian man with film star looks, he was totally taken aback. Shyam smiled. 'May I come in, Sam?'

Sam didn't move. 'What can I do for you?'

'I'd like to see my wife.'

'She's asleep. She doesn't want disturbing.'

'I'm sure she won't complain if she knows it's me. May I enter? Please. It's cold out here.' Grudgingly Sam moved his body so Shyam could come a few inches across the threshold. 'I'm afraid there's been a breakdown in communications. The British airports are shut, as you probably know, though I believe they're reopening today. I had to come via Paris. Is your sister well?'

'She's fine,' Sam growled.

'And she's also here.'

'No, she's back home in England.'

'Then there has been a misunderstanding.'

Gently but persistently, Shyam advanced into the house so that he was in the large open-plan reception space. 'What a lovely place. Is Chita upstairs? She sleeps like a log. We have two alarms at home – one is the radio, the other a persistent bell. Well, she has them in New York now, of course.' All the time he was talking, Shyam kept moving. At the threshold to the kitchen, he risked looking behind him, but the room was empty. 'I see you have a range. They're all the rage in London. My brother cooked our Christmas meal this year. It was a disaster. Do you cook? Chita, I think, is one of the world's worst cooks.'

'She shouldn't have to cook.'

'I agree. She is perfect as she is. That is why I married her.'

Sam said nothing. Shyam was inches from the stairs. Hearing that his wife was alone in this house with Sam made the hair on his neck stand on end. Bloody slime. She'd better be safe. He wondered what Sam had done with the gun. As he kept talking, he saw Lucky's shadow at the window. The front door was still ajar.

In mid-sentence he broke off and ran up to find his wife.

She was fast asleep in the double bed, one arm out. Her clothes were neatly folded on the chair. She was wearing the baby pink T-shirt they'd bought from a shop in Tobacco Dock. Shyam shut the door and jammed the chair under the handle.

He bent over her to check she was breathing. But before waking her, he instinctively lifted the duvet to see if her bottom half was covered. Shyam shook his wife gently and then with a fearful agitation. 'Chita, are you all right?' She mumbled and grumbled and rolled over on to her back but continued sleeping. 'Chita: wake. Please.'

She pushed his face away from her. 'Leave me alone. I'm sleeping.' Then, semiconscious, she suddenly opened her eyes. 'Shyam? *Shyam.* This is a dream! Are you real?' Her arms came out to him and then they were both laughing and crying and hugging and kissing until he heard the crashes down below.

'You stay here. Don't move.'

He kicked the chair out of the way and flew down the stairs to find his brother and Sam in combat. Sam had recovered the gun. Shyam was just in time to see him bring the barrel of it down on the back of Lucky's head. His brother was sent sprawling in a bloody heap on the rug.

'You *bastard.*' Shyam leaped across on to Sam's back, wrestling him to the floor. For his pains, he was hoisted over Sam's shoulders and dumped on his back. Sam bent to pick up his gun. As he straightened, Shyam kicked the weapon from his hands and, leaping to his feet, grabbed Sam around the neck. Sam bit his hand. Shyam fell, but he made up in speed, dexterity and tactics what he couldn't match with his bulk. He was back on his feet almost immediately and now the two men fought around the furniture.

172

Overhead, Shyam was aware of Chita moving around. Oh God, she's coming down. Using his peripheral vision, he knew his brother was still knocked out. Please let him be all right.

Sam kept diving for the gun. Again and again, Shyam kicked it from his reach. He felt wasted. I haven't slept in twenty-four hours! And yet the adrenaline coursing through his body kept him going.

In a moment of pure chance, Sam grabbed the pistol. Getting to his feet, he aimed it at his rival. 'I will never know why she married someone like you. I will never know what she sees in you.'

For a nanosecond, Shyam was unmoving.

But as Sam Raven pulled the trigger, the child who could once hit moving apples, and the young man who flicked Sellotape balls with perfect precision, leaped forward.

He grabbed the barrel and swung it upward so the bullet hit the central light fitting and ricocheted.

So the bullet hit the central light fitting and ricocheted: to explode with perfect precision in the centre of Sam Raven's chest.

Part Five

Chita came down the stairs as Sam aimed at Shyam. In that suspended millisecond, she saw her entire life rush by and knew it had no meaning without her husband in it. But she couldn't cry out. It was as if all the air had been sucked out of her. Instead she stopped, her mind still hazy, and watched uncomprehending as Shyam reached out and, with his bare hand, twisted the barrel upward, literally as the bullet shot out. It was extraordinary.

She didn't see the bullet hit the light, but in her line of sight she saw Sam take the blow and fall backward, an explosion of red suddenly flowering on his chest. And then, in slow motion, Shyam, filled with golden light, bending to check Sam's pulse before saying gently: 'Chita, call 911,' and going to Lucky.

She went to the phone as if in a dream. It was still dead. 'The lines are down, Shyam. They haven't worked since we arrived.'

'It's unplugged, Chita. Shola had the number checked from London.'

In a daze Chita had followed the line of the cable to the junction box. He was right. Frightened and confused, she'd reconnected it and dialled the emergency services. She noticed that the heating was on.

Twenty minutes later, when the ambulance arrived, Lucky was sitting up, groggy but apparently sound. He'd been all right. Slight concussion, a big bald patch where they shaved his hair to put in thirty stitches and a few days' medical surveillance.

In that time statements were taken and Brina Raven arrived in Colorado, but thankfully the police had kept them apart. It had been a fraught time as forensic experts took their fingerprints and DNA samples, worked Sam's home with a fine-tooth comb and questioned every movement made in the previous week.

But it had also been comforting to be quizzed like that: forced to answer the same questions again and again. It had made them confront what had happened and ask why. But it was also an excuse for Shyam to close the door to further discussion. 'We have relived the events more times than I can count. As far as I am concerned, Chita, there is nothing more to say.'

Afterwards, in New York, the three of them were put in an hotel on Fifth by Chita's company. She'd spent six weeks operating on autopilot to stabilise and replan the RAT contract with colleagues who kept a polite distance, as if her jinx was contagious.

Only Monica had been there at the end of a phone to put things into perspective and stop her sinking into a pit of self-loathing and despair. 'There's no point beating yourself about it, Chita. He's dead. If seeing his desk upsets you, avoid it. You're like the rape victim who thinks she was at fault. People are distant because the whole episode is beyond their understanding. They're ashamed on his behalf and embarrassed on yours.'

Even three months on, it remains beyond *my* understanding, Chita thought, as the 'Fasten Seatbelt' light came on. But the client's new tender has now been accepted, so everyone's happy. Our precious flat in the Docklands is cleared and being prettied up for sale. Spring has sprung. It's time to move on.

Slipping her hand into Shyam's, she watched her brother-in-law come down the aisle of the plane to find them, his hair still in a classic GI cut. 'Is everything all right, beautiful?'

Chita smiled up at him. 'Everything's fine. Sit down. Use the flight to get some sleep. It'll be all go from the minute we land.'

As Lucky returned to his seat, Chita wondered whether things could ever revert to the way they once were: temperate, trusting, uneventful. She pushed away the smiling image of Sam that was imprinted for ever on her subconscious. Crazy man. Where was the point at which the emphasis changed? Such waste. If only I could put the memory away. Like Shyam.

'We should talk, Shyam. This isn't healthy.'

'It's healthier than what went before.'

'You weren't responsible for Sam. It was a fluke.'

'I'm not frightened of taking the responsibility, Chita.'

'It's weeks now and you refuse to acknowledge what happened.'

'To acknowledge what exactly? My wife with another man?'

'Is that what you think?'

'No, of course not.' He'd taken her in his arms then. 'I'm so glad to have you safe and well. I don't care about Sam, Chita. I never did. It's only you I care about. His death wasn't planned but in the circumstances it was inevitable. That's all there is to be said. Let him die in our memories as well.'

'I love you so much, Shyam. More than you can even imagine.'

'And I you, Princess. Enough now. We're back together.'

'But I'm still torn in two.'

'Between him and me?'

'No. By the horror of it.'

'Concentrate on the future; look forward. Isn't that what you always tell others to do?'

He has benignly blocked all avenues of approach, Chita

thought as her husband dropped her hand and pulled out the in-flight magazine. Hearing the engines roar into life, she wondered bleakly what further surprises the future had in store.

Shyam's family had welcomed them with a joyfest of parties and feasting. Shivan and Kusum flew back specially, and the four brothers embraced for the first time in nearly fourteen years.

'I could not have imagined this,' Shyam said excitedly, bounding around the house like a schoolboy. 'We're all together again. It's as if time has stood still.'

'Yes – you're all a little older, but you still act like a bunch of kids.'

Shivan had doubled in size. 'He looks like our father,' Lucky told Chita as they sat out on the verandah together that first afternoon. 'I have never seen his features in my own face, but they must be there because Shivan and I are so similar.'

'Perhaps. You don't look at all alike any more.'

'And Bobby has aged.'

'He wears the responsibility like a curse. It's his albatross.'

'But now there is water to drink.'

'By the time the Ancient Mariner got water, everyone had died.'

Lucky jumped up. 'Lucky that Bobby doesn't sail. I'm going back in to reminisce and back-slap my brothers, and to minister to the needs of our ageing monkey. Are you coming, sister-in-law?'

'No. I'm still queasy from the flight. Let me enjoy the heat and the sounds and the smells.'

Chita remained there, remembering her first weeks sitting with Sujata on the verandah and receiving instructions on the

181

ways of the house and the men whose presence and needs dominated it. 'As Shyam's wife, Chita, this is your domain. Until his brothers leave, they too are your responsibility.'

'I know that, Auntyji.'

'Then why are you drooping the corners of your mouth? It's not that bad. They are quite capable of keeping themselves occupied. You only have to ensure there's food on the table and that the dobi returns their shirts in time.'

Tipping her head back, Chita left the sun breathe life and energy back into her. Is that my future now? Surely not. Shivan will return abroad, Lucky must find himself a wife and Bobby . . . he'll probably take himself off and live a little.

Listening to the laughter and seamless chatter inside, she contemplated the future with uncertainty. What will I do with myself once Shyam has got his teeth into the estate? He's uncomfortable with my interest. It's his baby.

Soon he'll expect me to have a real one.

Ah well. The pills have gone. Wait and see.

Pulling herself up, Chita coiled her hair, now past her shoulder blades, into a neat bun and went inside. This is *my* home and *my* family and I must be with them through this momentous time.

Was it on that first day that things started to go wrong? Chita wondered now. Because I couldn't be as gracious and smiling and *happy* as I should have been? But I *was*. I did my best. If I could just shake off this bloody bug I too would be rushing around yelping and teasing. Wouldn't I? Instead, it feels like another abrupt turn in life with no time to lay the past to rest and readjust. I loathe myself for being so lacklustre. And everyone else loathes me too.

Shyam put his head around the door. 'Do you want lunch or will you be spending the whole day in bed?'

'I've just thrown up. Shyam, I love you. You know that?'

'Of course. I'll tell the cook you don't want anything.'

Chita stared up at the ceiling, frightened of closing her eyes and seeing Sam framed there, alive and vital and then, suddenly, the flare of red and the life force gone.

She rolled onto her side in the foetal position. For the thousandth time she trawled through the litany of lies and manoeuvring; through Brina's strange outpourings and the emptiness afterwards.

'I am so sorry.'

'Sorry for who?' Chita looked up, startled. Shivan's wife, Kusum, was at the door. She came inside. 'Chitaji, you are always hiding. We've hardly seen you since your arrival. Have some lunch.'

'I'm not hungry, Kusum.'

'You know, Chita, it's hard for everyone. We have all been affected by the events in your life.'

'Then it's you that I'm sorry for.'

'Perhaps you should have considered the rest of us when you were gallivanting around the world for your job.'

'We all get it wrong sometimes. I couldn't foresee the future.'

'Did you even try? We choose our own paths, Chita.'

'I've travelled many paths since I married, Kusum, and always with my husband. But now I'm stranded at a crossroads and nobody will show me the map.'

'Then you are lost,' Kusum said, leaving the room.

The death of Sam, while just another statistic in the US, had received comprehensive coverage in the domestic press: 'Duel of the Hearts'; 'Love Triangle Exposed'; 'God-Fearing Hindus Slay Christmas Stalker'. There aren't many crimes of passion involving Indians abroad. It had been reported in Sri Lanka too, where Sam Raven still had family with presidential connections.

In Shyam's home town, and on the estate, and in the refinery where hundreds of workers whose parents and grandparents had worked for his family maintained the traditions, the stir continued. Gossip had been generated. And innuendo.

Chita was blessed with too much: great beauty, intelligence and the scion of a great household. In the eyes of those farther down the social chain, she was too good to be true.

So when it transpired that she'd been on Sam's turf for several months, and alone with him until the last, it was inevitable that they'd start speculating.

Her return did nothing to discourage their conjecture. Indeed they looked at this stylish Western girl who was quite different from the easternised copies one gets in the large conurbations of India, and it seemed to them that she had guilt writ large across her fecund body.

How could someone so lovely not be courted by others; and given Western mores, how was it possible that, having gone against her husband's advice and been spirited away by a handsome and powerful suitor, she *didn't* succumb to his seductive prowess?

They'd read the details of Sam's trail: the way he'd become obsessed with Chita at a Guy Fawkes party and hounded her American counterpart out of a job to deliberately make an opening for his intended wife and lover (though not necessarily in that order!). They admired the unerring way he'd lobbied the London bosses, insisting he needed her expertise. The cool calculation and lies behind their living together with no chaperone . . .

Indeed, even though no connection could be found between the closure of airports and Chita's departure for the Aspen 'love nest', they discussed the possibility of spells or enchantment. Evidence of a consciousness that supersedes, and superimposes itself on, life.

So, while they couldn't be precise about who did what to

whom, they read meaning into Brina's ranting outbursts on Doordarshan News and the methodical progression of Sam's behaviour.

How could Chita have repelled such advances unless she was charmed – and how could a girl from some hill family be charmed? She'd already been blessed with more than her fair share!

So began a sequence of cogitation and agitation that eventually transmitted itself to Shyam, and he knew not what to do.

'Shyam: *for God's sake.*' Lucky slapped his forehead with the flat of his hand. 'We have been back only four weeks. It will soon stop.'

'That's what you said last week and the week before. If anything, Lucky, it gets worse. It's undermining everyone and everything.'

'Only because you let it. It's arrant nonsense.'

'They did live together.'

'They shared a flat.'

'She didn't have to go.'

'She was foolish. That doesn't make her a criminal.'

'How do I know she was faithful?'

'Because she told you she was.' Lucky shook his head and started pacing the office. 'It's as if we've suddenly changed places, Shyam. You're talking about the woman with whom you've spent the last fourteen years of your life.'

'We're all susceptible to temptation, Lucky.'

'Have you ever succumbed to temptation?' When his brother didn't answer, Lucky went and stood over him. 'No. You haven't. So why should she? You are talking about idle gossip, Shyam. You cannot put it above your loyalty to your wife. I won't pretend I agree with all her actions, but they are always well meant.'

'The people are asking what proof there is.'

'Since you had already taken Chita's virginity, they will have to make do with her word. And if that isn't enough, you have evidence of Sam Raven's demented planning. Why should a man who has got what he wants scheme and lie as he did?'

'Because it wasn't enough. He wanted to *keep* her.'

'Is that what you really think? Why the hell can't the two of you talk about it? Instead of bearing grudges, tell her your feelings.'

Looking pained, Shyam rose and, brushing past Lucky, went to look out of the window. 'Feelings don't matter, Lucky. What is important is what I *know*. And I know that without the loyalty and respect of the people in this place, I will have thrown away everything my father held most dear.'

'I loved our father too, Shyam. I also obeyed him. That doesn't mean he was always right. Look at the damage caused by his will. We were riven as a family.'

'He was honouring a promise. And I promised that I would carry on his work. I don't want shame to be associated with his name.'

'*Shame?* Chita doesn't bring shame. She's a prize.'

'Of course Chita is a prize.' Shyam put his head in his hands like a man tormented. 'I have loved her from the first moment I set eyes on her. Even now, when I watch her walk across a room, there is a quickening of my heart. I can never not love Chita.'

'Then?'

'This isn't about love, Lucky. It's about duty. The two are not always the same. So much has happened that was outside my control, I no longer know what to think. But I do know what other people think. And I have a duty to them as much as I have a duty to Chita. That was always my destiny.'

* * *

186

'Was it a good honeymoon?'

'Forget the honeymoon. How's life at home?'

'Don't ask, Manju. Tell me about you.'

'There's not much scope for fall-out during a week of love in San Francisco, Chita. Are you and Shyam speaking?'

'No, not really.'

'I'm telling you – it's jealousy.'

'Not Shyam. The one thing we've always been sure of is mutual loyalty.'

'Chita – I'm a newly-wed and I still question mutual loyalty! Would you like me to talk to him? So many times I encouraged you to misbehave with the sexy Sam Raven and never once did you bite. I'll tell him.'

'No.' Chita sighed. 'Perhaps you're right about the jealousy – or resentment, perhaps, Manju. Maybe I've got off too lightly. I don't know. Something has changed.'

'Going over and over the details won't improve things, Chita. If your husband is hell bent on being difficult, let him. Clearly you cannot make things better. The short-term strategy must be to prevent them getting any worse.'

'What's wrong with Shyam, Lucky?'

'I don't know.'

'He's so distant. Is it just business or is there something more?'

'I don't know.'

'It's almost as if he's avoiding me.' Chita poured herself another glass of water. It helped keep her head clear. 'Have I done something wrong? Am I not showing enough interest in the estate? How can someone change overnight like that?'

'I don't know.'

She drank the water in one. 'Shall we walk? The flowers are beautiful at this time of year. At home I'd spend hours in the botanical gardens.' She diverted into the rose arbour.

'The gardener does such a good job here. I see him out even in the midday sun. Is it to do with Sam?'

'I don't know.'

'Don't lie.' They walked down to the fishpond, covered with netting to discourage predators. In the years they'd been gone, Bobby had had it enlarged and koi carp now guarded it aggressively.

'Does Sam's death haunt him?'

'In life, some outcomes are inevitable. We are taught to accept them.'

'I wish I shared your certainty.'

They stopped and watched the fish with feigned interest before moving on to the little gazebo where Sujata had regularly disappeared for gentle afternoons with her sewing box.

Here Chita, feeling a little faint, sat down. 'He comes to the bedroom only when he thinks I'm asleep. In the morning he finds reasons to leave as soon as I'm up. We don't talk and we don't make love.' She giggled. 'Don't look like that, Lucky. Shyam and I are husband and wife. It can't surprise you that we make love. Anyway, he's avoiding me.' She studied him carefully for a minute or two. 'And now you're doing the same. Why?'

'I don't know.'

'But you do know,' Chita said sharply. She burst into tears. 'You do know. The only one who doesn't know is me.'

'It is the only solution, Lucky. I love her more than anything. But the people are up in arms. They say there's no smoke without fire. When I think of the many times I counselled her to return but she wouldn't . . .'

'Because she'd given her word. You would have said the same.'

'I believe I would never have entered the commitment after so many warnings.'

'It all ended in victory. What does it matter?'

'A hollow victory, Lucky. It ended in battle and the death of a man. A man with whom Chita spent several months, alone. On that final morning she was in *his* bed in her underclothes. Didn't we read all about it in the newspapers?'

'We didn't need to read it, Shyam, we were there. You saw her. You found her. Don't add punishment to suffering.' Shyam shifted uncomfortably under Lucky's unflinching gaze. 'Brother, Chita is a clever woman. She could easily have lied and we would have been none the wiser. But as you say, Sam Raven was sleeping downstairs. Do you think if she'd accepted him he would arm himself and sleep in front of a dying fire?'

'I have re-examined events many times, Lucky. Each second of that terrible morning is imprinted in my mind. I've explained to people until I've run out of words. What am I supposed to do? It is my role to adjudicate when they are unhappy. And they are deeply unhappy. I cannot run the business without equanimity and respect. If my wife cannot command respect, how can I?'

'So you want me to take her back to England.'

'It's the only place. She will never fit in here again.'

'What is she to do there? Go to the temple and make vows every third day? Buy a Madhur Jaffrey book and finally learn how to cook curry? Return to the office where Sam Raven sowed the seeds of her destruction? This will kill her, Shyam. Her whole life – both our lives – have been dictated by our love and commitment to you. To reject her at the moment when she should be enjoying the fruits of her endeavours is . . .' Lucky's eyes filled with tears. In a corner, Honeybun, white haired and near death in his basket, put a hand over his eyes and started to shriek softly.

Lucky went to the door. His hand on the handle, he stopped. 'How are you going to explain this to her?'

Shyam stared blankly at his brother's back. 'I'm not going to explain, Lucky. How can I when I love her so much? You are.'

'He's gone where?'

'I don't know. The whole team – Aluwalla, Waragoda and Mudalige – have gone to the refineries for a few days.'

'Why didn't he tell me? I saw him last evening over dinner. He kissed me when I went to bed. I felt him in the night. Now you say he went this morning before breakfast?'

'It's true.'

Not for the first time in recent weeks Chita became tearful. I hate myself for being so emotional. It must drive them all mad . . .

'You're stressed, sister-in-law. Why don't we pack a bag and head back to Docklands for a croissant and shopping break.'

'Are you mad?'

'The flat's been redecorated.' Lucky put his hand in his pocket and pulled out a set of keys. 'We have instant access.' She shook her head. 'We need to go back anyway, Chita. Estate agents have to be visited, solicitors employed . . .'

'We did all that before we left.'

'We could go together.'

'Lucky: in ten weeks both my world and my husband have changed. Again. The last thing I want is a walk down Memory Lane.'

'It was his idea.'

'That I go to London? When did *you* decide to go?'

'Is it right for you to question your husband's will? Again? I've booked us on a flight tomorrow.'

'Tomorrow?' Chita studied her nails; her fingers; the lines on her palm, as if she could suddenly read what they meant. An expert would have noticed a flaw in the love line; the top one running across from the little finger and breaking into a V somewhere between the middle and index. But all Chita saw was the depth and clarity of them: qualities she misunderstood as suggesting a prodigious and clear path ahead. She waited for Lucky to make a joke or do something that would relieve the cold horror of what he had suggested. He distinguished himself with a rare silence. Realising it was no joke, she wondered how something so solid could unravel that quickly.

'Isn't a wife allowed a voice in this family, Lucky?'

'You've had your voice, Chita. It didn't bring us the finest of good fortune. Perhaps it's time to listen to your husband.'

'Is that what we're back to, brother-in-law? It's funny. Shyam and I have always believed there was a middle way where husband and wife attain an equanimity. An equivalence between them. It's not like Shyam to go straight back to the feudal system. It's not like *you*, Lucky.'

He wouldn't meet her eye. 'Pack a bag.'

'What's the hurry?'

'Strike while the iron's hot – isn't that what they say?'

'Is that the pressing iron, Lucky, or the branding one?'

She had packed just hand luggage. He sent her back to make up a suitcase. 'You never know what the weather's like. Take coats and jackets, shoes and boots.'

'It's summer. I'll take enough for two weeks.'

'No, two months. Better safe than sorry.'

She did as he said because whatever was propelling him could come only from Shyam, and since returning to India, Chita had become aware that she had lost her husband's ear as well as his support.

She pulled out clothes she'd never expected to wear again and packed the case quickly and methodically. There was something familiar and pleasurable about handling the fabrics and accessories that marked her life in England. Only two months and I'm going back.

She looked across at the dressing table, where her precious perfumes were arranged in a beautiful tableau of curves and colour and glass. No, I'll leave them here. I wish I knew what was going on. I'm too ill these days to argue. Ever since eating those prawns on the flight here. I am so tired and run down.

If Chita sensed Lucky's unease as they got into the car, she didn't say anything. If she was brought low by his jumpiness, his clear embarrassment, his inability to construct a sentence without becoming aphasic or making some Spoonerism, she chose to ignore it. Just as she did the fact that his luggage was just an overnight bag.

At the airport, she bought magazines and vomited in the toilet. She powdered her pale face in the mirror, noticing the huge bags under her eyes and the way her mouth was drawn. I'm looking old. She put on a smear of lipstick and straightened her back. Hell: Lucky's right. It'll be great to do some shopping.

Lucky had arranged a car at Heathrow. When she arrived back at the flat, everything was so utterly familiar Chita was no longer sure where home was. I was away in New York longer than I was in New Delhi. And I only ever spent the first few months of married life there anyway. Whereas I was here for fourteen years . . .

The flat looked sensational. She'd chosen her colours before they left. Creamy yellow for the main walls. Violet for the wall of windows and the kitchen area. Where she and Shyam slept, it was a muted grey, and Lucky's mezzanine looked totally different in baby pink. 'I'll feel like a bloody girly sleeping up here.'

'It wasn't meant for you.'

He looked away, and again she felt the frisson of fear. No. If he will not tell me, I won't ask.

'Why don't you ring Monica? Tell her you're back.'

'Is the phone connected?'

'What an idiot I am. I didn't think about it. I'll call NTL in the morning and have the line reinstated.'

'It's not worth it for a couple of weeks, Lucky. We both have mobiles. We can manage with those.'

'Where has Ambreen moved since getting married?'

'Somewhere in Surrey. I don't know where. What a shame we returned without warning. I would have loved to have got things for Shola and Jez and some hand-made toys for little Annie.'

'You missed Manju's wedding. Has she forgiven you?'

'Of course. She's my best friend. She understood.'

'You could fly to Michigan easily from here.'

Suddenly the insistent nature of her brother-in-law's questioning started to take on a curious shape. Chita felt cold. She caught his shame-filled gaze and something deep inside her crumpled and died. Taking several deep breaths, she lowered herself into a chair before finding the words. 'What is it, Lucky? Let's drop the pretence. I can see you're crying. This is clearly not an occasion for celebration.'

'How do I start, Chitaji?' She offered no help as he floundered. 'You must know people have been saying things.'

'Saying what?'

'About you. And Sam Raven. That it wasn't innocent.'

'But you know it was.'

'I know. You know. Shyam . . . knows. But . . .'

'Lucky, how long does he want me out of the way?' Her brother-in-law shrugged. 'That's why I'm here, isn't it? Because he wants me out of the way?' She forced herself up again: business tactics – you should always be at the same head level as your adversary.

She went and stood at the windows from which she'd surveyed the City of London for so many years. You think you know someone so well, then one day they do something that makes you realise how little you *really* know. I got it wrong with Sam – but then he was effectively a stranger. Shyam isn't a stranger. He is my twin soul. My destiny. Why couldn't *he* have told me?

It was a beautiful day. The sun glinted on the water and off the dome of St Paul's. What a blessing we didn't find a buyer. She could see the statue of Justice on the roof of the Old Bailey. Gathering her thoughts, Chita worked through the various permutations.

'I'm here for two months, is that it? It can't be worse than that, Lucky, because that's as bad as it gets.' A riverboat came motoring past with gold helium balloons attached to the rails: 'Ann and Bob Fifty Happy Years'. 'I don't know why Shyam couldn't just say this.' Chita started playing with the simple gold band on her ring finger. 'Sometimes, even if the problem is minor, it's easier to remove the source until people have accepted the major factors in a change. I know that. It's my job.' There was a bitter taste in her mouth. 'But *he* should have told me.'

Lucky was searching vainly through the cupboards. 'Where's the Scotch? I don't remember packing it.'

'I threw it. Everything we didn't take was either thrown or given away. The cupboards are bare.' And the poor doggy had none. She watched as he paced in a state of agitation. She was utterly calm. On the outside. Inside, she felt sick again.

'I'm not angry with you, Lucky,' Chita said, 'I'm sad.' She took his hands in hers. 'He told you to do it like this. I know that. I understand your relationship. You are the messenger only. I'm not going to shoot you.'

His hands gripped hers till they hurt. 'It's not that simple, Chita. If only it were.' She held her breath. 'He doesn't want you to come back, Chita. Ever.'

'What does that mean, exactly?' Did I really say that?

'It means that Shyam . . . Oh God, Chita – I love you as a sister. This is unbearable. Shyam loves you also. But his first duty is to our father, to our family – to the name; the estate.'

'He doesn't want me back? *Ever?*'

'Ever. I'm sorry.'

Chita tried to concentrate on his words but there was a sudden buzzing in her ears and everything went black. When she came to, she was lying in the bed she and Shyam had shared for so many years and her brother-in-law was sitting weeping in a chair beside her.

She insisted on driving him to the airport in the little runaround he bought her. He had offered her cash but she'd refused. There was still an account in London holding her savings and her substantial RAT bonus. 'I don't want your money,' she told him as they pulled on to the Heathrow slip road. 'You've given me the flat. That's enough.'

'I'll have the rest of your belongings sent on.'

'As you wish.' She hated herself for being businesslike but there was no other way to be, without falling apart. I have learned that it's safer to leave the introspection for when you're feeling strong. In the short term the only thing that matters is survival.

In the short-stay carpark, she helped Lucky find a trolley. 'I won't see you off, brother-in-law. Best we say goodbye here.'

'Chita . . .'

'I know. Shit happens.' She laughed ironically. 'A favourite Sam Raven saying.'

He clasped her to him. 'You are the best.' She said nothing.

Straightening the luggage trolley, Lucky headed for the walkway, turning to give her a final wave. She smiled, the foul taste back in her mouth again. 'Tell Shyam I love him,'

195

she said in a small whisper he couldn't hear. 'Tell Shyam I'll always love him.'

'Why do men do this? They declare undying love and the next minute they claim they've been unhappy for years and run off with another woman. My sister's husband left her and three children at one hour's notice. He'd never once complained.'

'There is no one else, Monica. I'm the one accused of breaking the marriage vows.'

'Same principle, Chita. Shyam closes the chapter without a word. *You* couldn't have done that. It goes against the grain of decency. I hate him for what he's done to you. How can he put rural tittle-tattle over his love for his wife?' She jabbed her fork in the air. 'If he walked past right now I'd stick this up his sanctimonious butt. Bastard.' She giggled. 'That made you smile.'

'Is there any contract work going?'

'Not a lot. Anyway, you can't come back. It would stir up all the Sam stuff again.' Monica leaned across the table and took Chita's hand in hers. 'However desperate you feel at this minute, retracing your steps isn't the answer. Every time I say Shyam's name you cry; every time I say Sam's, you blanch. You need to get away from memories.'

'How can I? One is my husband. The other, I thought, a friend.'

'Ah, well. Life would be deadly dull if we always got things right.'

'Shyam does.'

'Not this time.' Monica called for the bill. 'You look rough, Chita. Why don't you put the job-hunting on ice and destress? You can afford a couple of months off. I think you should see your GP.'

'And once I've finished a course of Nurofen, then what?'

'Who knows? Maybe your arsehole of a husband has done

you a favour by giving you a clean sheet. There aren't many women who get a new start at thirty-eight.'

Chita sat in the doctor's waiting room for an hour, despite a timed appointment. Looking over the other patients, she told herself off for feeling depressed. There were worn young women with listless children; elderly men who could barely walk; and a whole host of in-betweens who looked far worse off than her.

Closing her eyes, she made a mental list of her blessings:

- I have a home.
- I have my health.
- I can find work.
- I have no responsibilities to anyone but myself.
- I have known true and deep love.
- I have my parents.

Oh God, she thought. How am I going to tell Amma and Papaji? He's still so weak from his bronchitis. It will finish him off. She thought again about Shyam and was overwhelmed by his rejection.

It doesn't matter how much I pinch myself, this just doesn't feel real. I have become detached from reality. I don't even know who I am any more.

'You're being sick two or three times a day and you feel nauseous? How long has this been going on?'

Chita shrugged. 'I first noticed it on the flight home to India – just over three months ago. I tried various local potions but I couldn't shake it off. I thought it might ease in London, but it hasn't.'

'Could you be pregnant?'

'No. I came off the pill only a month before leaving London. I haven't yet restarted my monthly cycle.'

'Many women find they're most fertile when they come off the pill. I think we should do a test.'

'I am a little bloated, but on the scales I'm two pounds lighter than usual.'

'Because you're not keeping anything down.'

'I eat like a horse.'

'Let's see.' The doctor took out a little plastic bottle. 'Have you a full bladder? Can you manage a specimen?'

Chita returned a few minutes later with the sample and sat down wanly. 'Could it be anaemia, Doctor? My mother has problems with anaemia. I probably don't eat enough iron.'

The GP turned from the sink where she was putting sticks into Chita's urine. 'You're having a baby,' she said matter-of-factly.

There were many options that had gone through Chita's muddled mind, but this was not one of them. 'That can't be right, Doctor.'

'Why don't we check? Pop up on the couch for me and we'll have a listen.' She watched as Chita removed her coat and climbed up. 'It's certainly true that you've lost weight, but from where I'm looking, your stomach *is* distended. I would guess you're around sixteen weeks.'

'Maybe it's hormonal imbalance. I took oral contraception from the day we married. It must have an effect.'

She pulled up her blouse and the doctor rubbed gel on her abdomen and ran an electronic listening device across the space between her navel and her groin. 'Ah, yes. Here it is.'

There it was indeed: bu-boom bu-boom bu-boom. And then a little echo behind it.

Chita's mind went totally blank. She felt a surging rise of panic. Dear God, am I really pregnant? I'm having a baby? I'm having a baby! What the hell do I do now? The doctor continued moving the scope around. Chita noticed that the GP was smiling to herself. It was then that her other self kicked in, filling her with alarm and anxiety on behalf of this strange unformed creature who'd apparently taken root in her body when she least expected it.

Nothing must harm her child. *Her child.* A child of love, abandoned to fate. No. Not abandoned. You have your . . . mother.

Veering between euphoria and shock, she said in a whisper: 'Is everything all right? Is *it* all right?'

'Everything's fine,' the doctor said, smiling. She took Chita's hand. 'Congratulations. You're having twins.'

Part Six

Chita lay in bed, staring despairingly at the ceiling. The boys were being so noisy chasing each other up and down the stairs. She felt for the young couple next door who, as she and Shyam had once done, clearly slept late on Sundays after overworking all week.

Chita also overworked all week, but when you're a mother, particularly a single mother, there are no lie-ins. Weariness brought on by professional toil is heaped upon the aching tiredness that comes from being all things at all times to your children.

In recent years, even the saintly Chita has been known to blow. 'What the hell are you doing, boys? For goodness' sake show some respect for others.' She'd been known to threaten, to hand out the odd smack and then to huddle weeping in a corner like an abused woman hiding from the next blow. I am only human. And I am on my own.

Even the most virtuous crumble under the pressures of demand feeding and sleepless nights, of unremitting nappy changing, teaching and 'This little piggy went to market'. Sometimes she was filled with resentment after yet another scrap or tantrum. I know that's what makes them children and the rest of us adults, but it's too much to bear.

'At last I'm handing over the reins a little, Manju. I'm working full time three days a week. I've a lovely childminder who's happy to kick footballs and cook fish fingers.'

'Don't bore me with detail, Chita. Holly is only four weeks old.'

'Have you crow's-feet from the strain of labour?'

'Not the crow's-feet – the whole crow.'

'I'm sure you're looking great, Manju.'

'No, Chita, *you* still look great. I look like a worn woman of forty-four who has miraculously had her first child.'

Chita still turned heads: maturity had imbued her with a depth and a mystery that added to the allure. She was a woman in her prime.

Now she looked at the clock with half an eye. Only 7.30. Forcing herself out of bed, she went on to the landing and hugged the boys. 'Rustem. Shashi. Can we please have some quiet before the neighbours go crazy?' They looked peeved, but the noise subsided as she switched on the TV for early morning cartoons.

In the kitchen she made herself a cafetière of Colombian coffee. Chita loved it at weekends when everything was suddenly silent. The papers wouldn't be delivered till nine. She put on Radio Four and listened to the day's news.

The huge and fashionable loft had been sold six weeks before the boys arrived a month prematurely, by Caesarean section. On the day they exchanged contracts, she'd expected to feel sad and nostalgic. It was a pleasant surprise to discover that she was, instead, excited and hopeful for the first time in months.

If I look ahead, she'd told herself, all I can see is hope. So why bother looking backward and spoiling the picture?

She'd invested enough money for the three of them to live comfortably for a couple of years. The rest had gone on the small two-bedroomed house in a Kentish Town mews.

The new area was grubby and overcrowded despite its proximity to Hampstead Heath and Highgate village: a dustbowl in the valley, above which rose the foothills of urban civilisation.

The Northern Line Tube station was round the corner and

the trains ran along the bottom of the embankment beyond the back wall of their tiny garden. She'd expected to be irritated by the noise, but alone at night the rumble and accompanying tremor were strangely comforting. It also meant that if you looked out of the boys' bedroom window all you could see were the trees planted to deaden the noise. It was lovely in the summer.

This is an in-between place, Chita had thought as she painted the house from top to bottom, weighed down by babies but filled with the frantic energy of a woman in nesting mode. And it's only fifteen minutes' walk from our first London flat. Happy days.

She stirred sugar into her coffee. By Christmas she would have been 18 months with her current firm. Time enough to afford a long break with the boys. Amma and Papaji are so desperate to see them, and Rustem and Shashi have no memory of our last visit.

She rinsed her cup. A cold sun was already up. In the garden the first crocuses of spring were showing their heads. We'll take the bikes and go to Parliament Hill, she thought. A few hours of fresh air will soon wear them out.

It would take another hour or so for the caffeine to kick in. Furtively Chita slipped back to bed and napped. She'd learned the hard way to make the most of the short breaks before a boisterous five-year-old came up demanding breakfast, or justice after World War III had been declared over possession of a car or a train or a gun or something equally inconsequential.

A quick forty winks, Chita thought. But as soon as her head hit the pillow she was out for the count.

The letter had arrived in the morning post but by midday both boys continued to display a reluctance to open it.

Unable to stand the suspense, Chita took it from the mantelpiece. 'I cannot wait any longer. I'm going to open the envelope.' Rusty came and stood in front of her. He was almost her height, now. Shashi, so like his father, remained at the window, his face turned away from them. She opened the letter and broke into a broad smile as she scanned the single sheet.

Rusty punched the air. 'We've done it! Haven't we?'

Chita nodded.

Shashi said without turning: 'Both of us?'

'Of course, both of you.' Still he remained immobile as Rusty did a dance of celebration around the room. 'What's the matter Shush?' He shrugged. My darling son: eleven years old and I still can't get inside your head.

Chita walked across to him, putting a gentle arm across his shoulders. 'Congratulations. You've both won partial scholarships to the Milburn School in September.'

'You're sure we can afford it?'

'Yes. I've been working full time for three years now. We have no mortgage. It may be a squeeze at times, but it can be done.'

Outside, the middle-aged man who'd bought one of the garages was working on his old Rover 3000, rubbing wax into the retouched black paintwork and polishing the chrome. It reminded Chita of the ambassadorial cars back home, throwbacks to a time when motoring splendour was also reflected in size and weight.

In her mind's eye she saw Manju, pulling up in her precious Humber, and Lucky, on her first day in Shyam's house, getting out of his prewar Mercedes-Benz. What would Shyam make of his two sons? Both boys so luscious and fresh that even now they received Valentine's cards from girls in their class.

Like Lucky and Shivan, they were almost identical. If you looked at them very quickly you wouldn't know which was which. But Shashi had his father's curly hair and that same air of sobriety. He was constantly distracted and occasionally baffled by the strange ways of a changing world.

Rustem, on the other hand, had thick straight hair, like his mother. He was impetuous and joyful, but tempered with common sense and sensitivity. Chita instinctively understood him, whereas Shush took conscious effort and coaxing.

'Is it quite frightening to think of changing schools? Being the youngest instead of the oldest?' He nodded. 'You'll be fine, darling. Remember how easy it was at primary school? It's the same now. You'll have the fun without any of the responsibility.'

He, more than Rusty, feels the lack of a male role model. Of someone in whom he can recognise the seeds of his adult self. Poor darling. How much we, all of us, model ourselves on the parent or sibling or other close relation we feel most reflects our own personality: our outlook, our opinions, our talent and obsessions. My sons have only me . . .

Chita hugged him now despite his growing discomfort with intimacy. 'When you're taking exams in a few years' time, you'll wish you were eleven again.'

Suddenly, he hugged her fiercely – his head only just fitting under her elegant chin. 'I love you, Mum.'

'I love you too, my son. You'll never how much.'

* * *

Many times Chita had debated writing to Shyam or contacting one of his brothers to tell them about her sons, but each time she'd been discouraged by the fear of further cruelty upon cruelty. Although she could forgive Shyam his weakness in banishing her, she couldn't forget the pain of it. Because it still hurt. How could he just jettison me after half a lifetime? As if I were suddenly surplus to requirements. No explanation. No apology. No *respect*.

Over the years she had heard too many stories from women whose marriages suddenly disintegrated to think she was unique. She knew now that destiny does not automatically confer good luck. But how could Shyam, of all people, have behaved like that? As she left, he had been rewriting history to justify his behaviour. Who knew what stories he had spun during her absence?

Lust, Ambreen had said after her own husband left, is a stronger force than love for many men. 'They dress it up with meaning, but it's just sex.' In truth, if Shyam had met someone else I would have found it easier to stomach, Chita thought. There would have been a tangible reason. I could have moved on. But I can never achieve closure while the questions remain unanswered.

This deep insecurity had led her to be circumspect when discussing the children's provenance. Their parents' wedding photograph was on the boys' bedside table and Chita often told stories about the early years in London when she, Shyam and 'Uncle Lucky' shared a flat; but when they questioned Shyam's absence from their lives, she didn't answer. I cannot risk him rejecting you, Rustem and Shashi, flesh of my flesh. If for any reason he denies you are his . . . denies you the love you both deserve . . . I could not forgive myself.

'Does he know about us, Mother?'

'No, Rusty, he doesn't.'

'Why not?'

'It's a long story. I will tell it to you both when you are older. You see, the concepts are complex and the facts are confusing. You will understand better when you've lived a little.'

Initially the boys had found Shyam's absence romantic. They wove stories around him and his secret life as a pirate or an eco-warrior and even, given his good looks, a Bollywood star.

As they got older their mother's reticence was an irritation but she always managed to turn it into a game or a joke.

'Did he have a beard, Mum?'

'No, darling. Just some hairs on his chest.'

At one point she had consulted her parents and had been glad when they agreed that the boys' existence should be kept secret. 'What will happen if he contests paternity, Chita? A man who can cast aside his wife so easily is quite capable of claiming the boys have a different father.'

'We could do DNA.'

'What humiliation, child. Mud sticks. It would damage the boys.'

Manju continued to have a go at Chita. Ever since having Holly and then Grace within a year of each other, she felt very strongly on the subject. 'He should be supporting them financially, Chita. Why should you do it all?'

'Because I want to. Because I can. Because it's easier.'

'Is that fair on the boys?'

'We're doing fine.'

'Now. What about all those endless nights when they were ill? Colds, coughs, chickenpox . . . you never stopped. How you managed to study and start a new career while juggling their demands I will never know. You have no freedom of action or movement. Everything you do, Chita, you do for his children.'

'They're my children.'

'He should be ashamed that his wife had to do it alone.'

'He's ashamed enough of his wife, Manju. If he discovered she now specialised in family law, he'd have the last laugh.'

*   *   *

The next few weeks went by in a blur of Saturdays and Sundays spent on sports fields watching her sons playing football and basketball. The twins could run like the wind and turn on a sixpence. They were instinctive team players, constantly on the lookout for others as well as themselves. The same was true of their abilities in basketball – if either got possession, their team was guaranteed a point. Chita enjoyed watching them play, even though she never got into the games themselves.

She'd become quite friendly with some of the other parents. Two single fathers in particular would make a beeline for her. But while she happily engaged in small talk they could never get her to the next step. Years spent alone had toughened her up and made her wise to the ploys that once got her into so much trouble.

Afterwards she'd take the boys out for a pizza or a Chinese. Then it was home for homework and an evening of TV or videos, snuggled on the chesterfield: homage to happier days.

Chita enjoyed watching the boys jostling for space and favour. She never complained about their teasing or bickering. She retained her mother's words from the one time she'd complained about her own lack of freedom and solitude: 'Make the most of it, Chita. Time is an arrow that flies with unerring precision. They are only children for a short time. Each passing day takes them farther from you. One day you'll look up and they'll be gone.'

Resting on the sofa, she was filled with a sense of profound sadness. Don't ever leave me. I love you both so much. You are my world. With you, I have fulfilled my destiny.

Shush was sitting on her feet. Rusty was squashed up with her, so long and lanky now they only just fitted. Soon he, like his brother, would find this level of closeness too oppressive. But for the moment they adored her, and she them.

The boys turned on an old film: *What Women Want* – a stupid, juvenile fantasy that had Mel Gibson hearing the thoughts of the opposite sex. Chita found herself laughing despite the banal script.

'What do *you* want, Mum?'

'What do I want?' She was nonplussed. 'Nothing more than I already have, Shush. I'm very contented.'

'Don't you wish we had a bigger house, or a new car?'

'Then I'd have to work longer hours or we'd have to forgo holidays and visits to your grandparents. It's impossible and boring to have it all.'

'When you've told us about Papa and Lucky in London, it sounds like you had it all.'

'And look where it got us. Sometimes you have to lose the things you hold most dear to perceive the frailty of life.'

'Don't you miss him, Mum? Don't you yearn to tell him about *us*?'

'Yes and yes, my son. But as I said, sometimes you have to lose the things you hold most dear to perceive the frailty of life. And when you realise how fragile happiness is, the chasing of dreams doesn't hold out promise, but threats.'

The long Easter weekend was in April and Monica and Peter were going to Scotland to see his parents. 'Take our cottage early this year, Chita. It's lovely in spring.'

Chita and the boys collected the keys and headed up the A1 to Wisbech and then cross-country past the royal estate at Sandringham and the lavender farms in full glory. 'I can smell the sea,' Rusty said.

They'd been to Monica's cottage every summer since the boys were little. They got on well with Annie, but since crossing the threshold of puberty she was scathing about them on grounds of age and gender.

'We're here.'

The roadside garden with its profusion of budding foxgloves and hollyhocks took Chita's breath away as they rounded the corner and saw the house flame-lit by a mid-afternoon sun that blazed like a fireball.

'Can we go for a walk, Ma?'

'As soon as the food is put away.'

They headed across the back fields. Suddenly, ahead of them, a giant hare leaped from the long grass and was momentarily silhouetted against the orange of the sky.

'A March hare,' Shashi shouted.

'April. Is it lucky?' Rusty asked.

'I certainly feel lucky, don't you?' Chita took his hand, and they followed behind Shush, who, as ever when they were in the wilds, was setting the pace for them. He is in his element in the country – like his father. He would have loved Shyam's stories of their adventures on the estate. The picnics and the dares. What am I thinking? He would have been living them. Like being a member of the Famous Five.

Rusty now ran off and the boys started chasing each other across another field and then over dunes and on to the beach at Holme.

Cresting the rise, Chita was again filled with the sheer pleasure of the landscape there: the golden beach stretching out in either direction as far as the eye can see. A timeless place without the detritus of trippers – no ice-cream vendors or hamburger stalls. Just man and nature, and the odd dog, at one with each other.

The tide was out and the boys far ahead of her, pulling off shoes and socks and running into the waves. She could hear their squeals as the freezing water caught them by surprise.

In the old days they hadn't been allowed anywhere near the sea without supervision – there were rogue currents that swept children away. But now they were big and both were strong swimmers. They were free to do as they wished.

Chita laughed aloud as they rolled up their trousers for fear of chastisement. In the last two months they'd shot up even further. From a distance they didn't look like children but gawky young men fooled by a mirage into thinking it was summer. They looked like Shyam; like two Shyams.

She stopped for a while and watched them, no longer sure if her face was wet from the salt spray of the sea, or the salt of her tears.

They went to the aquarium at Hunstanton. Shush had already announced his wish to be a marine biologist. Rusty was less certain of his obsessions. 'Sometimes, Mum, I think I'd like to be a doctor in medical research, but what if I got involved in some project that I didn't agree with morally?' He stopped to watch the seals leaping for their morning fish. 'What if they wanted me to do something I didn't believe in, like human cloning?'

'By the time you grow up, much of that research will be complete.'

'Or gynaecology. I don't think I'd like that.'

For a moment Chita was taken back to a previous life, to the day her father had so proudly perambulated the room with her, his glittering young prize, as the well-dressed gynaecologist with the manicured hands popped a gulab jamun in his mouth.

'What do you know of gynaecology?'

'I think I might be a journalist. A proper one, I mean – for a newspaper or the BBC. I'd like to investigate frauds and wrongdoing. I'd like to expose corruption.'

'What do you know of corruption?'

Taking his hand, she pulled him along to the underwater tunnel where Shush was studying the sea mammals through the glass. 'Hi, Ma. Did you know that whales can store oxygen in their muscles for more than an hour? There are two types of whale – the toothed and the whaleboned, who have baleen hanging from their jaws like giant strainers.'

'*These* aren't whales, they're seals.'

'I know they're seals, Rusty. I was just telling you about whales because watching the seals made me think about them – doh.'

Afterwards they had the first of their two visits to the neighbouring fair. 'Don't you think you're both getting a little old for this?' Chita asked as she picked up a mat and joined them to walk up the helter-skelter.

'If we're too old, what does that make you, Mum?'

'This is my only ride. And the Waltzer.'

'Exactly.'

As always, Chita felt sick as she scrambled off the Waltzer, but she loved the adrenaline fix: the bumps and the circling and the car spinning so madly on its axis she always feared that at some point it must uncouple and go flying across the strand and into the sea.

Laughing at her, the boys stayed on for a second ride. Chita bought herself a coffee from one of the booths and followed their progress to the ghost train and back to the helter-skelter, while keeping warm.

The dark-skinned woman behind the counter said: 'On your own?' Chita nodded. 'It doesn't get any easier, does it? I've got five.'

'Five? How old?'

'Oh, all grown up now, but they never stop needing you. If it's not baby-sitting it's "Lend us fifty, Mum" or "Can I borrow the car?". If they'd told me all that in the first place I'd never have started.'

'But they're a joy too.'

'If they're that much of a joy, why don't the fathers stick around?'

*   *   *

That evening, they lit the new wood-burning stove Monica and Peter had had fitted in the sitting room and played Scrabble on the floor in front of it. 'I love open fires,' Rusty said.

'It isn't open, Rusty. It's behind doors.'

'You know what I mean, Shush.'

'You should be more precise.'

'Did you have them in India, Mum?'

'No. At home we had radiators, just like here.' Chita remembered the open fire in the bar at the Meridien: it had always seemed so pretentiously olde English. Unwittingly, the open fire in Colorado came to mind. A brief snapshot of Sam Raven laid out on the rug and reading the TV listings looking like a god. I might as well have succumbed for all the good it did. But . . . it wasn't right.

All the same, it had been a precious moment of closeness and companionship. There'd been a hiatus in the suspicion and gamesmanship that had dogged relations with Sam; it was an evening of true tranquillity. But it had led to the most awful day of her life. More awful even, she thought now, than coming with Lucky to London and being told her husband no longer wanted her.

Chita was implicated in Sam's death, because she'd had the option not to be there. He'd lied and schemed and cheated, but every step of the way she had foolishly given him the benefit of the doubt where someone else might have known better.

Shyam's rejection of her, on the other hand, was a matter between him and his conscience. She hadn't been consulted or asked to put her argument. She'd done nothing to invite it.

'Ha! Got the triple word. That's eighteen times three . . . is . . .'

'Fifty-four.' Chita wrote down Rusty's score. 'We're neck and neck – only six points in it.'

'Then we're not neck and neck.'

'Shush . . .'

He grinned. 'Sorry, Ma. I know. I mustn't be so anal.'

'Who taught you that term?'

'My brother.'

'Rusty?'

'I heard it on TV and looked it up. It's proper usage, isn't it?'

Chita shook her head. 'I can never win with the two of you.'

'Of course you can, Ma. You said yourself. We're neck and neck.'

Before they went back on the Monday, they made the annual pilgrimage to the country park. However old they got, the boys enjoyed feeding newborn lambs and watching the little piglets squealing around the sows' soft stomachs.

Going in, they bought cups of grass pellets to feed the sheep and goats. They queued for the trailer trip around the grounds with the old chap who used the same spiel year after year and still made them laugh.

They fed the deer that came to the sides of the vehicle, feeling the velvet on the antlers of the stags and stroking the heads of the fawns that jostled to nuzzle their overfull palms.

Sandwiched between them, Chita felt utterly at peace.

Afterwards they ate their picnic on grass that was still a little damp from overnight rain, and then went into the pottery, where each boy made a clay hand- and footprint: 'Another one for the collection.'

'We can hang them in the den.'

Initially the attic den had been Chita's idea for giving them separate bedrooms. Their shared space was cramped and unworkable, but they'd refused to be separated. Instead, they'd reorganised themselves, moving all belongings upstairs – the computer, the games, their stereo and books – and turning the room downstairs into a haven of sleep.

The downside was that it heralded a new phase in which Chita became excluded from some areas of their lives: the gossip and the teasing and, probably, a growing interest in girls. On the other hand, for the first time in over eleven years she had time to herself.

She could go to bed and read, or potter around the kitchen without them constantly coming in asking for things or demanding her presence. It left her confused. 'I don't know what to do with myself. I've not had such freedom in eleven years.'

'Time to get out and shake a leg.'

'I can do that now, but I'm too tired for a social life, Monica. Two nights out each month is my limit. Ambreen pops by on her way back from yoga on Wednesdays. That's as much as I can manage.'

'Don't you ever feel trapped, Chita?'

'Of course. Just because my face is impassive, it doesn't mean I'm not screaming inside.'

'Do you miss having a man around?'

'It's a permanent hole.'

'An unfilled hole.'

'Trust you.' They both got the giggles.

'Why don't you do something about it?' Monica said. 'The boys are about to do an Annie and cut loose. Get back on a dating website. Flirt. Have a little fun. You're so fantastically beautiful and elegant. Men would die for you.' A pause. 'Oh, shit.' Unintentionally, they both got the giggles again.

Watching her sons chasing each other around the play area meant for children half their age, Chita said to herself: 'Those are my men. Two is more than enough.'

In May, instead of booking the boys into a daily sports camp as she usually did during school breaks, Chita took the week off and they loafed around town, going to galleries and museums and finally to Debenhams where they were fitted for their new school uniforms. Chita ordered everything in bigger sizes for longer wear, including their blazers with the distinctive red-and-gold braiding.

'I look ridiculous, Mum. Like Charles Atlas.'

'You look lovely, Shush. Very handsome.'

'I hate the elasticated waistband on these trousers.'

'That's so they'll grow with you, Rusty.'

'A tie. Yuck.'

It took over two hours to get everything ordered, including extras Chita could not have imagined, like embroidered name tags and special games socks. By the time they left the store, her spirits and her funds were depleted. 'My goodness, we'll only just be able to afford the airfares to India this summer.'

'We're definitely going?'

'Of course.'

'You said you weren't sure.'

'I've told the partners I'm taking a month off.' Chita stopped momentarily by Oxford Circus Tube. 'Why don't we walk up Portland Place and into Regent's Park? We can get the bus there.'

They pushed their way purposefully through the throngs of shoppers, passing the Langham Hilton and Broadcasting House. 'I could be working there one day.'

'Let's hope so, Rustem. Anyway, the reason I think we should go to India this summer, even though it's only two years since the last visit, is that we can't anticipate how secondary school will change your interests and the demands made on your time. Also, I'd like to see Amma. Her arthritis is worse and Papa gets tired so easily.'

'Can we go riding again this time?'

'Of course. And you can borrow bicycles and go up into the hills with the Wijesingha children if you like.'

'We might not get on now we're older.'

'You got on fine last time. Anyway, it's an idea only.'

They passed the Chinese embassy and signed a petition demanding human rights for its citizens. A little farther on, they passed the Somali embassy. 'This is the street of oppressors. Many years ago, that's what your father called it. Nothing changes.'

'What does oppression mean, Mum?'

'It means withholding someone's rights. Denying them free-dom – whether it's of movement or action or thought.'

'So we're lucky because we're not oppressed.'

'Yes. Though having freedom counts for nothing if you're oppressed by conventions of your own making,' Chita added as an afterthought.

But the boys had run on ahead.

The summer came in a rush of heat waves and flash flooding. It was a prophetic time: amateur weather forecasters saw portents in the way the cloud formations were changing. The latest media astrologer pronounced that Mercury and Jupiter had declared war in the heavens. Great change was forecast. If not the clashing of two continents, the resounding boom of life at the speed of sound.

Two weeks before the end of term, Shashi fell awkwardly during a gym session and broke his left wrist. Encased in plaster to the elbow, he was often hot and uncomfortable, and every day things took on a complexity that none of them could have envisaged.

He was constantly pained. 'Now I can't get my T-shirt on!'

'Here.' Chita gently tugged the arm over his plaster. 'I'm sorry if that hurt. It's a good thing it's warm – imagine if you also had to put on coats and jumpers.'

'I haven't put my homework book in my rucksack.'

'Rusty, can you do that for him?'

'Why should I? He can do it perfectly well himself.'

'Just do it to help *me*.'

'He's turning us into his slaves. He's so bloody righteous.'

'If you don't want to help your injured brother, *Rustem*, don't,' Shashi said.

Chita shook her head. 'You've just proved his point.'

By the time the summer holidays hoved into view, they were all feeling ratty with each other. Chita sensed that part of it must be the boys' anxiety and sadness at leaving the local primary. Neither had a best friend because they had each other, but they were part of a wider group who played together at break and in the holidays.

Another component was an increasing sense of urgency about her own parents. Papa had never been the same since the latest heart surgery, and Amma's arthritic hands were starting to curl into permanent fists. As ever when she was feeling unsettled, Chita started to worry about where her duties lay.

She raised the matter with Manju when her best friend arrived in London for a six-day stay. Now in charge of developing literacy across the curriculum within her state, Manju was ostensibly in town to attend the launch of a new reading scheme at the European children's book fair. But within forty-eight hours she'd declared the whole enterprise a waste of time: 'Actually it's an old reading scheme dressed up with whizzy interactive Net aids. Not worth the money. And the other stuff on show I've already seen in the catalogues. No surprises.'

'Manju, what do you know about the Indian system?'

'The Indian system for English or for Hindi?'

'The Indian education system.'

'Are we again having the debate about whether or not you should return home and care for your ageing relations?' She laughed. 'Don't look at me like that. It's true. You raise this every six months and my response today is the same as always – I think the level of education here is as good as the good schools back home. Or, to answer your question – the good schools back home are as good as the good schools here. But it's not a question of the boys' education, is it, Chita? It's about lifestyle.'

Deftly Manju flashed her fork across Chita's plate and stole a mouthful of chocolate pudding. 'Sorry – a very Western habit and one you probably hate, but you know it's precisely the sort of social constraint that would choke the life from you at home.

'You've paid the price of duty many times over, Chita. First you land in England because of an old man's will. The second time, because of his son's insistence on piety and propriety above trust and self-knowledge. Our rules work against you. If you return, they may also work against your children.'

'But what is the right thing to do, Manju?'

'The right thing is what works in favour of the greater good.'

'That was Shyam's argument for getting rid of me.'

'He couldn't argue his way out of a paper bag. I hear he's a politician now. What a joke. Shyam got rid of you, my darling, because your story made people suspicious and mistrustful. He confused greater *happiness* with greater *goodness*.'

Before Chita could speak Manju held up her finger to silence her. 'Sometimes people have to suffer in order to learn – and the lesson justifies the suffering. For the greater good, Shyam should have displayed loyalty and humilty. By abandoning you, he fed ignorance and exposed his own weakness.'

Chita finished her pudding in silence, sticky with heat even though it was ten o'clock at night and they were sitting at a table outside the Hampstead restaurant.

Leaning back in the chair, Manju was struck by her friend's timeless grace. Hitting fifty and still head-turningly lovely.

She had on straight-cut slacks and a sleeveless white shirt showing off wonderfully fair and toned arms. How is it, Manju wondered, that even her hands are smooth? When did the concept of age change? When did it cease to be measured in years and become, instead, a series of interlocking and often interchangeable phases?

'What are you doing now?'

'Just checking my personal organiser. It's the boys' final school assembly tomorrow. I've had to change everything around.' Chita put away the Palm Pilot. 'What do I do about my parents, Manju? For all your proselytising, you were the one who gave up years of your youth to look after your mother.'

'My mother was threatening to die from the day I was born, Chita. I had such a burden of guilt there was no choice. I thought I had somehow caused her illness. I tell you, the therapists would make millions if they moved in on India. You're lucky. You don't have the same constraints. Don't create them.'

They paid the bill and strolled down Downshire Hill for Cokes in the pub. Chita called Ambreen to make sure that she was all right looking after the boys. Afterwards, she and Manju window-shopped along South End Green before cutting down silent back doubles to Kentish Town. Linking arms with her dearest friend, Chita said: 'Whoever would have thought that you and I would end up in the West? Me in England with twin sons, and you with an American husband and two little girls even naughtier than you were.'

Manju laughed. 'Fact is stranger than fiction. Don't forget to give your folks my love when you see them next week.'

They had come to the airport.

Walking into the unruly arrivals hall, she saw them standing behind a huge family group: Amma, Papaji and Uday, the servant boy, now a married man with four children, living in the little three-roomed annexe behind the main house and acting as driver, housekeeper and general factotum.

Chita struggled a few yards more with the wayward luggage trolley and then gave up. Abandoning it to the boys, she ran, arms outstretched, to her parents.

What is it about family that even when we're fifty our parents make us feel like kids again? Make us feel foolish or too precious so you half want to spoil the moment just because . . . well, just because you can – and the joy of being the child is you get forgiven again and again and again. It's the only *true* power we ever have.

The boys were hanging back, half through shyness and half as a function of their age – the dread of cuddles and kisses and cheeks pinched and very Indian comments like: 'Isn't your mother feeding you? Arms like sticks, no?'

Noticing Shashi's plaster, Amma was immediately concerned. Chita could feel him cringing behind the calm façade, but then, unexpectedly as always, the smile surfaced and he embraced his grandmother with joy.

Rusty, hopping from foot to foot, was equally uncertain of what to do. Bypassing them, he approached Papa and put out a hand. The old man burst out laughing. 'Am I such a stranger we have to shake? Give me a hug, Rustem – it may be the last chance you have.'

Chita had subconsciously noted her father's loss of weight. Now common sense told her this was a prelude to the end in a household where a healthy appetite and a tight waistband were compulsory. She felt the first frisson of fear in his company.

But this wasn't the moment for articulating worry. Chita laughed as Uday struggled past with the crazed trolley. Leaving the boys to follow with her parents, she helped him guide it to the old Mercedes shooting brake parked outside.

As Uday loaded the boot, she watched her parents quiz

their adored grandsons about school and about London. They answered self-consciously. Another couple of days and they'll be totally at ease.

She shouted to them: 'Come on. Let's get *going*.'

These are the four people I love most in all the world.

And Shyam, of course. Still. Somewhere deep inside.

But he is my past and they are my present and my future.

By the end of the first week, every friend, neighbour and relation within a fifty-mile radius had been to Chita's home to admire the boys and comment on the continuing success and timeless beauty of their mother. 'Papa and I are exhausted,' Amma said.

On the Monday, Chita drove down into the valley and to the private hospital where they'd arranged to have Shashi's plaster removed. Afterwards, she and the boys lunched at a Chinese restaurant.

'It feels odd eating Chinese in India.'

'I think it's better than the Chinese in England.'

'It's less gooey.'

'How's the wrist, Shashi?'

'It feels a bit stiff, but it works. I hate this wristband.'

'It's to warm your muscles until they loosen. The doctor says it helps get the movement back more easily.'

'When can I play basketball again?'

'When it feels normal.'

'What's normal?'

'I've no idea. I'm sure you'll recognise it when it happens.'

They got home late in the evening. Her parents were dozing on the verandah. Her father went to bed at the same time as the boys. Chita sat with Amma. The sky was so black it was blue. The stars were like random halogen lights and the moon was almost full. The air was still and so fresh it seared the nostrils.

'Amma,' Chita said, 'I think it's time we shut the doors to the world and just enjoyed this time together quietly.'

'Enjoy time quietly with two active boys?'

'They can look after themselves. They love the woodland and the Wijesingha children are there to come up with new adventures.'

'You know, Chita, there's a three-day poetry and story-telling competition in Bangalore next week. Children between the ages of ten and sixteen are coming from all over the country to recite.'

'It's too long a drive.'

'The car is comfortable. We can spend one night with cousin Jyoti in Madurai. I think the boys would enjoy it. They've never read Tagore or *Omar Khayyam*. They could even take part. I have a copy of the Ramayana by my bed – imagine them reading or performing a scene in those lovely English voices ... they'd win the gold prize.' Seeing her daughter's face, Amma smiled. 'It's just an idea. Why don't you let me take them? It's such a treat for me and an important part of their heritage. You stay here and spoil your father. He's very ill, Chita, as you've already realised.'

'But Amma, what about *your* health?'

'I'm old, Chita, not ill. I have arthritis only. My hands are no longer much use, but I'm strong. I'll be here for a long, long time. Your father has a weak heart. Since the last stroke, he has deteriorated badly. They say nothing can be done.'

Chita hugged her mother. 'If you don't mind taking the boys, Amma, I'm sure they'd love it. And I'd like time alone with Papaji. I haven't had that since I was a child.'

Far from finding the idea boring, the boys were delighted to go with their grandmother and dramatically declaimed and Anglicised long passages from the Ramayana on the endless drive. 'I *am* going to enter you in this competition,' Amma said. 'You will win. I am sure of that. It's good for you to understand your culture.'

That evening they stayed with her cousin Jyoti in a small cramped house at the foot of a hill. 'You have always been at the top and we have been at the bottom,' Jyoti joked.

'The view is better at the top, but the food is better at the bottom,' Amma said as she and the boys ripped into fresh parathas, the creamiest dahl and enough varieties of curry to feed a temple crowd through Diwali. 'Your boy Shanthi looks well in the photos.'

'He's a journalist now. You know that, of course. He did the big Hitarachi exposé in the *Times of India*. I was terrified – waiting for gundas to appear and smash the house to pieces.' Jyoti turned to the boys. 'Bribery scandals are rife in India and very difficult to prove. I was worried my son's life was endangered.'

'I want to be a journalist when I grow up.'

'Do you, Rustem? Perhaps Shanthi will help you with the rhyming in your script when he gets back. He'll be here soon.'

They arrived in Bangalore the following evening. After booking into a small guest-house, Amma headed straight for the competition office. The organisers were less than enthusiastic. 'We have a full complement. Names were put down three months ago.'

'Three months ago, I didn't know these boys would be here.'

'That is not our concern, madam.'

'But it is *my* concern. They have come all the way from London.'

'To take part in this competition?'

'Rustem, come here. Let him read you a passage. Read, boy.' Purple with embarrassment, Rustem read a few lines. 'Now Shashi, take a turn.' His face averted from that of the bemused official, Shashi, too, read. 'It is *their* Ramayana. You saw how beautifully they perform, and with such meaning.'

'There is no space. I could only fit them in at the end.'

'Then fit them at the end.'

And so it was that, squirming with the horror of it all, the boys were entered for the competition and their grandmother, in whom they suddenly recognised their own mother's quietly determined quality, sent them packing to bed with the advice that they must rest their minds and their voices in order to plan for success.

'Papa? Are you awake?'

'I'm always awake. But sometimes I close my eyes.'

Chita sat on the edge of the bed and put a cool hand on his hot forehead. 'You're running a temperature.'

'I overheat.'

'I'll get a wet flannel and bring it down a bit.'

She moved the cold compress around his face and noticed an easing of the tension in his body. 'I'm sorry I don't see more of you, Papa.'

'I too. But more than that, Chita, I'm sorry your life has been so difficult. It is not as we would have wished it. Your mother and I had such dreams for you. God blessed us with you, our only child.'

'My life's fine, Papa.'

'Yes, I know. The boys are all anyone could wish, and you continue to earn well. But what every parent wants for their child, Chita, is security and protection. I would like to die knowing you are loved and being cared for. That – how would you put it? – the buck doesn't always stop with you.' He struggled to sit up in the bed. 'The ideal in life is to share the hardship and responsibility as well as the pleasures and rewards. It's why we marry.'

'I'm strong, Papa. Women are. We may not like taking on

227

every duty but we do seem to have a unique gift for doing just that. Perhaps because there's no choice.'

'It is a Western way.'

'And an Eastern way. I'm proof of that.'

'Your mother and I share everything.'

'Because you can. It's not so easy when the demands of others are constantly encroaching on your plans and your lifestyle. Something, or someone, has to give.'

'You should never have worked.'

'I'm educated, Papa. I need the stimulation. He loved me for it.'

'But not its consequences.'

'That isn't my fault.'

'But it *is* your problem, child.'

'I don't see my life as a problem.'

'Then what?'

Chita struggled, trying to find an answer. 'We all have ideals. They define us. They provide the framework for our lives and so we incorporate them into our expectations. But within that frame, the picture is always changing and so is control. Despite the best intentions, things don't always work out as planned. Every day I do *my* best and look ahead with hope. That's as much as I can do.'

She took and kissed her father's feathery hand. 'On that basis, Papa, my life is not the problem, but the solution.'

On the third day, Amma picked up the day's programme and flicked through. 'Ayee!' The booklet fell from her bent hands and she cupped her mouth in shock. Rustem and Shashi, rewriting their lines for maximum effect, looked up to see the old lady literally immobile, frozen in time and space like a Rodin sculpture.

'What is it, Narnie?' Rusty ran and picked up the pamphlet.

Shush approached their grandmother gingerly. 'Are you all right, Narnie?' She didn't respond. Gently he took her arm and led her to a chair. 'Are you sick?' She sat silently, eyes glazed.

Rusty thumbed the programme but he didn't notice that a visiting politician to the state had been invited to present the prize after the judges reached their decision. If he had, he might have stopped at the name of the popular and self-effacing businessman turned professional socialist.

A revered man who was also, by a strange coincidence, their father.

Shashi: This is the story of Rama and Sita.
Rustem: About trust and duty and making life sweeter.
Shashi: The son of a king, and another king's daughter.
Rustem: Falling in love, just like they oughter.
Shashi: Rama breaks Krishna's bow, a sign of great might.
Rustem: This is a bloke you'd avoid late at night.
Shashi: He shoots moving apples, he's sharp eyed and clever.
Rustem: And she's a princess who will love him for ever.
Shashi: Gaily they marry but soon there's bad news.
Rustem: His brother inherits and Rama will lose
Shashi: his right to the throne for fourteen long years.
Rustem: He runs to the forest and bathes in warm tears.
Shashi: The beautiful Sita remains by his side,
Rustem: 'As shadow to substance, so I'll be your bride.'
Shashi: Another young brother, one half of twins
Rustem: joins them in exile. The story begins.

Sitting in the front row looking up at these beautiful boys reciting so cleverly their own version of the Ramayana, Shyam felt strangely discomfited. He looked behind him, scanning the faces for Lucky, who he knew was here somewhere. No sign.

Turning his attention back to the boys, he had a violent sense of déjà vu so compulsive that his heart literally skipped a beat.

They were nothing to him so it didn't make sense. Two teenagers by the look of it, tall and gangly, from a different state and speaking in accents he hadn't heard for years.

He scanned the entry sheet but the information was limited to their names. Funnily enough they shared his surname, but that was the only connection. He frowned. Next to him, his fellow judges watched with rapt attention.

Shashi: A little while after they've thus relocated
           the new king comes by and some home truths are stated.
Rustem: He'll keep the throne warm till his brother comes back.
           But at that point, he says, 'Please give me the sack.'
Shashi: And so in the forest they start a new life.
           Rama, Laxmana and Sita, the wife.
Rustem: The men go out huntin', shootin' and fishin'.
           While Sita's at home doing the washing.
Shashi: And so things remain for many long years
           until in the trees a she-demon appears.

At this point the boys changed position. Shashi kneeled on the stage while Rustem, bending, spoke down to him in a husky voice.

Rustem: 'I think you're gorgeous, come be my mate.'
Shashi: 'I'm happily married to my first serious date.'
Rustem: 'But I am so pretty and funny and clever!'
Shashi: 'I have a wife and we're pledged for ever.'

Both boys moved back to a standing position. Shyam felt the sweat break out on his back. I used to know this story so well.

Oh God, those first days on Inderdates – Chita and I – we were Rama and Sita . . .

Chita. Why? Why did it have to happen? What went wrong?

He caught his breath. I am undone by the resonances here. It's too close to the bone. It permeates my marrow. I feel so . . . uncomfortable. It must be the heat. Damn Lucky. Where is he?

Rustem: The she-demon leaves in a puff of hot smoke.
And goes home to her brother, a well hard bloke.
Shashi: In fact he's a devil. A cruel king from Lanka.
He's got twenty heads, and his full name is Ravana.
Rustem: When his horrible sister tells him of Sita,
he decides she's the dame who will make his life neater.
Shashi: He heads for the forest and then tries to woo her.
He sends a gold deer in a bid to undo her.
Rustem: The trick nearly works and the men are alarmed.
They draw her a circle within which it's charmed.
Shashi: 'Do not step out. Inside there you're safe.'
Protected from harm and pillage and rape.
Rustem: But the devil's determined and so he makes magic.
He appears as a beggar and the outcome is tragic.
Shashi: He asks the good Sita to give him some alms.
She steps out of the circle and cancels the charm.

Again the boys changed position; this time Rustem kneeled and Shashi talked down. They had not had time to memorise the whole skit and so, at this point, there was a co-ordinated pulling out and reading from the script. Amma, standing in the wings in a state of near-collapse, watched Shyam as he fidgeted with his collar and ran his hands constantly through the thick grey curls that, as ever, needed a cut. The audience, however, was absolutely still.

Shashi: 'Undone by your goodness! Now Sita, you're mine.
              Here with me in Lanka, we're bound for all time.'
Rustem: 'Don't kid yourself, Ravana, you may have me here
              but Rama's the man to whom I stay dear.'
Shashi: 'Sweet lady, I'll wait. I'm in no hurry.
              The longer you're with me, the more weight I'll carry.'
Rustem: 'You cannot tempt me, my heart is elsewhere.
              I'll be faithful to Rama, that much I can swear!'

As the boys returned to the narrators' positions, Lucky walked up the aisle to find his brother. Approaching the stage, he heard the wonderful declamations and was struck by the silence in the hall.

Close to, he saw two boys so like the young Shyam that, for a moment, he thought he was hallucinating.

Shashi: Magicked away with not one single clue,
              Laxmana and Rama knew not what to do.
Rustem: They scoured the states all around them in vain
              with a quiet desperation to see her again.
Shashi: The monkey band came – Hanuman and his mates.
              'Just leave it with us, boys, we'll put on our skates.'
Rustem: They found Sita in Lanka, her face etched with sadness.
              'Don't worry, Princess, you'll be freed from this madness.'
Shashi: The monkeys and Rama started a war.
              They snatched Sita back and settled the score.
Rustem: In a show of such force it remains quite heroic
              Rama vanquished his foe with a blow that was stoic.
Shashi: Ravana collapsed, his many heads choking.
              Lanka was freed as the bad spell was broken.
Rustem: 'I love you,' cried Rama, kissing his bride.
              'For ever more now, you will be at my side.'

The boys paused for effect.

Shashi: It is here with great sadness we have to relate
          'They were happy thereafter' is not Sita's fate.
Rustem: When Rama returned to become rightful King,
          his subjects all claimed she should not wear his ring.
Shashi: How can you prove she was faithful? they said.
          She was gone a long time from the marital bed!
Rustem: Good Rama, confused, thought they made sense.
          Laxmana was sent to dispatch Sita hence.
Shashi: She returned to the forest and death called her name.
          Depressed and dejected she—

'No!' Shyam jumped up from his seat. He thought he was going
to choke. A few feet away, Lucky was frozen to the spot. He
watched as his brother, in slow motion, tried to push his chair
back and leave the judging area.

On the stage the boys had stopped, not sure what to do.

Suddenly a man in the audience shouted at Shyam: 'Be quiet
and let them carry on!'

Lucky moved quickly to the judges' table. He steadied
Shyam's elbow and whispered in his ear: 'For God's sake sit
down, brother. Don't make a fool of yourself.'

'Who are they, Lucky?'

'Work that out for yourself.'

Shoving Shyam gently but firmly back into his seat, Lucky
smiled at his nephews. 'Your performance is very moving.
Please continue.'

'Let's do it from the hermit,' Shashi whispered to Rustem.

Rustem: The hermit gave Sita a room in his home
          and it was there that her twin sons were born.
Shashi: Two boys, Kusa, Lava, the spit of their dad,
          she watched them both grow, and good followed bad.

233

Rustem: Meanwhile the hermit was writing their story.
　　　　Love and adventure, mistrust and glory.
Shashi: He called it the Ramayana. They read
　　　　a verse of it nightly before going to bed.
Rustem: And when a poetry contest was called
　　　　they spoke it aloud and all were enthralled.
Shashi: Including King Rama, who realised just then
　　　　that these were his sons, now almost men.
Rustem: He cried for their mother—

Even though he was sitting, Shyam felt his legs give way beneath him. He slumped from the emotion of it all and, for a moment, everything stopped, including the performance.

He is looking at two boys who are built in his likeness, and though his name is Shyam, not Rama, and hers is Chita, not Sita, he knows these boys, whoever they are, are really Kusa and Lava. Well, they're not Kusa and Lava but . . .

But they are his sons.

Shyam sees it in the structure of their cheekbones, the cut of their chin, the length of their fingers. The tears start to come because he also sees Chita. She's in the shape of their eyes and the way they smile, as they're smiling now, worried that he will shout at them or tell them to stop. It's in the cadence of their voices and the grace of their stance.

Shyam tries to get up and everyone around him is clearly embarrassed. His beloved brother is again at his side, ready to pick up the slack. 'Stay, Shyam,' he says now. 'It's time to do the right thing.'

Conclusion

Chita heard the boys' excited voices as they climbed out of the car. Jumping up from her father's bedside, she ran to the front door. It had been a difficult few days. It was almost as if, having waited to see her and spend time with her alone, Papa had let go.

She'd spent most of the time sitting sentinel while he slept. Uday's wife had assured her that Papa had occasional episodes of extreme fatigue, but it frightened Chita. Especially because, in their first week there, he had been so active, meeting and greeting and doing everything expected of him. Since the departure of Amma and the boys, it was as if his life force had started to drain.

Chita had called the GP and Papa's drugs had been topped up, but there was nothing else to be done. 'He is no worse than before,' Dr Uppuma had said. 'It is merely his ability to cope that is changing.'

'It's not the end?'

'Not yet. But he travels a one-way road, Chita. I think you know that.'

It was a relief therefore to hear sounds of life and laughter. Her mother was talking to someone at the gate. The boys were teasing each other as they ambled up the path.

She galloped towards her sons, grabbing them in a bear hug and covering their faces with kisses. 'So how did it go? Why didn't you ring?'

'We won.'

'You won? What did you win? The book tokens? The CDs?'

'No, Ma – we won the gold prize!'

'The gold prize? No! Really?' She checked their faces for signs of amusement but all she saw was pleasure. 'How can that be? You only learned the story the day before you left.'

'We wrote most of it ourselves and Shanthi, Aunty Jyoti's son, did the grown-up bits for us. It was brilliant. They went wild.'

Chita stepped back and studied them with pride. 'It's changed you. You both seem more confident. Older. You know, you boys never fail to amaze me.' She put her arms out. 'I love you so much.'

As she spoke, her mother was coming up the path with a strange man. Chita, looking past her sons, was struck by the familiar slope of his shoulders, though it took a few seconds for her to make out the soft lips and sharp cheeks now hidden behind a thick beard.

'Hello, Lucky,' she said without missing a beat. 'Were you just passing?'

'He's desperate to see you, Chita. You have no idea of what he's going through. Seeing the boys was the biggest shock of his life.'

'Not any bigger than carrying them, or giving birth to them, or raising them single-handedly for twelve years, thousands of miles from my friends and family, I can assure you.'

She got up and walked to the window, looking out on to the back garden where she and Shyam had gone walking that first time. How many years ago was it now? Twenty-seven. Twenty-seven! What a momentous day that was. I have never once regretted it despite everything that has happened.

'He's their father.'

'Surely that can't be right? Wasn't I banished for sleeping with Sam Raven? How can he be sure?'

'It was a mistake, Chita. We all know that.'

'Does *he* know that, Lucky?'

'He does. Now.'

'And you?'

'I knew then, Chita. He wouldn't listen. He believed his duty was to the masses and if they didn't believe, then you had to go.'

She nodded. 'It is only the capacity for wisdom that is God-given, not wisdom itself. Shyam is a great warrior. He is instinctively protective and selfless. But he has no understanding of women.'

'What man does, Chita? Isn't that the historic complaint?'

'But we understand *you* so well. That's why we stay through thick and thin. It's what keeps us dutiful to the last. Is it really too much to ask that sometimes you try to take on our perspective?' She laughed dryly. 'Don't answer that, Lucky.'

'He *is* a great warrior. He has fought the most protracted battles for human and civil rights. He's a hero.'

'He *is* a hero. He is an idealist who upholds his ideals. That is why I have never stopped loving him. Never. Not once. But ideals have to be underpinned with qualities like trust and kindness and mercy.'

'He's learned that lesson. Now.'

'From the Ramayana.'

'It was how the Lord Rama learned the same lesson, Chita.'

She extended their stay by a week even though it gave the boys just two days to readjust before starting their new school. After tearful goodbyes, they took the flight north.

'Tell me I'll see you again, Papaji.'

'In my bones I believe it, Chita, but they are old bones.'

'I love you more than words can say.'

'You think I don't know that?'

She clung to him then, smelling the pomade in his hair and the Wright's Coal Tar soap he loved so well on his body. 'If

I could have chosen from every man in the universe, I would still have chosen you to be my father, Papa. You're everything a girl could want.'

'Then I wish there could have been two like me. One to father you and a younger version to marry you.'

'The boys adore you. You're such a wonderful role model.'

'And so are you, child. You have been both mother and father to them. Nothing that happens in the future will change that.'

Amma wept as they went through to departures. 'Take care, my child. Go with your mind, not your heart.'

'Can't I go with both?'

'Only if it's what you want, Chita.'

Chita smiled and took her mother's hands. 'I don't know what I want, Amma. But I'm glad I've got you.'

On the flight to Delhi, Chita got the boys to recite their poem to her together. She loved hearing it again and again.

King Rama's heart swelled when his wife came in sight.
'My love, I have missed you with all of my might.
'You gave me your hand, and that trust I abused.
'I know now with hindsight that you were misused.'
He wished her to love him as she had once done,
This woman who'd borne him two perfect young sons.
And love him she did, with all of her heart,
Despite what he'd done and their years apart.
But she also had pride as befits royal blood.
She wanted to show that she'd always been good.
'It's important you know I have been true and pure,
And there's only one way I can prove it for sure.
Light me a fire and through it I'll walk.
If my feet burn then you've reason to talk.
But if they don't—

240

'Mum? Mum!' Rusty stopped in mid-sentence. 'She's fallen asleep. Now she'll be out for the whole journey. How does she do that?'

Shashi pushed a frond of hair from his mother's face. 'She's tired.'

'And scared.'

'I'm scared too. Aren't you?'

Rusty shrugged. 'I don't know. Part of me's excited because at last I'll meet my dad. But there's another bit of me that says he may be your dad but he's also a complete stranger.'

'It is just like their story, though, isn't it? Now she's told us.'

'Except she won't be walking through fire.' Rusty caught his brother's quizzical look and felt suddenly uneasy. 'She won't walk through fire. Will she?'

Shashi shrugged. 'There are a lot of . . . what's the word Lucky kept using when he first met us?'

'Resonances,' Rusty said. 'There are a lot of resonances.'

They drove to the big estate house that was to have been her marital home in India.

Shyam came to the door to meet them. He was in crumpled cream linen trousers and a blue shirt. He looked devastating. Her heart leaped. Physical feelings, longings she hadn't had for so long she'd forgotten their existence, suddenly exploded into life. It was as if her body had been taken over by someone else.

But it hadn't. And as he watched her walk towards him in a loose-fitting lilac shift dress, every curve and every movement was so familiar Shyam yearned to take her in his arms and kiss her and undress her and make love to her at that very moment.

The ache of longing that used to overcome him at the thought of her had become the ache of loss over the years.

It was so much a part of him he hadn't realised until now that it could be pegged to a single event – a single person, who, despite being absent for so long, remained an intrinsic part of his physical and emotional whole.

There had never been anyone else for him, either. How could there be? She stopped now, in front of him, their two sons standing curiously behind her. Shyam regretted that he was on the step as he seemed to be looking down on them all.

'Chita.'

'Shyam.'

'I have tea inside.'

'And sympathy?'

He smiled, unsure whether it was humour or irony.

'Hello, boys.'

'Hello.' They didn't know what to call him.

Shyam ushered them into the house. The whole place was painted white with a handful of colourful pieces. A man's home.

There was a housekeeper. She had made a creditable spread but nobody seemed capable of eating, not even the boys.

Lucky somehow kept the conversation going, and afterwards he offered to take the twins to meet the horses. 'We have two shires from England – enormous fellows. Let's see if we can get you on them. You do ride?'

They sat in silence for a few minutes. She concentrated on a point somewhere in the middle distance and he studied his hands. Finally he said: 'I'm sorry, Chita.'

'Is that it?'

'I'm sorry because I love you so much. I have been unjust and cruel beyond measure.' She didn't respond. 'I don't know what else to say.'

'You didn't mean it, Shyam.'

'I was rash. Easily swayed.'

'You thought you were doing the right thing. That's an important consideration.'

'But I didn't do the right thing. I love you, Chita.'

'I love you too.'

But though they both meant it, neither looked at the other or made any form of physical contact. Because they had learned that love, on its own, doesn't have any substance. It's the boring detail, the smallprint of life, our compassion, understanding, trust and loyalty, which imbue love with value.

'I want you back.'

'I can't come back while you think I betrayed you.'

'I know you didn't betray me. I was a fool. I bowed to pressure.'

'Because part of you believed it was possible.'

'Anything is possible, Chita. What I didn't consider was whether it was *probable*. Clearly it was not.'

Finally she looked at him. 'We can't go back.'

'We have children.'

'We have children irrespective of whether we're together or not.'

'I have a right to see them.'

'They are free to do as they wish. I will not stop them.'

'They should be raised in India.'

'They are raised as *Indians*.'

'This is their home.'

'Isn't home where the heart is?'

'Their hearts could be here, Chita. With ours.'

'Their hearts are whole, not broken. Let's keep them like that.'

'We could be happy again.'

She frowned away the tears. 'I haven't seen you in twelve years.'

'You're still beautiful.'

'What has that to do with it?'

'I've missed you so badly.'

She noticed he was twisting his wedding ring. So he still wears it. Like me. Matching gold bands: slim, simple, significant.

'I want you so much, Chita. You belong here.'

'I've changed, Shyam. I'm a different woman.'

'Tell me what I must do to convince you.'

'It's not about convincing me. It's about convincing others. You know, Shyam, the boys have recited the Ramayana to me every day. I have even considered doing a Sita, and walking through fire for you. That's how crazy and impotent this whole situation makes me feel. But you and I are not gods, and I know that fire burns even the most innocent. Without that facility to prove myself, I cannot stay here.'

'You'll feel differently after a few days, Chita. It's all new.'

'Geographically, yes. Emotionally, no.'

'What are you saying, Chita?'

'I'm your wife.' She held out her hand. 'See, like you, I still wear my ring. I have always believed in the sanctity of marriage.' She kissed the gold band. 'I have never looked elsewhere and I never will. But you and I cannot function on the same continent. By sending me back to England you placed us in different worlds and I am no longer able to exist in yours.'

'The boys . . .'

'The boys will come back here, Shyam. If not tomorrow, then in a few years' time. Of that I am certain.'

'But you . . .'

'I have been true to you, and to myself. That is enough.'

She reached across the table and took his hand. She went to raise it to her lips but then changed her mind. 'Let's go and find the boys,' she said, rising gracefully from her seat.

*   *   *

244

'It's all been a bit of a shock to our systems.'

'It certainly has, Lucky.'

'You know that everyone – absolutely everyone – accepts that the allegations were wrong. They've seen the boys, they've seen you. Shyam has washed every ounce of his dirty linen in public, even at the risk of his political career.'

'I'm grateful for that.'

'Nobody can be in any doubt that you were wronged.'

'Thank you. Really.'

'But you still won't stay? What about destiny?'

'I've remained loyal to Shyam through thick and thin, Lucky. Mainly thin, and twelve years invisible. I've fulfilled my destiny.'

He laughed. 'You *are* the dutiful wife, Sita. Chita.'

She watched as he put their luggage on the British Airways luggage belt and felt a deep rush of pleasure at the thought of returning home. Home to the forest. To a poky little house in Kentish Town where she and her boys had love and trust and laughter. More than enough.

She handed over the three tickets and passports for checking.

'Thanks for everything, Lucky. You're a really good person.'

'You'll be coming back to India?'

'To see Amma and Papa, yes.'

'And Shyam?'

'The boys can visit on their own. They're big enough.'

'So we won't see you?'

She kissed him and thanked him. 'No, Lucky, you won't see me, but I'm out there, ever faithful, ever loving.'

Chita picked up her hand luggage and, calling the boys, disappeared through the doors, into the departure lounge. As if by magic.

*   *   *

Sita walked through the flame and her feet were so soft
They shouted her name and held her aloft.
It is true what she says, this dutiful wife.
To prove us all wrong she risked her own life.
Now look at her, love her, rejoice that she's ours,
Let us anoint her and dress her in flowers –
A queen to our king and mother of twins,
Aren't we all glad to acknowledge our sins!
Sita bowed to them all and took King Rama's hand.
'I am so happy now you understand.
The duty of woman's to love and obey.
All my life I have tried to do as you say.
At last you have seen that I repaid your trust.
In all future dealings I know you'll be just.'
She called to the earth: 'I've been faithful and calm,
Open beneath me, and let me come home.'
And as she spoke the ground rumbled beneath.
A small but deep chasm formed at her feet.
Mother earth did her bidding. She never returned.
The dutiful woman whose feet did not burn.